Dory Lee Maske

Published by Dory Lee Maske, 2024.

Cold Land
by Dory Lee Maske
Copyright © 2024 by Dory Lee Maske
All rights reserved
Cover design by Jan Orsini
Draft2Digital Edition 2024
Discover other titles by Dory Lee Maske at Smashwords.com
https://www.smashwords.com/profile/view/DoryLeeMaske

This is a work of fiction. Similarities to real people, places, or events are entirely coincidental.

COLD LAND

First edition. November 21, 2024.

Copyright © 2024 Dory Lee Maske.

ISBN: 979-8227872869

Written by Dory Lee Maske.

This book is dedicated to my two sons, Paul and Todd.

List of Characters

<u>Ambassadors of the *By Grace*:</u>
Joshua – from the Christian Bible, Book of Joshua
Daniel – from the Christian Bible, Book of Daniel
Jonah – from the Christian Bible, Book of Jonah
Deborah – from the Christian Bible, Judges 4 and 5
Lydia – Acts, Chapter 16 Christian Bible
Rahab – Joshua 2:1 Christian Bible
Uriah: 2 Samuel 11:3, 1 Chronicles 11, 2 Samuel 23 Christian Bible
By Grace – New Jerusalem spaceship
<u>Miners from Swage</u>
Daco – leader of mining excursion
Aldo – Daco's adolescent son
Bran – Daco's brother
Onri – adult son of Tull and Dray
Pheebs – miner
Mica – adult daughter of Tull and Dray
Bonanza – Daco's spaceship
<u>Jangle Clan – Jhar's Clan on Cold Land</u>
Jhar - daughter of Singe
Grum – cousin of Jhar
Sim – Jhar's younger brother
Cray – Jangle clan leader
<u>Sylvan Clan - Clan next to Jangle</u>
Dunk – friend of Jhar
Darp – Dunk's father
Romm – Sylvan leader
<u>Flag Clan</u>
Stan – Flag Clan leader
Swarm – Flag Clan member
<u>Brite Clan</u>

Chai – Brite Clan leader
Chi – Brite Clan member
Biologists from Swage:
Mona – biologist from Swage
Soma – Mona's exploration partner
Professor Stern – Chief Biologist
Seeker – Biologists' spaceship
Cold Land Creatures:
Skallon – larger than moose-sized herd animals with thick fur and horns

Ripcons – badger-sized carnivors with huge jaws and rows of sharp teeth

Skippers – fish that resemble edible fish found on the planet Swage

Swipes – large black-feathred carrion birds on Cold Land

Twinks – small swallow-sized birds that fly in huge flocks over Cold Land

Horids – Large bear-like predators that live on land but hunt in the sea

Therefore, we are ambassadors for Christ, God making his appeal through us.
2 Corinthians 5:20

Preface

This story takes place after the Rapture and the seven terrible years of the Tribulation. As promised, God, after his second coming, has set up His New Earth and the incredible city of New Jerusalem. The promised thousand year millennium began 402 years ago. God has provided a fleet of spaceships to send out into His universe and the believing Body of Christ are His ambassadors.

The ship *By Grace* is one of these ships which are set apart to visit areas of concern throughout the universe. Humanity in all its constructs is given the gift of free will. But free will includes the opportunity to make bad choices.

Cold Land

Chapter 1

Year 402 of The Lord's Millennium
Joshua

Joshua, a solid man with a soldier's bearing, walked briskly along the gold-paved street that bordered the River of Life. The trees on either side of the river stood heavy-laden with fruit as always. This month they held bright yellow-orange apricots bursting with juice. The leaves around the fruit glowed with healing nutrients. Joshua had not eaten yet this morning, hadn't wanted to take the time, so he plucked off an apricot to eat as he walked. The river that ran between the rows of fruit trees made a pleasant rippling sound, but there was power in it. Two fishermen cast their nets over the waters as they joked with one another. A giraffe lowered its tall neck down to the level of the stream to take a drink.

Joshua would normally stop to enjoy the scene, but this morning his mind was full of urgent business. He had received the following new directive from his God and King:

A situation has arisen in the star system Trance of the Sculpture galaxy. The planet Swage, with an orbit close to its star, has been destroyed by a massive solar flare. Survivors from Swage are currently mining asteroid M275JR. They hope to resettle on planet Cold Land, known to Swagians as planet Bando. Hostilities probable. Timely intervention needed as asteroid's path lies close to Cold Land's south sea and tidal flooding affecting a large area is unavoidable. Use discretion and minimal intervention necessary to resolve crisis. Crew will include yourself as commander, Uriah as pilot, Deborah, Lydia, Daniel, Jonah and Rahab. You, Deborah and Lydia will be dropped at the asteroid to talk to the Swagian miners. Remaining three will land on planet Cold Land to assess the possibilities for a peaceful transition. Thank you, Joshua, for your continuing service to our universe. Yeshua, High King of New Jerusalem

After considering the sparse guidelines of this new assignment, Joshua's thoughts centered on the crew chosen to accompany him. Often he could glean more insights about the mission by noting who God had chosen for it than he could from the information provided.

Uriah had been chosen pilot. Uriah was born a Hittite on the Old Earth thousands of years ago. Though Hittites were enemies of the Jews at that time, no one was more trustworthy than Uriah once he threw in with Israel. He was a dedicated soldier, loyal to God and even to King David, who wronged him. Joshua could easily trust his ship to Uriah. He wouldn't give another thought to the flight through space knowing Uriah was at the helm.

There would be two phases to this mission. Half the crew would be dropped on an asteroid and the other half flown to a planet that circled its star barely within the orbital distance that was neither too hot, not too cold to sustain life, the so-called Goldilocks Zone. It was brutally cold year-round, with permanent ice on the polar caps.

He would be with Deborah and Lydia, the first trio to drop down from the ship. Why would God choose two generals – himself and Deborah? Would they encounter warring factions? Were they headed for a battle zone?

And Lydia? What had she to do with conflict? Lydia had been one of the first to accept God into her life on the basis of faith alone. God had opened her heart and she had believed the Apostle Paul's message. She had taken advantage of the new path to salvation provided by Christ's amazing accomplishment: making himself a living sacrifice to shoulder the sins of the world and redeem all those who accepted his offer of salvation. A more gentle and gracious soul than Lydia would be difficult to find. So how did she fit into a mission that required two generals and the soldier pilot, Uriah?

Joshua shook his head. Only God knew. He looked around at the beauty of the city he would soon be leaving, wanting to inscribe it in his mind – a buffer against whatever was waiting out there in space.

God's radiance shone all around him in the shimmering gold of the avenues, the iridescent glow of the pearl gates, and the luminescent sky.

A pride of lions crossed the gold-paved street in front of him, heading for the grassy verge beside the river. Close behind them, a group of pet goats with their young caretaker fairly bounced along the same path. They headed for the low hanging fruit of the fecund trees lining the riverbank.

He was happy to see Lydia and Deborah waiting outside the Museum of Ancient Antiquities, throwing out breadcrumbs to the red and green parrots that nested in the fruit trees. He had asked the two women to meet him here as soon as they could.

Lydia waved when she saw him. She was wearing a white scoop-necked blouse and tan skirt that complemented her Mediterranean skin color. She maintained the features of her original Greek roots in her resurrected body, just as Joshua and Deborah still looked much as they had in ancient Israel—medium builds, brown complexions, dark hair and eyes. While there were few changes in their outward appearance, within was a different story. No life-giving blood ran through veins to bring oxygen to their lungs. Now their life blood was the Spirit of God and their bodies were immortal.

Deborah was wearing the clothes she always wore for travel—a long-sleeved shirt and cargo pants with lots of pockets. What looked to be a heavy backpack hung from her wide shoulders. She seemed perplexed, standing straight and tapping the toe of her boot on the pavement. "Do we need something from the museum?" she asked.

"We need to dress like those we are sent to help," Joshua said. "Our assignment involves mortals whose life source is blood. Unlike us, they still need the oxygen spacesuits provide to survive."

"I remember those days," Lydia said, smiling. "But don't our new subjects have oxygen on their planet?"

"Back on their planet they did, of course, but just now they are mining an asteroid, with only a scant atmosphere. I'll tell you all I know soon, but right now we need to find the appropriate spacesuits."

"Where are the others in our crew?" Deborah asked.

"They're already on board the *By Grace*," Joshua said. "They'll be landing on the planet Cold Land which has a breathable atmosphere. Their new bodies won't be a cause for suspicion there."

They entered the museum where ancient artifacts of every sort were on display, often staged in a setting appropriate to their time in history. A group of school children filed past an exhibit of war drums and trumpets, led by a docent dressed in clothes from the Old Earth Middle Ages.

Joshua thought he recognized the docent. When she glanced his way, she smiled. "Anna," he called out.

"Mordecai told me to watch for you," Anna said, coming closer. "He is monitoring activity in the Ships of the Seas wing. He wants you to meet him there."

"You are looking very historical," Joshua noted.

"I am dressed as Eleanor of Aquitaine," Anna said, smiling.

Joshua waved at the children as he headed for the Ship's wing of the museum with Lydia and Deborah close behind.

They found Mordecai giving orders to a group of robots pulling up the floorboards of a large hall. Other specialized bots were moving small round willow and animal skin boats from the Stone Age of human history to a holding area within the museum.

"Welcome, Joshua, Lydia and Deborah," Mordecai said. "I received your message and have been researching spacesuits."

"What is happening here?" Deborah asked, looking around at the activity.

"We are installing an underfloor sea that will underlie the whole of the ship's wing. We have brought back many of the extinct sea creatures from Old Earth's early sea life. I thought such a sea, covered in a glass floor, might be helpful to ambassadors sent out to nascent star systems in their assessments of conditions for intelligent life."

"I'm eager to see it myself," Lydia said.

"I know you are pressed for time," Mordecai said, "and I think I may have located what you will need on level 749."

"Thank you, Mordecai. We need to dress in a manner similar to a race of Swagian mortals whose level of technology enables them to fly only as far as their neighboring planet," Joshua said. "They are presently stranded on an asteroid that necessitates the wearing of spacesuits."

The curator nodded. "Of course," he said. "I have located just such a suit. Follow me please."

As they walked into a transparent graphene elevator, they could see through to the elevator shaft where a cinematic program of spectacular proportions played out. A kaleidoscope of galaxies with multicolored nebulae from which stars coalesced before their eyes was projected on the walls surrounding them. They were unaware of motion until they felt their elevator come to a gradual stop.

At floor 749, the three stepped out and followed Mordecai past rows of spacesuits – some armored, some winged, and some bristling with weapons.

Deborah stopped to inspect a suit with a built-in plasma caster gun. She held up the arm that held the plasma gun, saying, "Now this is formidable space suit."

Lydia lingered at the next rack to feel the thin metal feathers of a winged harness. "Look at this one. These wings are works of art." She held the tip of one wing and moved it in a wave motion. The little feathers made a breathy sound like jostled cutlery.

Mordecai coughed politely to draw their attention to a group of suits made in the twenty-first century A.D. on the Old Earth. "These seem appropriate," he said, pointing toward some white padded suits.

"They are called AxEMU or Axiom extravehicular mobility units. They're made with flexible joint inserts for maximum mobility. The headgear has the added benefit of a switch at the neck ring to deactivate the electromagnetic seal and enable easy removal of the helmet. It was first used in the exploration of the southern region of the Old Earth's moon."

Joshua checked the suit from top to bottom, lifting each boot in turn to judge the weight. "Perfect," he said. "You are a learned man, Mordecai. The museum is lucky to have you. Do you need a scan for our measurements?"

"We already have all your measurements on file," Mordecai said.

"Can you have three sent to our ship, level three?" Joshua asked. "We need to leave as soon as possible."

"Certainly," Mordecai said. "Level three, *Jehovah rapha*. The Lord Heals. Anything else I can help you with?"

"No, that should do it," Joshua said.

Mordecai shook hands with Joshua. "God speed to you and your crew."

Lydia and Deborah each gave the museum curator a hug before heading back to the elevator.

"We can always count on Mordecai," Deborah said.

They exited the inertia elevator at level 50 where a bridge crossed to the entrance to the Sky Tube. As they crossed the bridge they looked down at their golden city one last time. Far below, tiny people moved like ants along the sparkling River of Life. The city, 2225 kilometers high, wide and long, was a perfect cube terraced with vines and flowers in bloom. Around the complex stretched the outer wall complete with twelve pearl gates, honoring the twelve tribes of Israel. The ambassadors didn't know how long they would be gone. They lived to serve, but they would miss New Jerusalem every day they were away.

The three walked the short distance to the Sky Tube that would transport them to the top of the exosphere, the highest level of New Jerusalem, where their spaceship waited. The Sky Tube was essentially a vacuum tube with inner pods that traveled at a speed of 25,000 km/hr. As they entered a pod, the surrounding bumpers filled with compressed air and an electromagnetic pulse provided the initial thrust needed to send them streaking skyward. Cool air within the pod was supplied by liquid nitrogen stored below the floor of the pod. They were whisked up soundlessly and friction-free amid a colorful light show.

The *By Grace* gleamed on her landing pad. She had seven levels of torus shaped peridot wheels stacked one above the other at 2.5 meter intervals, each secured independently to a central shaft with large titanium spokes that acted as tunnels radiating out from the central hub. At the lowest level of the shaft, titanium landing gear spread out like spider legs to support the ship when docked. The legs would contract to curve around the central shaft when in flight. The vivid green crystalline wheels turned slowly, each torus dotted with viewing portals on its outer wall. At 76 meters across, with a matching height, the ship weighed in at over 500 tons. Powered by an anti-matter engine, she could reach 116 million km/hr with very small increments of timed thrusts.

Joshua, Lydia and Deborah boarded their ship through the shuttered hatch that spun open at the sound of Joshua's voice. Uriah came out from behind the anti-matter containment unit and nodded at them. He was a tall, muscular man who rarely smiled, but could be counted on to do his job.

"A distant destination, I see from my orders," Uriah said.

"Yes, a far galaxy," Joshua confirmed. "We'll be strapping in on level three. Where are Daniel, Rahab and Jonah?"

"Level seven," Uriah said. "And your space suits are in your lockers on level three. Are we ready to climb?"

"Give us a minute to settle in," Joshua said. "I'll signal you."

Uriah nodded and turned toward the bridge.

Joshua, Deborah and Lydia entered the central shaft and stepped onto the waiting escalade, rising to level three where they stepped off into a spoke tunnel that led to a viewing room. From the observation portal they could look down on the curvature of the new earth. They saw only clouds below that marked the dividing line between the atmosphere and the exosphere. In the distance other platforms held docked spaceships awaiting their own crews to fly to trouble spots throughout the universe. They strapped themselves into large reclining chairs and Joshua nodded at the screen on the arm of his chair. "At your pleasure, Uriah."

"Aye, aye, Commander. Initiating ascent," Uriah announced to the ship at large.

The ship rose slowly, like a helium-filled balloon. It would follow one of millions of God's superhighways, adhering to magnetic lines of space curvature, slipping through worm holes, delving into alternate dimensions that bypassed time and space to shorten their journey, all the while maintaining the slight simulated gravity of the slowly turning wheels.

"Please, don't keep us in suspense any longer," Lydia said. "What is our mission?"

Joshua looked down at the comm link and diary built into the arm of his chair. "We'll be dropped inside asteroid M275JR in the star system Trance of the Sculptor galaxy," he said. "It is currently the residence of a group of miners from the planet Swage."

"They live in the asteroid?" Deborah asked, her curiosity aroused.

"Temporarily," Joshua said. "They have wrapped their asteroid in carbon nano fiber, blasted out an opening large enough to land their shp inside and are now mining it from the inside out."

"Quite advanced in their technology then," Lydia noted.

"Yes, industrially developed," Joshua said. "Unfortunately, while en route to their asteroid, they watched their home planet Swage burn up in a gigantic solar storm."

Lydia's hands flew to her face. "How horrible," she cried. "They have no home to return to. Are we sent to rescue them?"

"No," Joshua said. "There is a neighboring planet which they call Bando, though the residents of that planet call it Cold Land. These Swagian survivors hope to travel to Bando and carve out a place for themselves, though they know the Bando residents will attempt to kill any aliens that set foot on their planet. They plan to safeguard their new homestead with their superior technology—they will use force if necessary."

"How many live on this planet Bando?" Deborah asked.

"About fifteen million. They call themselves Cold Land clansmen. They are shepherds who follow their herds. The planet is only warm enough to support grasslands around its equator. Its upright axis means no seasons. The grasslands are held by clans in great equatorial squares that circle the globe – each 200 kilometer-wide square belongs to one clan. The creatures they herd, skallon, provide most of their needs: food, clothing and tools. They migrate from one corner to another, following their herds. Each clan guards their square of land fiercely and is unfriendly with neighboring clans."

"Do these miners hope to take over pasturelands and become shepherds?" Lydia asked.

"Doubtful," Joshua replied. "But the remainder of the planet is covered with ice and snow year-round. Very different from their lost tropical planet, Swage."

"I can see we will need to find some areas of potential compromise," Deborah said. "Is there a way no one loses?"

"Yes, I believe there may be, but it is up to us to figure out what that is," Joshua said. "And, there is also a possibility everyone will lose."

"Why is that?" Lydia asked.

"The asteroid the miners are riding will soon swing by very close to Bando. It will fly over the top of an ice-covered sea south of the grasslands and tidal forces on Bando could cause a break-up of the asteroid over the sea. A resulting tsunami would flood four clans and their pasturelands. It will mean the death of both the people and livestock in its path."

"How much time do we have?" Deborah asked.

"Based on the speed and orbit of the asteroid and our own projected travel time, we should have approximately four Cold Land days and nights, once we arrive," Joshua replied.

"Not much leeway," Deborah said.

Joshua nodded, staring at the backpack she held on her lap. "What's in the backpack?" he asked.

Deborah smiled. "A talking Book and the specifications for building translators. They arrived just this morning. God evidently cares very much about these people we are sent to help."

"I have the same feeling," Joshua said. "I'm eager to meet the stranded miners."

Chapter 2

Daco

Daco looked up with weary but loving eyes at his ship, *Bonanza*. It wasn't a beautiful ship, but a utilitarian one serving its purpose as a home away from home for the thirty-four miners on board. It was three stories high, hill-shaped with a cargo hold 30 meters wide at the bottom, galley dining and sleeping in the middle and navigation on top. On the port side was a top to bottom shaft with a service elevator on one side and empty space on the other. There was a ladder affixed to the port side wall. The shaft could accommodate floating, jumping or climbing from one level to another depending on the gravity situation of their landing site.

Swagian astronauts had learned two centuries ago that asteroids were usually slammed-together rocks and accretions of rocks on collision courses in space. That being the case, they were fairly easy to break apart with rockets. But that was not what miners wanted. They needed to mine the large asteroids. So the *Bonanza* carried both rockets to blow holes large enough to allow entry of the ship into the center of the asteroid and carbon nanofiber wraps to hold the rock accretions together from the outside. A final tug of the wrap would generally send the asteroid spinning and supply enough gravity to land their ships inside the asteroids. If this trick didn't work, they relied on corkscrew anchors to drill down and hold them in place. Adhering to the asteroid had the added benefit of providing a fuel-free ride through space inside the amassed rocks while they mined the ores they took from it to be sold back on their home planet, Swage. But now, of course, there was no Swage. Their planet had been swallowed up in a solar flare.

Daco sighed and walked on to the hatch of the cargo hold. He pressed his palm flat on the sensor beside the air lock to activate the hatch. The light on the pad changed from red to green as the door slid open with a raspy grinding sound. He stepped inside and waited again as the outer door closed and a mixture of oxygen and nitrogen filled the airlock. The inner door lifted and Daco turned left into the cargo bay.

As his eyes adjusted to the dim light of the hold, he pulled off his environmental suit and his mag boots. The spin they had given the asteroid after wrapping it provided just enough momentum to allow the feeling of light gravity within the ship, making the mag boots an unnecessary precaution while inside. He emptied his pockets of his newly found items: a few chunks of high-grade iron ore, some magnesium scrapings and carbon dust that could be smelted down together to craft the outer shells of plasma grenades.

He headed for the darkest area of the hold where he was growing edible moss and fungi. A wave of elation passed through his chest when he saw that some of his fungi were popping out of the mulch he had fertilized with processed human waste. With a little luck, they would not starve before they were close enough to the planet Bando to attempt the jump.

His group of miners was all that was left of the planet Swage. It hurt too much to think of his beautiful warm planet and all those millions vanished in one angry outburst of flame from their star mother. He thought instead of his son, just twelve years old, who had come along on this trip, his first mission as an apprentice miner. His precious son, Aldo, who had escaped the fiery death of his homeland. Daco had been Aldo's only parent for three years since his wife had died of a fever. At least she had been spared the end that had taken everyone on the planet. Aldo was his life now – the person that made it worth hanging on in this cold asteroid wasteland.

Daco harvested a section of moss and left the fungi to mature. They still had food left in storage, but precious little. It was time to call a meeting of the miners. They would need to decide on a date to make the jump and plan their move to Bando. They would likely have to fight for their right to settle there.

Daco heard the airlock grinding into action and waited to see who was returning to the ship. It was his brother, Bran, who came through, shivering. Bran was a big man who looked very much like Daco – blue-black skin, a tall slender body, a prominent nose that jutted out from his forehead and a short fringe of dark hair atop his head. Daco smiled and reached out to cuff his brother on the shoulder.

"Bran, what news?"

Bran shrugged and lowered the two buckets of ice he carried to the floor of the cargo hold. "It is freezing out there and ugly to boot, though that is hardly news. I don't suppose it will be any less freezing on Bando should we by some miracle make it there."

Daco smiled even though there was little to smile about. It was true. Bando was a planet of ice and snow where the primitive pale-skinned population followed herds of bovines called skallon and tribes protected their grazing lands with all the fierceness their sticks and stones provided. Other Swage miners had landed on Bando just long enough to load up on the abundant supply of copper ore, but not long enough for the fierce hairy people of Bando to catch them in the act.

Swage had been the planet orbiting closest to its star, a tropical paradise full of jungles, quiet pools, colorful plants and animals of every sort. Daco searched his mind for something less painful than the loss of his home to think about. "I believe we are close enough now to decide on a day," he said softly. "If we wait too long we will be weak with hunger. Of course, if we jump too soon, we will not have the fuel to make it all the way."

Bran nodded. "I have been thinking the same thoughts. We can meet tonight after our meal." His eyes searched the dark cargo hold. "Has Aldo returned?"

"No." Daco felt his shoulders tightening. "Wasn't he with you?"

"Yes, he filled his two buckets with ice quickly and asked if he could go to look more closely at a cave with limestone pillars we had passed this morning. I gave him permission and told him to look only from the outside of the cave, to return to the ship afterwards and to bring his buckets with him."

"So you left before he did?" Daco asked, worry creeping into his voice.

"Yes, but I stopped on the way back to look at an area that showed traces of copper on an outcropping."

Just as Daco became concerned, he heard the hiss of air as the airlock filled. When the inner door lifted he let out the breath he had been holding. There stood Aldo with a bucket in each hand and dark eyes that danced with excitement.

"There are visitors on our asteroid," Aldo said.

"What?" Daco grabbed the two buckets from his son's hands and set them down so he could pull his son into his arms. His son had his mother's beautiful smile, but his father's height and prominent nose. He was already nearly two meters tall. "What kind of visitors?"

"People, I think, though it's hard to say. They had on some manner of suits that covered their heads and bodies, but different from our suits and breathers."

"What were they doing? Could you tell?" Bran asked.

"They seemed to just be wandering around, looking at things," Aldo said.

"Did they see you?" Daco asked.

"I don't think so. They weren't looking in my direction."

Daco and Bran shared a glance that was part apprehension and part curiosity.

"How far from our ship were they?" Bran asked.

"As far as the limestone cave. I could look out and see them but I don't think they saw me."

"You weren't supposed to enter the cave," Bran said.

"I only went as far as the first pillar." Aldo looked down at his feet.

"Should we go to check them out or wait for the others?" Bran asked.

"How many were there?" Daco asked his son.

"Three of them."

"Do you think they were armed?" Bran asked.

Aldo shrugged. "Hard to tell. They weren't carrying any weapons in their hands. If they had them, they were hidden inside their suits."

"Were the suits very different from ours?" Daco persisted.

"I don't know. It could have been material we haven't seen before. At least it was new to me. It was white and a little puffy."

"I think we should go have a look," Bran said.

Daco sucked in a deep breath, thinking. "Let's wait until a few more return from the ice deposits. Someone must have seen something. They had to have a ship to get here. I don't want to leave Aldo here alone. I'll pick three others to go with me."

"I should go with you," Aldo said. "I can show you where I saw them."

Daco shook his head slowly. "I know where the limestone cave is. You've done well to tell us all of this. But now I need you to stay behind with your uncle."

An unspoken acknowledgment passed between the two brothers. If Daco should fail to return, Bran would assume the role of father to Aldo.

Daco moved to the area of the cargo hold where their weapons were stored. He pulled a laser gun, a blaster and two plasma grenades from the rack before turning at the sound of the airlock door lifting.

Tull and Dray entered the cargo hold with four ice-filled buckets between them. They were heads of a family of miners that Daco had known all his life. Their grown son and daughter, Onri and Mica, also worked with them sometimes, and luckily, were aboard for this expedition.

Tull smiled and raised his hands in the air, still holding the buckets. "No need for weapons," he teased. "Only ice in the buckets."

Daco tried to relax. "It seems we have uninvited guests on our asteroid. Aldo saw them out by the limestone cave. I thought I should go out and introduce myself."

"How is that possible?" Dray asked, her expression turning concerned. "We saw no ship land."

"I believe I will go along with you," Tull said, setting down his pails of ice.

"As shall I," Dray insisted.

Tull shrugged. "Best pull down a few more of those grenades."

Chapter 3

Daco

Daco, Tull and Tull's wife Dray returned late that night, but all aboard the spacecraft were still awake and alert. They had delayed their evening meal and were in the act of forming a rescue mission when they heard the airlock outside the ship began to cycle.

As soon as Daco walked through the airlock his brother pulled him into a crushing embrace. Daco shook his head as he absorbed the warmth of his brother's hug. "We couldn't find them."

This was not implausible. Their asteroid was large, over 300 kilometers in diameter with many craters and caves. It even had a very thin atmosphere of its own.

"Perhaps they've left on the same ship that brought them here?" Bran offered.

"Perhaps," Daco agreed. "Much as I feared the threat their presence represented, I now feel the loss of what might have been an opportunity. We know we're not alone in the universe – the Bando people prove that – but these visitors? How did they get here? Where have they come from? We know they're not from Swage."

Daco waited a moment for the lump in his throat to subside. Speaking the name of his lost planet threatened to send him down a well of despair he would be unable to climb out of.

"Maybe. We don't know that for sure," Dray said. "Is it possible another group from Swage was off planet at the time of the star flare?"

Murmurs of hope surged through the group of assembled miners.

The whispers stopped abruptly at the sound of an intruder alert going off on the ship's alarm system. Daco turned on the camera that showed the area directly outside the ship's lower hatch. Three people in spacesuits waved at the lens of the camera.

"Could they be other survivors from Swage? Is it possible?" Tull asked.

"Only one way to find out," Bran said.

Daco secured his laser gun in its chest holder before putting a restraining hand on his brother's shoulder. "Don't open the air lock just yet. I'll go up the tophatch and come around behind them. If I give the signal, you may open the lock."

After donning his breather and mag boots, Daco climbed up to the hatch at the top of the ship and pushed it open, knowing there would be no sound that carried to the newcomers since there was not enough atmosphere to carry sound. He slid down the curve of the ship to the small platform above the hand holds lining the ship's port side.

When he reached the ground he stepped carefully through the icy slush, circling wide behind the visitors.

He threw a pebble at the tallest of the three that bounced off the person's helmet. All three turned around and Daco motioned with his drawn gun that they should put their hands in the air.

Three sets of hands dropped baskets they were holding and rose quickly. Daco dared to hope they were brethren, though they wore suits unfamiliar to him, just as Aldo had said.

"Are you Swagian?" Daco asked, coming near enough to touch his helmet to the tall one's helmet to carry the sound of his voice. .

"No, but we come in peace," a deep voice replied.

"Who are you and why are you here?" Daco asked.

"We are passersby who noticed your ship," the voice said.

"You speak Swagian?"

"We speak all tongues."

Daco took a moment to consider and then signaled to the camera above the hatch, moving his fist in an upward curve.

A moment later the inner door to the cargo hold opened to allow three people wearing unfamiliar spacesuits and holding baskets of orange items to enter. Daco followed close behind with his hand held lightly over his holstered gun.

"I hope I don't appear rude," Daco said, "seeing as you have come apparently bearing gifts – but you have not as yet told me where you come from."

"We come from a distant galaxy on a spacecraft of a different design, and we come to be of service," the voice of a woman answered.

"How is it you speak our language?" Tull asked. His tone mirrored his astonishment. "Even the Bandos, our neighbors, don't share our speech."

"We wear translators," the male voice said. "They pick up your brain waves and translate your thoughts and speech into our ears and automatically translate our responses into your speech."

"What a wonder," Aldo said, amid similar outbursts from all the assembled miners.

"Will you join us for a meal?" Daco asked.

"We would be delighted," a second woman's voice replied.

The assemblage jumped or climbed up, a few at a time, to the galley level where they crowded together on benches and chairs around a very large oval table.

Bowls of moss together with their precious dwindling stores brought from Swage and the gift baskets of fruit soon covered the table.

"Please help yourselves, everyone. We finally have something to celebrate," Daco said. "We are, perhaps, too many to introduce ourselves one by one but I will make a start. I am Daco, leader of this mining troupe. Bran beside me is my brother and Aldo is my son. My wife Fila passed away from fever before we, ahh..." A tense pause ensued before Daco was able to continue. "Before we all became homeless."

"I am Deborah," said the woman wearing a backpack, "and with me are Joshua and Lydia. We are on a mission of discovery and thankfully, still have a home to return to. We are truly sorry for your loss. You mentioned you have neighbors? A nearby planet perhaps?"

"Yes, we have neighbors," Daco affirmed, "but they are primitive, warring tribes. They speak a multitude of tongues, superstitious people with no knowledge of our former home, Swage. We have always left them alone; their planet Bando is a very cold world, dissimilar to the warm jungles of Swage."

"But now, surely, you will want to ask their permission to settle there," Deborah said.

Daco supposed his actual plan of taking a piece of the planet by whatever means necessary would seem unjust to these newcomers and he wondered if they could hear these thoughts amid his brain waves. "They are not a people who would welcome strangers from another world."

"Perhaps they would," Lydia said in a soft voice. "Perhap if you offered a school whereby they could learn your advanced technology and improve their own lives..." Her voice trailed off.

Daco shook his head. "I doubt they would be receptive." He smiled at the newcomers, wishing they would remove their suits, at least from their faces. "We, however, are of a different mind. We would welcome any instruction you would care to give us in your own technology – especially in the area of those translators that have made us instantly like-minded."

Joshua laughed. "That could possibly be arranged. He removed his faceplate to reveal a light brown complexion and a face different but not totally unlike their own. Joshua had facial hair – a trimmed beard and eyebrows as well as a dark mat of hair atop his head. He looked to be about thirty years old. Daco saw no gill slits in Joshua's neck and wondered if these new people were confined to life outside the water.

Joshua picked up a fruit from the basket he had brought. "This is from our homeland. You may want to take a small bite at first, to see if it agrees with you. I will take the first bite to show that we speak truth when we say we come in peace." He bit into the fruit that looked similar to those that grew in the jungles of Swage. The fruit had a thin dull orange skin on the outside with a bright orange interior that dripped juice. It was about the size of a fist.

Daco reached for a fruit from the same basket. He took a tentative small bite and a smile spread across his face. "This is the most delicious thing I have ever eaten."

Soon everyone was reaching for fruit from the baskets. Fruit even better than that which grew on Swage. How was such a thing possible?

"I don't suppose it would be possible for us to return with you to your world beyond our galaxy?" Daco asked.

"Our mission is not authorized to grant us that freedom," Joshua said with a touch of sadness. "But I believe we might offer you the technology involved in producing the translators. It is a thing you might have developed on your own, had you put your minds to it."

Joshua popped one from his ear and handed it to Daco.

As soon as Daco put it in his ear, he was aware of thoughts all around him. He was so overwhelmed he almost removed it. But he stopped himself long enough to at least test it. He cleared his throat as he looked around the table and said, "These other bowls on the table hold moss and fungi we have managed to grow here in the dark spaces of the ship's cargo bay." He was amazed to hear his own voice speaking in a foreign language.

The guests nodded and the two women removed their faceplates to reveal tan-colored faces with eyebrows and long brown hair cascading from the tops of their heads down to their shoulders. One wore small gold hoops hanging from her ears. All three took bits of moss into their mouths, chewing thoughtfully.

Daco removed the earpiece and a new idea took shape in his mind. Perhaps these foreigners were right – if he could speak the language of the Bandos they might hope to strike a peaceful agreement. Could they trade access to their higher technology for a place to settle on Bando?

Daco noticed the visitors did not take a second helping of moss and he sighed, wondering what their homeland must be like.

Chapter 4

Daco

Daco, Bran and Aldo gave up their beds that night to their visitors. They slept together on the floor of the cargo hold, making a comfortable nest of spare blankets and warm clothing.

Though it was late according to their Swage internal clocks, they stayed awake for some time going over the day's surprising events.

Daco spoke into the darkness, "Do you think the visitors might be correct in thinking we could avoid violence and come to an agreement with one of the Bando tribes?" He could sense Bran's tension through the quilts that separated them.

"They don't know the Bandos as we do. Other Swage miners have attempted in the past to trade with them. Those overtures were always met with threats and violence. They tried to set fire to our spaceships," Bran said.

"Certainly that has always been the case," Daco said, "but we had no way of telling them why we had come. These translators could make a difference. Joshua has agreed to help me make one to use as a prototype for manufacturing more."

"I am not sure people who cannot live peacefully with others of their own species can be trusted to keep the peace with those from another planet," Bran said.

"What do the Bandos look like?" Aldo asked. "Have you ever seen one?"

"No," his father admitted. "I have only heard stories that warned me against going there. The Bando people are white skinned and dress in the furs of the skallon they herd. They have lots of blonde hair all over their faces and bodies, especially the men. The women sometimes weave their hair into elaborate patterns. Grassland on the planet is limited to equatorial regions. Most of their land is covered with white flakes of snow piled up into hillocks. Each tribe guards their wide green pastureland from other tribes who would like to steal it and increase their own herds."

"If we showed no interest in having their grasslands, perhaps they wouldn't fear us," Aldo said.

Bran laughed. "Leave it to children to sniff out a truth."

"Yes, thank you, Aldo," Daco said. "It's an important observation and one worth stating at the onset. I believe with the help of the translators we have some hope of doing just that. And now we must sleep to have clear heads for beginning a new trade tomorrow—learning how to manufacture those amazing translators."

Daco could feel Aldo nestling closer into the blankets beside him.

The next morning all the miners made quick work of the remaining fruit the visitors had brought. They lingered at the table over tea to see what new revelations might come from the mouths of the foreigners.

"I should like a tour of the ship if such a thing is allowed," Deborah said.

Dray spoke up. "It would be my honor to guide you. Perhaps my husband Tull, our son Onri and our daughter Mica should come along. Tull is our specialist on fusion core engineering. He could explain that part of the ship much better than I."

Tull chuckled. "Onri is as much a specialist as I am. But thank you for the compliment."

Onri shrugged. "I had thought to stay and learn more about the manufacture of translators, but I will certainly go if I'm needed."

"Don't go," Daco said, putting his hand on Onri's shoulder. "I am likely out of my depth when it comes to this advanced technology. If only we had some of our elite team from Swage aboard."

"Onri could have been one of the elite," Tull boasted. "It is only love of family that kept him with us. Both our children are adults now, but both have chosen to be miners."

Onri blushed. "Now you give our visitors false hope about my capabilities. It is only interest, not gifts, which plead my case."

"All the same, I want you here," Daco said. "You have a younger mind, more capable of retention."

"Then let's begin," Joshua said. "Might we use this table to lay out the specifications?"

The other miners thanked the visitors for the breakfast fruits and lingered only long enough to ask if there were any metals those building translators might need them to find on the asteroid.

"Be on the lookout for platinum and gold," Joshua said.

A few giggles and murmurs erupted from the assembly. "Of course it would be the very scarce ones that are needed," one miner grumbled as he left the table.

Joshua spread out a handful of printed specifications on the table. Onri immediately leaned over the diagrams, taking pictures with his wrist diary's camera. "Some of these miniatures resemble tiny tuning forks," he said.

"Yes, a similar resonance tool to scan brain waves," Joshua said, smiling his approval. "I can see you have some knowledge of sound transfer."

"I have always been interested in resonance. I used to play a stringed instrument back on Swage."

"That interest will serve you well here," Joshua said.

"I should enjoy hearing you play your instrument," Lydia said.

Onri smiled. "I would be happy to play for you. Several of us play instruments. Perhaps tonight after our meal?"

"Wonderful," Lydia said.

"Now we begin," Joshua said. "I can see from your ship that you are familiar with the making of acrylics."

"Yes, we had many deposits of crude oil and tar back on Swage and learned to make synthetics such as acrylic and polyethylene from them long ago," Daco said. "I don't know if such deposits exist on Bando."

"If your solar system is old enough for such deposits on one planet, any others with ancient life likely have them as well," Lydia said. "But you must use them wisely lest you run out. They may be deeply buried."

"Your knowledge of all things past and present overwhelms me," Daco said. "I wish we had something to offer here that might tempt you to stay and teach us just as you advise us to communicate what we have learned to the Bandos."

"All things in their time," Lydia said. "Do your people have things or ideas they hold sacred?"

"Not things so much as people. We all value our families most and we remember to honor our ancestors in stories and songs," Daco said.

"And how do you view death?" Lydia asked.

"We believe our spirits live on in the spirit world with the spirits of our ancestors."

"And to whom do you credit the creation of all things seen and unseen?" Lydia asked, seemingly fixated on this topic rather than the building of a prototype translator

Daco looked at his brother to see if he might have an answer.

"We don't know," Bran said. "Perhaps all things have spirits and can move from spirit to its physical representation when convenient or necessary. Rather like the difference between these diagrams of translators and the physical product after manufacture."

Lydia nodded. "A most interesting view. However, we will leave you a diagram of another possibility before we take our leave." She paused and pulled forward a schematic. "And now to the business at hand. We will begin with the hard wiring."

Chapter 5

Daco

That evening, the thirty-four miners and their three visitors assembled once again around the big oval table. Daco stood up holding the translator they had fabricated during the day. "We had to take part of the handle of a small knife for the acrylic body," he said. "The gold comes from one of my wife's nose rings and the platinum from her wrist diary. She would be happy to know we put her things to good use were she still among us."

"True, true," a few of the miners said, holding up their glasses of ice water.

"I will pass it around so that each of you might witness this marvel of technology," Daco continued. "As soon as we are established on Bando, we will begin mass production. I feel certain the people of Bando will pay to be able to understand their neighboring tribes whom they currently view as enemies."

As each miner placed the translator in an ear and spoke a few words, each smiled to hear his or her own voice speaking a foreign language.

"Any reports from the field?" Daco asked.

A miner named Pheebs stood up. "We found lithium on the star-facing interior of the asteroid," he said.

"Excellent," Daco said. "Were you able to harvest the bulk of it?"

"Yes," Pheebs said. "But we didn't use explosives. That fissure we noticed near our entrance hole is getting larger."

"Good thinking," Daco said. "We don't want to cause a break-up."

Deborah spoke up. "I noticed on my tour of the ship today that your energy source is internal confinement fusion burning pellets made of helium and hydrogen isotopes."

"Of course," Daco said. "Are you suggesting that there are other better alternatives?"

Deborah smiled. "I am not here to judge what is best for you, only to observe and serve. We may know of other alternatives but, everything in its time. And for now you have what you need to fuel your reactor."

Daco decided that he would have to be content with that answer, but how he wished he could gain access to the vast store of knowledge these space travelers seemed to hold. As the translator returned to him from its journey around the table, he considered fitting it to his ear in hopes of reading the minds of his visitors. Just as quickly, Deborah stared at him and shook her head – she had likely been reading his thoughts. He pocketed the translator.

"After dinner we will entertain our visitors with an evening of music," Daco said. "I hope all of you who play will bring out your instruments and join in. Now, eat what is before you and hope for better days to come."

They dug into the moss, fungi and dried food before them as hope settled all around.

That evening Onri and his sister Mica played their stringed instruments as others joined in with horns and drums. The music brought memories of warm waters ringed with vibrantly colored flowers. Rushing waterfalls and shady trees lived in their memories. Some imagined the silence before dawn as their star rose like a flaming red ball in a violet sky. The same mother star that had turned on her children.

As the miners began to yawn, sleepy but reluctant to call an end to such a cozy evening, Deborah stood up. "We have a gift for you." She reached down below the bench she sat on and brought up a wooden box. Opening the lid, she pulled out a heavy book – a thing the miners had seen only in museums on their home planet.

Deborah placed the book on the table. "This is a history of our God's chosen people, filled with prophecies that are fulfilled in the second section of the book. If you study the book carefully, certain truths will eventually be revealed. Truths that will set you free. As you will see, the book is written in an ancient language but as I run my fingers over the words…" Deborah traced her fingers over a few words in the book and a deep voice came from the book speaking in an ancient language.

"That is the voice of the Jewish ancestors," Deborah said. "But as each of you runs your fingers over the words, the book will speak to you in your own language."

Deborah slid the book from her place at the table over to Daco who sat next to her. "Would you care to give it a try?"

"I very much would," Daco said. He turned to the first page and slowly drew his finger across the words at the top of the page.

"In the beginning God created the heavens and the earth. Now the earth was formless and empty, darkness was over the surface of the deep, and the Spirit of God was hovering over the waters."

Daco lifted his finger from the page and stared wide-eyed at Deborah "How is such a marvel possible?"

Deborah smiled. "It is quite marvelous, isn't it? You must handle it with care. In time you will have scholars who will want to learn the original language and others who will want to teach the content of the book. There are lessons to be learned from the failings of the Jewish nation and the possibility of redemption for all. There are secrets revealed. This book will tell you much about us and by extension – much about yourselves."

"This is a gift we cannot hope to match," Daco said. "In fact, we have little to offer."

"Your gratitude is a gift to us," Deborah said. "You will be very busy establishing yourselves into a new life on Bando. But in time you will turn to this book and try to unearth its secrets. In doing so, you will learn a great deal. And I hope you will remember us in all our frailty – with fondness."

"But you speak as though you are saying farewell," Daco said. "Surely it is not yet time to take your leave. Couldn't you follow us to Bando? Perhaps speak to them as you have to us?"

"You are correct," Joshua said. "We are saying farewell. Our ship waits. But there are others of us even now who are looking into affairs on Bando. Our friends will do their best to lay the groundwork that will create an opening of sorts for all of you when you reach Bando."

"We can never hope to thank you enough for all you have done, nor do we know why you have concerned yourselves with our situation," Daco said. "Is there a reason for your concern?"

"Yes," Deborah said, "there must certainly be a reason, but we, like you, do not know what that reason is. We only go where we are sent."

With those enigmatic words, the three visitors stood and took their leave.

"May God look with favor on you all," Lydia said as they climbed down the ladder to leave by the door of the cargo bay.

Daco followed them out the hatch, hoping to see their ship before they boarded, but the three suddenly disappeared and he caught only a fleeting glimpse of a ship of seven light green turning wheels glowing in the sky before it, too, vanished.

After their guests' departure, the miners looked at one another in wonder.

"What have we just stood witness to?" Bran asked his brother.

"I don't know," Daco said, but in days to come we will look to one another for confirmation. We will ask, *did we really see and hear what we thought we did*? And we will affirm it, one to another."

Daco carefully placed the book back in its box and knocked his kuckles atop the table to make sure he had everyone's attention.

"Bran and I have counted the remaining stores of food. We have also checked the orbits of Bando and our asteroid. In three days' time we will be out of food, but those same three days should bring us close enough to Bando to make the jump."

"Three days," Tull shouted, raising his fist in the air.

"Three days." The remaining miners took up the chant.

Chapter 6

Jhar

Jhar plodded through a snow bank trying to reach the place where one large rock sat atop another, appearing to be precariously balanced but in fact, set firmly together. She had been gathering mong leaves in the pasture, and left her work at dusk to keep this meeting at the boundary marker between Jangle and Sylvan land.

"Dunk, are you there?" She spoke softly into the biting wind, hoping her words would carry, but only as far as her friend's ears.

She felt a gentle tap on her shoulder and whirled around to look into the smiling face of her friend Dunk.

"Where did you come from? You should be coming from the Sylvan direction."

"I came across your tracks in the snow. I've been following you since our red star settled below the horizon."

"You might have saved me some time wallowing through the snow." Jhar tried for an angry face but couldn't manage it. She was too happy to see her friend.

Dunk continued to smile and smoothed her hair. He seemed to be infatuated with her long white-blonde tresses. "I wanted to surprise you."

"As long as it is only me you surprise. One of these days someone will see us together and our friendship will melt like the snow when our star shines through the clouds."

"I will always be your friend," Dunk said solemnly.

"Our tribes are sworn enemies. The leaders wouldn't allow it. You know that."

"I know it but I don't accept it," Dunk said.

Jhar let out a deeply held sigh. "What news have you?"

Dunk put his hands up with his fingers's splayed out – his defensive gesture. "Don't blame me, but one of our clan saw your cousin Grum move a boundary marker from your pasture to ours. He increased the size of your pasture by at least two shanks."

Jhar wanted to protest, but moving a marker sounded like something her cousin might do. "Who saw him do it?" Jhar asked.

"What does it matter?" Dunk said with a shrug.

"It doesn't, but it matters that you don't want to tell me who it was," Jhar said.

Dunk closed his eyes for a moment. "All right. It was our leader's son. He doesn't know you and I are friends. If he had told me first I would have made him keep it a secret, but he told his father, Romm. Now Romm is planning a reprisal raid on your clan."

Jhar kicked a stone out of the slush where she stood. "Will he try to kill Grum?"

"Yes," Dunk said. He pulled his purple cap down over his ears. His light blue eyes reflected his concern. "They plan to come at night with weapons to find him."

"Tonight?" Jhar asked.

"No, tomorrow. I shouldn't tell you. My father was one chosen for the raid. Now you will warn your clan and my father might be killed."

Jhar shook her head. "I don't know what to do. If I tell my family they will hide Grum and be ready with their own weapons. I don't want you to lose your father but I don't want Grum's family to be defenseless when the attack comes." She yanked at her hair. "Why must we live like this?"

"I don't know," Dunk said. "Your cousin is an idiot."

"I know," Jhar said. "But should he die for being an idiot?"

Dunk shrugged. "People have died for less."

"Could you try to dissuade them? Ask for a trade item instead? I have a bag full of the scrapes you use to make your purple dye." She looked at her friend with hopeful eyes.

"I could ask, but you know how serious an offense it is to move a boundary marker."

Jhar nodded. "I do."

They both knew a decrease in the area of pasture squares meant smaller herds in an already minimal patch. The skallon provided their meat, their weapons, their clothing, the tools made from their horns and bones. Already their herds were barely able to provide for all the members of individual clans.

"What would you do if our places were reversed? Would you warn your family?" Jhar asked.

"I don't know what I would do, so I know how you are feeling. I promise whatever decision you make, I will still be your friend. Always and forever," Dunk said.

"I will throw the stones," she said. "That way I can blame fate."

The stones were any three flat rocks they could hold in their hands. On one side a mark was made. They threw the stones in the air when they wanted the fates to make a decision. If two or more fell with the marked side up, the answer was no. If two or more fell with the unmarked side up the answer was yes.

"Shall I find some stones?" Dunk asked.

"No, I have some in our dugout. I'll throw them when I return home. It's better you don't know how they fall. That way you won't be tempted to tell your clan."

"I could tell them I warned you," Dunk said.

"But you won't. Because you don't know if I will pass on that warning and neither do I. We'll both leave it to the fates to decide. It's better that way."

"But will you promise me that you will be nowhere near Grum tomorrow night, no matter how the stones fall?" Dunk asked.

"I don't want to be a coward," Jhar said.

"Nor do I," Dunk said. "But I promise I won't be one of the raiders. Can't you do as much for me?"

Jhar nodded, "Yes, I see your reasoning. I will do as you ask this one time."

"It is enough," Dunk said, cupping her face with his large hand. "And we will meet here at the same time two days from now, no matter what happens? No matter who dies?"

"Yes," Jhar said in a resolute tone. "No matter the outcome." She turned to walk back to her pasture before she could change her mind.

Jhar reached her family dugout in twilight. She found her mother outside the dugout cooking a skallon pelt in melt water studded with a few copper chips to make green dye. Green was the color of her clan. They wore green skallon-hair capes and green caps. Dunk's clan wore purple, but the scrapes used to make the purple dye were not plentiful. They clung tightly to the tops of rocks in a few places. She wondered if Dunk might try to argue for a trade item rather than a reprisal raid.

"Do you want my help with the dye?" Jhar asked her mother.

"No, but you can start our meal. "Cut up some meat. I see you have gathered mong leaves we can wrap around the meat. The coals inside the fire ring should still be hot."

Jhar walked down into the cave they called home. It had been dug deep enough to allow a man to stand upright. The walls held holes for mong leaf torches. Inside, a large communal fire pit for dining was vented overhead with a small hole to let out the smoke. Off to the sides each member of the family had a sleeping alcove.

Taking up a skallon bone knife, she cut the meat in small enough pieces that even the youngest in her family could eat them. Her older sister Gem should be returning with the little ones soon. They had been out collecting dried skallon dung for fuel to burn during the freezing night.

When she finished with the meat and wrapped it in mong leaves to set on the hot coals, she went to her cot made of skallon hides. Under the cot was the skallon's skull that held the three stones.

Jhar closed her eyes and held the marked stones in front of her at arm's length. She jumbled them up and sent them flying. Once they had landed she took a deep breath before looking at the result. All three stones landed with the mark up. The answer was no. She would not tell anyone what Dunk had told her. No warning for Grum or his family. Could she live with that decision? She decided she must. Anyway, it was not her decision. The fates had decided for her.

Chapter 7

Joshua

As Joshua, Deborah and Lydia walked toward the opening of the hole the miners had blasted into the asteroid, Joshua spoke into his wrist diary. "Prepare for tractor beam evacuation. Ready here for line of sight activation."

They all looked up at the sky searching for their ship. Suddenly a green glow was visible above them. "There it is," Lydia said, pointing up at the night sky.

Deborah triggered the light on her wrist diary and shined it skyward.

"Prepare for tractor beam extraction," Uriah's deep voice rumbled out from Joshua's wrist diary microphone.

Joshua put his right arm around Lydia's shoulders and his left arm around Deborah's, pulling them close to his body. "Ready for extraction," he said.

The three were suddenly enveloped in a beam of blue light that both lifted and destructured their atoms to neutrinos small enough to fly through the walls of their ship.

They materialized on the sixth deck of the *By Grace* and found Daniel, Rahab and Jonah waiting for them.

"Welcome home," Daniel said.

They all hugged one another and finally settled down on the comfortable couches to drink tea and eat toast with honey.

"Tell us everything," Rahab said. "Are the miners good people?"

"Yes," Lydia said. "In spite of the terrible loss of their planet, they are trying to carry on."

"Their leader, Daco, was prepared to go in, laser guns at the ready," Joshua said, "but he saw right away that the translators could provide an alternative."

"And they have one savant among them," Deborah added. "His name is Onri. He understood immediately that the ability to digitize a brain held more possibilities than understanding one another's languages."

"Where are they on the ladder of technology?" Jonah asked.

"At the lower range of stage one," Deborah replied. "They have pellet fusion and are advanced in laser use, but seem to have stagnated there. Probably life on Swage was easy. Swage must have been a beautiful place to live – tropical in climate with abundant water and resources."

"Bando will challenge them," Rahab said. "It is cold and forbidding by all accounts."

"Yes," Joshua said. "And the people there are hardened by the conditions."

"Our primary focus is a young woman," Rahab said. "She is not a leader, in fact, she is a rule breaker. Much like myself."

Joshua smiled. "Do you have a plan for approaching her?"

"A broad plan," Rahab said. "Jonah and Daniel think it best that I try to befriend her. They don't want to scare her away. I think they don't need to worry. I have a feeling she is not easily frightened."

Lydia smiled. "Like you," she remarked.

"Yes," Rahab agreed. "I have a feeling we could become good friends."

"So, are these Bando people rigid in their rules?" Joshua asked.

"Extremely rigid," Daniel answered. "Their rules, like our ancient laws and traditions, serve only to highlight their shortcomings. And we should stop calling them Bandos. That is what the Swage people named them. They call themselves Cold Land people."

"What rule has this young woman broken?" Lydia asked.

"She has a friend in a neighboring clan," Rahab said.

"And that is not allowed?" Deborah asked.

"Certainly not," Jonah said. "Everyone outside their clan is viewed as an enemy. The pastureland on Cold Land is divided up by clans that circle the globe. Each clan has enough grassland to feed their herds, but no more. And their herds of skallon provide for all their needs – food, clothes, tools, blankets. They weave torches and baskets from the various grasses that grow in their pastures and eat the leaves of the mong plants that flourish there."

"The skallon they herd are fearsome animals," Rahab said. "They are bigger then the moose of our planet and quite fierce. They are coveed in thick brown hair with long beards and huge twisting horns. It is only because the Cold Land people are with them every day from birth to death that they do not attack them."

"It sounds as though you have all done your homework," Joshua said. "We will be landing there soon, I think."

"We plan to stay out of your way," Deborah said. "Our part is finished. We have laid the groundwork for a peaceful transition on the side of the miners. I believe your part will be harder."

"I have a good feeling about my girl, Jhar," Rahab said. "I think she will be the key to making this work."

"I'm going to pay Uriah a visit," Joshua stated. "It sounds as if your strategy is a good one. We're ready to help if help is needed."

Joshua found Uriah outside the electromagnetic containment area for the antimatter fuel.

"The tractor beam you sent was flawless," Joshua said. "We all arrived intact."

"Good," Uriah was a man of few words..

"Have you decided on a landing site?"

"Yes, I have pinpointed the Jangle's square of pastureland on the equator and plan to land at the southern border where they're grazing their herds just now. We'll be entering Cold Land's orbit soon. Our orbital path will take us over the South Sea area if you want to have a look."

"Yes, I do want to see what is happening there. All good with our antimatter supply?" he asked, looking at the electromagnetic coils that surrounded the antimatter particles and kept them isolated from everything else on the ship. If even one small antimatter ion came in contact with a common bit of matter, the explosion would be horrendous.

"Everything is secure," Uriah said. "No cause for concern here."

"I never worry when you are in charge."

"Nor I when you are commander," Uriah stated.

Joshua thought he may have seen just a hint of a smile on Uriah's face, but he couldn't be sure.

Joshua took the escalade back to the sixth level, feeling comfort in his re-digitized body. His five friends were still there as he had left them, making contingency plans.

"Uriah says we will be flying over the South Sea area soon. We may be able to see early signs of rising water," Joshua said.

They all looked to the projection walls as Joshua called up a telescopic view of the planet below.

"I see it," Jonah said, "that flat area of ice surrounded by higher layers of snow and ice."

"Yes, I see a gentle heaving as though the sea is breathing," Daniel noted.

"The asteroid is unstable. There is one deep fissure that could give way under pressure from Cold Land's tida forces as the asteroid draws near," Joshua said.

"I noticed that as well," Deborah agreed. A great chunk of the asteroid falling into the South Sea would cause a massive tsunami."

"It will take the miners another day or two to arrive here," Joshua said. "And the asteroid won't be far behind them. We're on a tight timeline, but with luck and God's help it will all come together. The miners will see immediately that the sea is in danger of flooding. They will be heroes for warning the inhabitants."

"Our plan is devised to be only a nudge in the direction of peace," Deborah warned. "No interference with free will in any clan's decisions," she mummured.

"As always," Joshua said.

"It never hurts to add prayer to the mix," Lydia said.

"Pray without ceasing in all your words and actions," Joshua said, sowing comfort by repeating one of their key directives.

"We live to serve," Daniel uttered the customary response.

"Amen," the others chorused.

Chapter 8

Jhar

The day of the anticipated reprisal left Jhar in an unsettled state. She found her thoughts so jumbled she couldn't concentrate. As she dressed her youngest brother in green skallon-skin pants and a green cape her eyes kept drifting to the pile of scrapes near the fire pit. Scrapes that might be accepted with gratitude by the Sylvans.

She stopped midway through fastening her brother's boots and stared straight ahead.

"Jhar sad?" her five-year old brother asked.

Jhar smiled. "No, not sad. Just thinking."

"Thinking we'll eat soon?"

Jhar kissed her brother Sim on top of his fine golden hair. "No. Thinking of taking scrapes for a trade."

"Trade for food?"

"Trade for goodwill."

"What is goodwill?" Sim asked.

"Something we need more of."

Sim looked at her with light blue eyes. Steady eyes. He would be a good shepherd when he grew up. All the people of Cold Land were tall and muscular, light-skinned and covered with blonde hair. The skallon they tended were huge and as fierce as the Cold Land people who depended on them for food and clothing. Sim would be no different.

"Go find sister Gem. She'll need your help picking up skallon droppings for the fires. She said she would be by the curve in the stream this morning."

As Sim ran off to find his sister, Jhar packed the scrapes into a skin bag. Surely, if she took the scrapes to Dunk's clan and offered them as a gift, they would consider it a kindness and be inclined to show compassion for her cousin Grum. Perhaps they would wound him, but leave him alive. She would not be breaking her promise to Dunk if she said nothing about the planned reprisal. She could offer at first to trade the scrapes, but then say, "Just take them – I have no use for the purple color they make." But how could she explain knowing their tongue? Better not to say anything at all.

Draping the bag over her shoulder, she went to find her mother.

Jhar's mother was harvesting ice at the southern edge of the pasture to melt for water this morning.

"Mother," Jhar called out. "I think I will take these scrapes to trade with the Sylvans. Perhaps they will give me something useful in return."

Mother scowled. "I doubt the Sylvans have anything useful, but I suppose you could try." She was quiet for a moment, thinking. "The Sylvans can't be trusted," she said. "Take Mutt with you in case they try to steal your scrapes. He's out with the skallon today."

"Yes, Mother, I'll find Mutt," Jhar said.

Jhar found her brother Mutt in the pasture, standing between a newborn skallon calf and a ripcon, beating the ripcon with the bleached-out leg bone of a skallon.

The ripcons were savage knee-high animals with stocky builds, shaggy black fur and short bushy tails. They had large heads that housed huge jaws full of sharp white teeth that could snap shut with all the power of a strongly swung club. They burrowed into the permafrost, living on other small burrowing animals. Ripcons would not attack a full grown skallon because an adult skallon would stomp even the largest ripcon to death with its large hooves. However, newborn skallon were a favorite food of the creatures. Mutt had his hands full. She wouldn't bother him or take him away from his important work.

The pastures were green and thick where she walked. Wild flowers and weeds struggled for sunlight within the tall grass. She loved the vast open views of the green pastures studded with rocky outcrops. Her grandmother had always called Jhar her wanderer. Jhar supposed it was her curiosity that led her to study and collect things. She liked to watch the flocks of flying twinks make patterns in the sky. No bigger than her fist, individually, in flocks they could blot out the sun. They came out in the evenings to eat insects, massing together to intimidate the large-winged black swipes, birds the size of ripcons who ate the flesh of carrion.

Jhar's curiosity also led her to experiment with things like the bits of mossy scrapes she found on rocks. Dunk had told her they used the green sticky scrapes to make the purple dye for their capes. She had made a pot of purple dye to verify it. Though scrapes were becoming rare on Sylvan land, Jangle pastures still held plenty.

As she walked toward the Sylvan pasture land, she rehearsed what she would do. She would simply hold out the bag of mossy scrapes she had harvested from the sides and tops of rocks strewn throughout the pastures. If Dunk was there, she would pretend not to know him.

A movement overhead caught her attention. Was it a flock of twinks? This was not the right time of day for twinks to fly. And it was not the proper shape for a swipe. It seemed a collection of circular-shaped green rings.

The small thing in the air grew larger and larger. It was now the size of a ripcon. Jhar had heard stories about large structures flying through the air and setting down on Cold Land, but she thought them fables. How could a large structure move of its own accord, let alone fly through the air like a bird?

Jhar kept watching from behind a waist-high rock. The flying thing grew in size and clarity. She wondered if Mutt was seeing this same flying object.

The structure was composed of interlocking spinning wheels. All of the revolving rings seemed to have eyes embedded into their sides. What could it be? Her curiosity outweighed her fear. She knew she should run back to her dugout or at least find a bigger rock to hide behind. Instead she stood mesmerized as insect legs unwond from a central cylinder and spread out to to touch the ground. The whirring noise the ship made gradually softened as some of the interlocking wheels began to slow. Eventually one wheel stopped moving. An opening appeared at the base of the column. It was a small hole that grew larger until it formed an empty arch large enough for a person to step through.

After a moment, a line of three people walked through the opening. They were smaller than Jangles, with brown skin. Two had dark beards and appeared to be men. They both wore tan colored pants and had shirts that appeared much too thin to keep them warm. One had a red shirt and the other a blue shirt. The last person had no facial hair but long dark hair on her head that had been woven into a long braid. She wore a yellow shirt that hung below her knees and no pants. She must be freezing.

One of the people waved in her direction.

Jhar knew she was doing a stupid thing – a thing her cousin Grum might do, but her curiosity won out as usual. She stepped out from behind her rock and waved back.

The three people walked toward her.

"Hello," the one in a yellow shirt said in a woman's voice. "We are new to this planet. Can you tell us who we should report to?"

Report to? Jhar thought. There was no one in charge of the planet. And if there were someone in charge, that person would surely tell them to leave. There were no resources to share on Cold Land. How could these people think they would be welcomed on someone else's land? She could take them to the Jangle leader Cray, but he had no authority over the whole planet.

Setting aside her hostile instincts, Jhar answered the question. "There is no one to report to, but many who would kill you for landing here. You will not be allowed to stay here. We are not accustomed to having visitors."

"I see," the woman said in a soothing voice.

Jhar thought it incredible that this foreign woman spoke her language. Each clan had its own language and she had learned Dunk's dialect only because it was similar to her own. They had been friends learning from one another since childhood. How could these strangers possibly know the language unless some Jangle had taught it to them?

"Where have you come from?" Jhar asked, wondering if they were those who came from time to time to steal ores and leave.

"We come from a far away galaxy on a mission of discovery," the woman said.

Jhar didn't know the meaning of a far galaxy but she supposed it meant somewhere out in the stars.

"Are snow and cold new to you?" she asked.

"It is infrequent on our planet, but not unknown," the woman said.

"I would advise you to go somewhere else then," Jhar said. "There is not much more to discover here."

"Would you like to come aboard our ship and look around?" the woman asked.

They could be kidnappers, Jhar thought. *Sometimes one of the warring clans would kidnap someone and hold that person hostage until their demands were met.*

"We are not kidnappers," the woman said, as though she could hear Jhar's thoughts.

Jhar threw her hands in the air in an "I don't care who you are" gesture.

The woman moved closer, leaving the two men standing close to the flying thing. "Are you carrying an item to trade in that bag?" the woman asked.

Perhaps this woman really could hear her thoughts.

"Yes, I can read minds," the woman said. "My name is Rahab and I was once in a situation similar to yours."

"Similar how?" Jhar asked before she could stop herself.

"I had to decide where my loyalties lay. I had to choose one side and betray the other."

Jhar took a deep breath. "How did you decide?"

"Would you like to come aboard where it is warmer? We could have some fruit and go over both situations."

Jhar knew this was definitely a move her idiot cousin Grum might make, but found her feet were moving toward the opening of the thing with flying crystalline wheels dotted with shining eyes. She was at least a hand's width taller and a foot's width broader than these strangers and probably stronger, she told herself, and she desperately wanted to see the inside of this ship.

Chapter 9

Jhar

They walked through the entrance to the spaceship where an inner round room housed a platform. The platform, with side bars jutting out from a metal framework, sat a little above the level of the floor.

"This becomes a moving escalade," Rahab said. "Step up onto it."

As she stepped onto the platform, the three aliens joined her and Rahab said, "Level six."

Jhar had a moment of panic as the platform began to move up with all of them standing on it. She held tightly to a bar at the side. The platform moved up the heights of several skallon and came to a stop.

"Here we are," Rahab said. "Just through this tunnel."

The tunnel opened onto a room that gave off a soft green glow.

"We have some fruit and tea to share with you," Rahab said. "Won't you have a seat?"

Rahab sat on one of the soft white couches, but Jhar was drawn to inspect what appeared to be a hole in the wall, but on closer examination was actually an invisible part of the wall. She could look right through it.

Jhar looked at the distant entrance to her family dugout through the transparent wall oval. Everything below appeared so small. She could see her brother, still guarding the newborn skallon. He seemed to be looking in her direction. She could see her mother walking toward their dugout carrying bags of ice. She could see approximately where Dunk's pasture began, though she could not make out the boundary markers. She turned when she realized Rahab was speaking to her.

"Come and sit beside me. Eat some fruit."

Jhar sat and picked up a slice of fruit, sniffing it and noting the soft texture. She licked it with her tongue and was amazed. What was this new sensation that delighted her mouth?

"It is called sweet," Rahab said.

Jhar took a bite and nearly swooned as the sweetness flooded her senses. She ate three pieces greedily before wiping her hand on her trousers and looking back at Rahab.

"You brought this sweet thing from your home?" Jhar asked.

"We did," Rahab said.

Rahab's face and arms were tan-colored and her hair was very dark. She had brown eyes that seemed to twinkle with amusement. Jhar thought Rahab's face pleasing, though she had little facial hair, just a bit over each eye. Jhar had soft blond hair that covered her face but it did not grow long as a man's hair did.

The two quiet alien men had coloring similar to the woman, faces with beards and dark hair on their heads.

Jhar looked closely at Rahab. "You said you had once been in a situation similar to mine, but how can that be? Our lives are nothing alike. This feels more like a dream that is foreign to my life. How can there be structures that fly through the air and food that is too delicious to be real. None of this is anything like my life. Even the air around me feels uncold, yet there is no fire pit."

Rahab nodded. "I have lived in times when I wondered at what was happening around me. My people at that time heard stories of the God who was able to hold back the waters of a mighty river to allow his chosen people to cross on dry land. This God was against my people. I had to choose whether to help his people or my own people."

"How did you choose?" Jhar asked.

"I suppose I chose on the basis of the situation at hand," Rahab said. "Two men came to me intending to spy on our city of Jericho. I knew if I turned them over to my king they would be killed. They had done nothing to make me hate them. They had treated me more kindly than my own people did. I wanted to save them."

"So what did you do?"

"I hid them on the roof of my house and lied to my king. I told him they had been with me, but they had already left. I advised him to send his men out looking for the spies in the wrong direction."

Jhar nodded. "In my case the boy whose life I hope to save has done something very wrong. He has moved a boundary marker and the penalty for that is death."

"That is a severe penalty," one of the men noted.

"This is Jonah who speaks to you," Rahab said. "Jonah knows from experience that God is forgiving of those who truly repent of their trespasses."

Jonah smiled at Jhar. "God sent me to tell my enemies that if they did not repent, their city would be destroyed. I didn't want to go. I wanted them all to die because they were enemies to my people. But God insisted."

Rahab laughed. "Yes, he showed Jonah that it is best to obey orders from God."

"We have nothing like your God who holds back water here," Jhar said, "so I decided to leave it to fate to decide whether or not to tell my clan what I knew was about to happen."

"And yet you are now on your way with a gift for your enemies?" Rahab asked.

Jhar shrugged. "They plan to kill my cousin Grum tonight. I thought if I showed kindness to them, they might have some compassion on my idiot cousin."

"I think that's sound reasoning," the second man said. He had eyes the color of skallon hair and a long reddish brown beard. He seemed to be holding back a smile. "I am Daniel. I lived in a time when my people were forced from their land and taken to live in a foreign city at the mercy of their captors. And yet I showed my new king kindness. I interpreted a dream for him with God's help. He was grateful and was kind to me and my brothers in return."

"The Sylvans are enemies to my clan," Jhar said, "but I am friends with one of them and he is the one who told me that my cousin Grum moved a boundary marker. That is the sum of my problem."

"Your friendship is at odds with your clan?" Daniel asked.

"Very much so," Jhar said. "Neither of our clans would allow such a friendship if they knew about it. There are rules against it."

"It is not an easy thing to go against your people," Rahab said. "In my case, I felt I had no choice."

Jhar listened but saw no answer to her own problem. "Do you think my plan of offering a gift to my enemies is a good idea?"

"How important is your friendship with this member of an enemy clan to you?" Rahab asked.

"Very important," Jhar said. "You see, he only told me about the reprisal raid that will take place tonight because he cares about me. He asked me to promise I wouldn't be near my cousin's dugout tonight where I would be in danger if fighting breaks out when they come to kill Grum. They have the right because he did move the boundary marker."

"Yes, I see," Rahab said. "He does not want you to be harmed if fighting breaks out."

"What if we were to come with you when you deliver your gift?" Daniel asked.

Jhar's eyes widened in surprise. "You would come with me? I was half way to convincing myself that none of this is real, that you must all be part of some fantastic dream."

They all laughed at that idea. Rahab covered Jhar's hand with her own. "I assure you we are quite real. And I for one can understand your dilemma. We are often unsure of the best course of action in difficult situations. I find it helps to pray and ask God for his help in making a decision."

"And does this God of yours answer you?"

"God spoke directly to me," Jonah said.

"I prayed every day and especially when my life was in danger," Daniel said, "and God sent his angels to protect me."

"I had orders from God," Jonah said. "When I didn't want to do as He bade me, He showed me how much trouble I could bring down on myself by refusing to obey Him."

"And I," Rahab said, "feared a God who was powerful enough to hold back the waters of a great river, so I helped those who had come to spy out the strength of our city."

"Do you think your God has sent you to help me?"

"In fact," Rahab said, "that is exactly what I think."

"Then please do come with me," Jhar said. "After seeing the three of you the Sylvans may forget all about my idiot cousin."

Chapter 10

Jhar

Jhar and the visiters walked off the *By Grace* carrying gifts – Jhar with her skin bag full of scrapes and the visitors carrying baskets full of delicious fruit. "I will translate for you if you want, since I have learned the Sylvan language from my friend Dunk."

"That won't be necessary," Rahab said, "we're all wearing translators. It's how we're able to speak and understand your language."

"Translators? What are translators?" Jhar asked

Rahab pulled a small device from her pocket. "Put it in your ear and you will hear yourself speaking our language."

Jhar stuck the small object in her ear and said, "I really don't think..." She heard herself speaking words she didn't understand in a voice free of clicks, whistles, humming and smacks. "This is hard to believe."

Rahab nodded. "It makes our lives so much easier. We visit many different forms of life in our travels and each has its own unique way of communicating."

"I could speak to any clan on Cold Planet with one of these and they would understand me?" Jhar asked.

"Yes," Rahab said.

"Can I trade you a skallon for one of these?"

Rahab laughed. "Not us, but perhaps some arrangement could soon be made to provide these to all of Cold Land."

"What arrangement?" Jhar demanded.

"All things in their time," Daniel said in a firm but kind voice. "You can use that one for now."

They continued walking east past small groups of grazing skallon. In the distance, they could see a few green-caped herders standing close to skallon calves.

When they reached the border of Sylvan's pastureland, they crossed a stream of melt water where a group of adult skallon stood drinking. One big male who stood over twice as tall as the visitors was eyeing them suspiciously. The thick brown hair on his shoulders stood up in a hostile warning.

"Show no fear," Jhar warned her new friends. "The skallon will smell your foreign scent and try to stomp you to death if they smell fear."

"No worries," Daniel said. "We are not afraid."

"The Sylvan clan leader is called Romm," Jhar said. "He will probably be at the council dugout. It's close by."

Before they reached the council dugout they were met by a group of Sylvan men carrying rocks and clubs fashioned from skallon bones. They were all large, muscular men, at least two heads taller than the aliens. Jhar knew they could have passed for Jangles had their capes been green instead of purple. Leader Romm spoke for the group. "You dare to come onto Sylvan land bringing hairless strangers from off planet? Is it not violation enough that one of your clan moved a boundary marker? Why should we not kill you all where you stand?"

"We come bringing gifts and mean you no harm," Jhar said in a steady voice.

"How do you speak our language?" Romm asked.

"We are wearing translators," Jonah said in a deep voice that gave Romm pause.

Jhar sensed that her translator was able to pick up things like fear and hope. She felt fear coming from the Sylvan leader.

Romm seemed to recover quickly and resumed his attack. "And you come in foreign clothes of many colors to hide your clan membership? You can only be from some unnatural place with evil intent to hide behind such disguises." The big man bared his teeth at Jonah.

"We come from another star system," Daniel said, "and these clothes are common on our planet. We all belong to the same clan and have no need of color coding. But we don't come with evil intent. We are on a voyage of discovery. Your planet is new to us."

"Ha! You lie," Romm shouted. "Others have come in ships through the air. They take what they want and leave."

"There are others that have flying ships as we do," Jonah said. "In fact, one of their ships will land here as soon as tomorrow. But they wish to trade with you – not take what they want and leave."

"I have brought you scrapes to make purple dye," Jhar said, holding out her skin bag full of the mossy scrapings from the tops of rocks.

"Why would you do that?" Romm demanded in a suspicious voice.

"Because I have no use for them. We Jangles wear green, not purple, and we have all the copper we need for green dye." She didn't dare to tell him the real reason—that she hoped a gift might make him less likely to kill her cousin, Grum.

Romm took the skin bag and opened it. He pulled out a handful of scrapes to look more closely at them. "I will take them off your hands," he said, handing the bag to the man beside him. "Why have you brought these off landers onto our pasturelands?"

"They gave me fruit. It is very good. They wanted to meet you and give you fruit as well."

"It is likely poisoned," Romm stated.

"Pick up any one you choose from the basket and give it to me," Jhar said. "I will eat it."

Romm chose a fruit from the bottom of the basket. It was a deep yellow color with little brown dots, soft to the touch.

Jhar bit out a big chunk, trapping the juicy runoff with her fingers and licking them dry as well. Nor did she stop with one bite, but finished the fruit off with a good deal of lip-smacking.

Romm turned to the man who held the sack of scrapes and motioned for him to try a fruit. The man took one from the top and took a cautious bite. His eyes widened in delight as he made quick work of the delicious fruit.

Soon all the men in the hostile group were eating the fruit and putting more in the pockets of their trousers.

"You may come to our council dugout and tell us more about what you are doing here on Cold Land." Romm addressed the visitors in a distinctly less belligerent tone.

The Sylvan council dugout looked similar to that of the Jangles. It was a cave dug out of a snow bank which burrowed down into the permafrost. The fire pit in the middle of the largest space still held glowing coals. Bones of butchered skallon meat lay scattered outside the pit.

Jhar noticed they had no skallon hide rugs set around the fire pit for seating as they did in the Jangle council dugout. The Sylvan men sat on their capes. The smoke vent in the ceiling of the cave had not been lined with hides as her family's dugout vent was, making for a colder eating area.

The Sylvan leader revived the fire with patties of dried dung and everyone took a seat on the ground around the pit. "You may help yourselves to some skallon meat," he said, pushing pieces of meat wrapped in mong leaves toward the visitors with a long skallon leg bone.

"What have you discovered so far on this voyage of discovery?" Romm asked the visitors after everyone was seated and eating.

"We have discovered a group of miners on an asteroid," Daniel answered, "and now we have discovered your planet of shepherds with their herds of skallon on a very cold planet," Daniel answered.

Romm turned to his right to consult with the man seated next to him before turning again to Daniel. "What is an asteroid?"

"It's a very large rock mass that flies in a path of its own but does not have the atmosphere and resources necessary to support life," Daniel said.

"And yet these miners live there?" Romm asked.

"They were mining the rock for ore useful to them, like the copper the Jangles use to dye their capes and caps. They brought with them their own air to breathe and food to eat."

"Are they the ones who will visit our planet tomorrow?" Romm asked.

"The very same," Daniel said, the hint of a smile in his voice. "You seem a perceptive man."

Romm grunted. "It is plain to see you are up to some mischief." He devoured another fruit. "Why are they coming here where they know they will not be welcome?"

"They wish to trade with you on a permanent basis," Daniel said.

"Permanent? Then they do come to steal our pastures?"

"I doubt they are interested in your pastures," Daniel said. "They are miners, not herders."

"How could they live without skallon?" Romm asked.

"They grow fungi and moss in the moist dark of their ship," Daniel said. "They use the metals they find to build things like flying spaceships. They have recently learned to manufacture translators. You might find it to your advantage to trade a bit of skallon meat with them from time to time in exchange for some of the things they manufacture. You might even wish to sell them some of your unusable land outside the pastures. I think you will find they have much useful information to offer. But of course we will never know as we are only here briefly on our voyage of discovery."

"We would be willing to trade you unusable land for your fruit," Romm said.

Jhar could feel the hope in his voice as he spoke and wished she could find a way to keep her borrowed translator.

"Alas, we must return to our planet," Daniel said, "but what excess of fruit we have, we plan to leave with Jhar, so you might be able to frame a trade with her as long as the fruit lasts." Daniel stood up.

"You are leaving now?" Romm said.

"It is time. We have fulfilled our mission which is not to interfere, but only to suggest."

As the group left the council dugout, Romm pulled Jhar aside. "We will come tonight to make a trade," he said. "Tell your leader that one of your clan has moved a boundary marker and is in danger of losing his life."

Jhar nodded and left with the visitors. She couldn't suppress a small but hopeful smile.

Chapter 11

Jhar

As Jhar and the visitors rounded a snow bank and caught sight of their ship, Jhar took off at a run. Members of her clan were throwing stones at the ship and her brother was attempting to set a pile of dung and dried mong leaves aflame by striking a piece of flint with a stone.

"Stop! Stop what you are doing," she shouted. "These people are friends. They come in peace."

Her clan leader, Cray, scowled at her. Her father stood beside their leader, his hands full of stones. "Come away from those aliens," her father yelled.

The three visitors walked calmly toward the entrance to their ship. At a word from Rahab, the overlapping metal blades shuttered open in a counterclockwise direction to admit them.

"We will be taking our leave now," Daniel said.

"I will send down the fruit before we leave," Rahab called out to Jhar.

"What are they talking about?" Cray, their clan leader asked. "What is fruit? How is it they speak our language?"

"Fruit is a tasty new food." Jhar twisted her hands in frustration. "But this is about Grum. He broke a rule. The Sylvans will come tonight to kill him." She realized her words were rushing out. She grabbed the hair on her head, frustrated. "Why are you so quick to anger? So bent on killing?"

"Get a hold of yourself, Jhar," her father said. "You're making no sense. These people are from the darkness. We know nothing of them. They're not our clan. If they are truly leaving, we won't kill them."

Jhar sighed and tried to calm down. She watched as ten large baskets of fruit were pushed from the open hatch of the ship into the icy slush outside. Then the hatch closed with a soft purr that sounded like the end of a dream.

A loud whirring noise drifted over the crowd of Jangles as the great wheels of the ship began to turn. It lifted gracefully into the air.

"What is this evil they have left us?" Leader Cray asked, staring at the fruit.

Jhar lifted her chin high. "No one is allowed to touch these baskets. The fruit could save Grum's life. The Sylvans want this fruit. They may spare Grum's life to get it, even though he moved a boundary marker.With that announcement she turned her back on her clan and went to stand guard over her baskets of fruit.

Although her father continued to stare at her as though she might be possessed by an evil spirit, others looked at Grum who stood with his hands full of rocks and his face full of fear.

"Is this accusation true?" Cray asked.

Grum shrugged. "We have a lot of skallon calves. We need more grass for their mothers."

"You know the penalty for moving a boundary marker is death," Cray said.

"I didn't think anyone saw me," Grum said, beginning to tremble. "Will you let the Sylvans kill me?"

"I should kill you myself for bringing this trouble on us," the leader said, "but first I need to know why this spaceship came here."

"What were you doing with those strangers?" Cray asked, turning again to Jhar.

"I was on my way to trade some scrapes I had gathered. I thought the Sylvans might give me something useful in return." She glanced up to see that the visitors' ship was already the size of a swipe receding into the sky. "The ship landed and the visitors came outside the ship, waving at me."

"Why didn't you run back to the safety of your clan?" her father asked.

"They spoke our language – a thing not even our neighboring clans can do. And they seemed friendly."

"Yes, it was odd that they spoke our language," her father agreed.

"They invited me into their ship for a meal."

"And you accepted?" her father asked, seemingly horrified at the idea.

"Not at first, but they were so polite, so happy to meet me." Here Jhar hesitated. She didn't want to admit that they seemed able to read her mind for fear her friendship with Dunk would also be revealed. "I guess I wanted to see the inside of their ship," she said instead.

"So you did go inside," Cray said. He seemed astonished by her foolishness.

"Yes, I did," Jhar said, standing straighter. She refused to be bullied for her actions.

"And what did you see inside the flying ship?" her leader prodded.

"Curved white walls. A platform that moved up and down to different levels of the ship. We stepped on the platform and rose up to a high level. Then we walked through a cave into a place with soft white cots. I saw that those eyes on the wheels were transparent places in the walls. It was like looking through clear ice. I could see all our pasture land. I saw my brother guarding a newborn calf from a ripcon and my mother packing ice in a bag. They looked tiny from such a height."

"This is most unsettling," her father said. "They could have killed you."

"Do you know why they brought you inside their ship?" Cray asked.

"I think I served to satisfy their wish to discover new people and places. We sat on cots and they told me stories from their lives. They said they were on a voyage of discovery, visiting different star systems.

They gave me fruit to eat and offered to go with me when I went to trade my scrapes with the Sylvans."

"Unbelievable," the leader said.

"And yet, true," Jhar stated. "And they did go with me to the Sylvan pastureland."

"And what happened there?" The leader's eyes were already as big as skallon eyes.

"The Sylvan leader Romm threatened to kill us all, much as you have done. But he took my scrapes as a gift and offered nothing in trade."

"Why didn't they kill the visitors?" her father asked.

"They were surprised the visitors spoke their language, just as they spoke ours. They saw that I was not afraid to eat the fruit the visitors brought as gifts, so they ate some, too. They liked the fruit so much they invited us to their council dugout and that is where they told us one of their clan saw Grum move a boundary marker and they would come to kill him tonight."

Her father let out a sigh. "They have the right you know."

"I know," Jhar said. "But then the visitors said they would be leaving soon but they would give extra fruit for me to keep. As we were leaving, the Sylvan leader pulled me aside and hinted that he might spare Grum's life in exchange for more fruit."

Everyone's eyes turned to the baskets of fruit that Jhar guarded.

"They liked the fruit that much?" her father asked.

Before she could answer, the leader asked, "How could the Sylvan leader speak to you? He doesn't speak our language."

"The visitors wore translators in their ears. The translators allow them to speak and understand any language. They let me borrow one but I returned it when we left the Sylvans."

"This is some kind of dark art," Cray said. "They must have put a spell on you. You heard the Sylvan leader say they would come tonight to trade for Grum's life?"

"Yes," Jhar said, "And I heard the visitors tell the Sylvan leader, Romm, that the asteroid miners would come soon to trade with them."

"What is this new nonsense?" her father said.

"It may be nonsence, but it is what they said. The miners will come soon in their own spaceship."

Leader Cray shook his head as though to clear his thoughts. He looked up to follow the visitors' spaceship, but it was already gone. Then he turned to stare at the fruit the visitors had left behind. "I will taste this fruit. If it is as good as you say, we will go to our own council dugout and I will hear this account of a second spaceship which will arrive soon."

Cray picked out an orange-yellow fruit and sniffed it. He took a small bite. A smile crossed his face. "I believe Jhar speaks the truth. You may all taste of it, but save enough to ransom Grum's life."

Chapter 12

Daco

As their ship, *Bonanza,* settled into an orbit around Bando, Daco removed the restraints that kept him safe as the ship decelerated. He kicked his anchored crash couch to send himself floating in the direction of his son Aldo.

"All good?" he asked Aldo.

"All good," Aldo replied. "Are we there?"

"Yes, we're there. Now we need to find a place to land," Daco said. "Do you want to come along while I check on the others?"

"Yes," Aldo said, "I want to see what Bando looks like."

They floated around the sleeping quarters chatting with other miners huddled around viewing portals

Can you see anything?" Aldo asked burrowing through a group of miners to look out a portal.

"Only clouds," Pheebs said, lifting the boy to viewing height.

Bran came sailing through the air fast enough to bump into his brother. "It looks as though Socom has got us here," he said.

Daco nodded. "Aldo and I are on our way to the bridge now to look out at possible landing spots. Do you want to come along?"

"I wouldn't miss it," Bran said. "Our new home."

"Hopefully," Daco said. "It won't be a welcoming place if the stories we've heard from those who dared to visit are correct."

"It's not like we have another choice," Bran said.

"No, not like that at all," Daco agreed.

As Daco, Bran and Aldo crowded around the pilot's seat, Socom stretched and pointed at the screens. "Not the best time for us to arrive," he said.

"What do you mean?" Daco asked

"See that ice down there?" Socom said. "The asteroid is still coming closer and its pull is having an effect on the sea ice. It's causing the sea below the ice to rise. But that tidal pull is small compared to the tidal force this planet will have on the asteroid. We all saw the rift our explosives revealed on the unbanded side of the asteroid. It could well break apart when it get a little closer."

"Did we cause the rift?" Aldo asked.

"Not necessarily. Most asteroids are loose accumulations of smashed together rocks. They all have rifts." Socom yawned.

"You've been awake over thirty hours," Daco said. "Why don't you go get some sleep. The possibility of the asteroid breaking up over the sea changes things. We really should warn the people here that a hunk of the asteroid falling into the sea could cause a flood that would sweep over several clans' pastures. I calculated the asteroid wasn't on a collision course with the planet, but I hadn't considered the tidal forces a near miss would create. Nor did I realize there was a sea below all that ice."

Socom nodded. "I could use an hour or so of sleep, but I will need to be there when you discuss a landing site. Will you wake me up when you have decided whether or not to warn the Bandos?"

"I will," Daco said. "How would you vote? We will need consensus on whether or not to warn the people down below."

"I will stand with the majority," Socom said. "It may put our own people in danger if we try to warn them. They may blame us for the catastrophe. Wake me up when you have hashed it out with the other miners." Socom stood up with one last look at the screen before him. "We are in orbit now and a break in the clouds could tell us more, but the break is unlikely. He pressed a section on one of the screens. Here is an infared view that might be more helpful."

Socom floated out the entrance to the bridge, ruffling Aldo's scant hair on his way. He was shorter than most Swagians, but no one ever doubted his competence and expertise both as a miner and a pilot.

Daco took Socom's place in the pilot's seat and scanned through the various imaging programs, making notes on his wrist diary. He sighed. "No doubt about it, there is every likelihood of a break-up over the sea."

Bran was busy doing calculations on his own wrist diary. "If that half kilometer rift section falls into the sea, it will generate a tsunami that will flood an eight hundred kilometer wide swath of grasslands north of it."

"And we could be partly to blame for creating the fissure," Daco said.

"We are not to blame," Bran said. "That fissure had to be there before we came along."

"But we widened it with our explosives."

"Perhaps," Bran said. "In any case, we must decide on whether or not to warn the locals. If we do land to warn them, it needs to be a very brief landing."

"Yes, I'm sure you are right about that," Daco said. "What other factors do we need to consider?"

"We need to consider what to do if they don't believe us," Aldo said.

Daco smiled. "An almost certain possibility, and one I have no ready answer for." He stood up from the pilot's chair.

"We need to call an emergency meeting of the miners," Daco said. "All except Socom. Let him sleep as long as possible."

The miners met around the large oval dining table. They floated in, by ones and twos, happy to have made it this far and to have at least the chance of a future.

Daco smiled at his fellow miners. "We are in orbit around Bando. Socom is sleeping now so he won't be joining us. He leaves it to the rest of us to make a very important decision."

The miners nodded agreeably.

"This will be a new world and there is much to consider as we make decisions that are important to our survival as all who remain of Swage. Unfortunately, something is happening now that must push those decisions into the future."

Daco looked at the alarmed faces around him before continuing and decided to dampen the dangers as much as he could.

"We were able to manage this jump into Bando's orbit thanks to the path our asteroid was on. But we failed to consider other aspects of the asteroid's close pass by the planet."

"Tidal forces," Onri said. He blushed, perhaps realizing he had spoken his thoughts out loud.

Daco nodded. "Yes, tidal forces," he said, as he looked at the young scholar. "Tell us what you know of tidal forces."

Onri continued to blush. "I only know what is common knowledge," he said. "We all remember the rise and fall of our own seas back on Swage when one of our two moons would pass by. Here on Bando there is no moon, but the close passage of such a large body as our asteroid will have some effect. Any large bodies of water that may exist on the planet will feel the pull of the asteroid's advance and will rise accordingly. And Bando's pull on the asteroid will be even more pronounced. The bigger and denser the body, the greater its pull. Do we know of seas on Bando? It's so covered in ice and snow they may not be visible."

"As it turns out, there is a southern sea," Daco said. "We can see it only because the sea ice atop it is already beginning to bulge out. As the asteroid draws near, we fear the fissure we saw on the asteroid will give way and a chunk at least a half a kilometer wide will be drawn down into the sea producing a tsunami that will roll north toward the southern regions of the pasturelands in its path."

"We won't be able to land?" Onri's mother, Dray asked.

"We will be able to land," Daco assured her. "The question is, where and when?"

"We must warn the inhabitants," Onri blurted out.

"We would very much like to do so," Daco said. "But we might be putting ourselves in harm's way if we try to. The inhabitants are primitive, suspicious people. They will likely blame us for such a catastrophic event – they aren't familiar with tidal forces, having no moon of their own. It would be safer to land on the other side of the planet – the side which will not be so affected."

"But if there's a chance that we could save lives by landing on this side…" Onri's voice drifted off into silence.

"Of course we must warn them," Onri's father, Tull said. "We have three translators now. Onri finished two more on the way here. We will be able to tell them what is about to happen."

Onri smiled and nodded.

"What if they don't believe it or try to blame us for it?" Pheebs asked. "They are already known to try to attack anyone who lands on Bando. We could just stay in orbit until the flood subsides and then offer to help with the cleanup."

Several miners seemed to like this option better, nodding along with Pheebs' words.

"I admit I feel as Onri does," Daco said. "I would like to take a chance on warning them to save lives, but we have to put it to a vote. And we have to make the decision before the flood makes the decision for us. All in favor of landing on the pastures in danger, and trying to warn the inhabitants, raise your hand."

Somewhat reluctantly, all the miners except Pheebs raised their hands.

Chapter 13

Jhar

Jhar was not happy with her leader, Cray. He had given her clan permission to eat the fruit the visitors had specifically given to her. Not to Cray and not to the clan.

She should have been the one to decide who could eat the fruit and how much they were allowed to eat. Cray's order of 'save enough to ransom Grum's life' was vague and out of line.

"You may each have one piece of fruit," she said, standing in front of the baskets with her arms stretched out wide to protect what was hers.

Her clan members did as she commanded for the most part. She watched as her idiot cousin Grum stuck a second fruit inside his shirt. He would surely find some eventual way of getting himself killed.

But she needed her clan members' help to transport the baskets to the council dugout, so she kept the peace and designated the job of carrying the large baskets to the strongest.

They walked in a line to the southern tip of their pastureland where a warren of dugouts housed the Jangle clan. None dared to take up any of their pastureland for housing. It was too precious. The clan needed as many skallon as the grass could sustain to feed and clothe themselves. So they burrowed like other burrowing animals into the snowbanks and permafrost at the end of the pasture to sleep and eat, but spent most of their days outside with their herds.

That was not to say their dugouts were without comforts. Each family member had his or her cot made of soft skallon pelts, blankets made of the same, tools fashioned from bones and stones, baskets woven from mong leaves, sewn garments made from the hair and hides of skallons, games made from bone chips and pebbles. It was a good life and Jhar had no complaints.

As the procession of basket-carriers and other clan members walked toward the council dugout, they picked up more clan relatives along the way. Her sister Gem along with her younger brothers and sisters left off their dung collecting to walk beside Jhar.

"What is all this?" Gem demanded. "What's in these baskets and where are you going?"

We're headed for the council dugout. You will have all your questions answered there," Jhar said. "In the meantime, have one of these fruits to eat and give one to each of the children."

Gem looked at the fruit with narrowed eyes. "You're sure it's safe to eat this strange food?"

"Yes, I'm sure," Jhar said.

Gobbling the fruit kept her family from any more questions until they reached the council dugout and crowded inside around the large fire pit. So many clan members had squeezed into the dugout they had to make three rows of bodies around the pit.

Coals were stirred to life as more dried dung patties were added, bringing the temperature in the cavern to a cozy level that had the younger children yawning and stretching out on the skallon-hair rugs for naps.

Cray stood up. He was a big man—wide-shouldered, with a long golden beard and blonde hair that covered all of his body, except his dark blue eyes. He had a large family and was related to Jhar through a maternal great-grandmother. Everyone in the clan was related one way or another. He smiled at the assembled group. "I trust everyone has had a taste of the fruit left by our visitors," he said.

Nods all around.

"It seems the visitors left more than fruit. They also left a message – whether for warning or threat – we don't know." He looked at Jhar. "Jhar, please tell us how the message came about and what you know of its meaning."

Jhar stood up and looked around. It seemed most of Jangle was present. "I took a bag of scrapes to trade with the Sylvan clan," she began.

Everyone listened closely as she recounted her meeting with the aliens and the Sylvans. She included her tour of the visitors' spaceship, the translators they wore, the Sylvan offer to sell unusable land to the visitors in exchange for fruit. She left out any mention of Dunk and stopped when she got to the part about the miners who were soon to visit. Were they a threat to her home, or a help as the fruit givers had been? She didn't know. But the fruit givers had not warned that she should be wary of them. She continued her story.

"When Romm, the leader of the Sylvans, asked the visitors what they had found so far on their voyage of discovery, they said that besides coming to our planet, Cold Land, they had visited a group of miners living on an asteroid. Then Romm asked what an asteroid was and they said it was a very large pile of rocks floating through the sky but without the air and other things needed to keep people alive."

She saw many mouths open, ready to ask the obvious question and held up her hand in a stop motion. "The miners have a spaceship so they likely live inside it. For food they grow moss and fungi inside their spaceship."

Jhar took a breath. "When the Sylvan leader asked to trade a skallon for one of the visitors' translators, they said no, but hinted that these miners would be coming here soon and they would perhaps trade a translator for a skallon. They make such things as translators out of the metal they mine."

Jhar looked at Cray. "It was then that the visitors told Romm that the miners would want to trade here on a permanent basis and it might be good for the Sylvans to sell the miners a piece of their land."

A gasp went up from those seated around the fire pit. Selling land on Cold Land to strangers would have been unthinkable a few moments ago.

"And did Romm say he would do this?" Cray asked in an angry voice.

"No, he said nothing, but it seemed like he was thinking of doing it. And he said he might trade unusable land to the visitors in exchange for fruit or a translator."

"This is a serious thing," Cray said. "Selling pasture land to outsiders affects the entire planet – not just the Sylvans. "It's a thing that would necessitate a Grand Council of the clans. Many would refuse to come to such a meeting or even think about such a request. Romm had no right to offer those fruit givers a piece of land on Cold Land."

"But he did," Jhar noted. "Maybe Romm planned to offer ice-covered land and only pretend he owned it."

"If the Sylvans were to offer land they pretended to own to these miners, it would give them an unfair advantage over other clans," Cray considered aloud. "They could then trade more easily than the rest of us who can't speak other clan languages."

"Maybe we should offer to sell unusable land to the miners so that we could have that advantage," Jhar's brother Mutt said.

Cray shook his head. "No, we would bring a clan war down on our heads. It is unlawful."

"Will we go to war with the Sylvans if they sell unusable land to the miners?" Jhar's father asked.

Cray looked as though he was getting one of his severe headaches. "I don't know. I suppose we would have to. But the Sylvans will come tonight to kill Grum. Maybe we can talk with them then about their intentions."

Jhar felt her leader's gaze shift to her. "Do you remember any of the words you learned when wearing the translator? Do you think you could talk to the Sylvans?"

Jhar nodded as the promise she had made to Dunk flashed through her mind. She had promised to stay away from Grum tonight.

"Maybe we could meet them here, and keep Grum away until we have talked about the miners," she said.

"Yes, Grum is a separate issue," Cray said, grimacing as he pinched his forehead with his fingers.

Prow, one of her brother's friends, came running into the dugout, panting as he tried to catch his breath. "Another spaceship has landed," he cried out.

Chapter 14

Joshua

"Wasn't it just wonderful the way everything came together so quickly?" Lydia said. She sat with her friends looking out a viewing bubble as the planets of another star system flashed by.

Daniel nodded. "The Swagians are likely turning out translators as fast as they can and the Bandos will be standing in line to buy them."

"I liked our girl, Jhar," Rahab chimed in. "I hope things work out for her and her friend from the purple tribe. She had some starch in her."

"Do you think they'll survive the flood?" Jonah asked, his face crinkling a bit with worry lines."

"Of course," Deborah said. "Daco and his bunch will warn them and both clans will move themselves and their flocks north."

"If Daco gets a chance to tell them," Jonah said. "Those Jangles are pretty quick to take offense. We were lucky they had nothing bigger or badder than stones and bones to fling at our ship."

"We were due an easy assignment, don't you agree?" Rahab asked.

"Perhaps we're getting better at it," Deborah said, leaning back comfortably on her couch, a cup of tea in her hand. "How many hundreds of years have we been doing this?"

"Four hundred, give or take," Lydia said.

"Six hundred to go, and then what?" Daniel mused.

"Then the reckoning," I suppose," Jonah said. "Joshua, what do you suppose? You've been awfully quiet."

Joshua remained quiet, studying his wrist diary. He frowned and looked up. "It seems we may have left too soon. Another group of Swagians has just landed on Cold Land. A group of biologists who have been traveling months to get there. They hope to catalog and study the cold climate predators of the planet."

"Are they aware they have no home to return to?" Lydia asked.

"Likely not," Joshua said. "Their communications would have been cut off suddenly while they were on their way to Cold Land."

"Do you think they will see what's about to happen at the South Sea before it's too late?" Rahab asked.

"They should see it soon if they look out to sea," Joshua said

"Where have they landed?" Jonah asked.

"The north shore of the South Sea," Joshua said.

"We have to go back," Daniel said.

"Yes," Joshua agreed. "I'll speak to Uriah. In the meantime, we need to come up with a few contingency plans."

The group was quiet with heavy thoughts as they prayed for help and guidance.

"Anyone have an answer from God?" Lydia asked hopefully.

A slow shaking of heads followed.

"We may not get there before the flood," Jonah said. "There may be nothing we can do."

"The Swagian miners are smart," Deborah argued. "They will make sure the Sylvans and Jangles move to the north of their pasturelands. They are on the asteroid that will cause the flood. I'm sure they will fly over the South Sea before they land. As for the biologists, we don't know much about them. Scholars tend to see only the project they are working on. Narrow focus."

"If their project is the South Sea, they should notice pretty quickly that the ice is cracking and the sea is rising," Jonah said.

"True," Daniel said, "but will they be able to react quickly enough?" He stressed the last word in his sentence.

"The Swagians airships are capable of fairly quick reactions," Deborah said. "I paid special attention to the level of technology aboard the *Bonanza*. It used lithium-enhanced fuel pellet drop technology with magneto bottle and laser array fires. I would guess that the biologists' ship is of similar design. Of course it is nowhere close to the anti-matter fuel and space curvature-binding technology the *By Grace* employs, but it should allow a quick takeoff when they realize the danger."

"*If* they realize the danger," Jonah groused.

They could feel their ship adjusting course as Joshua returned.

"So, do we have a plan as yet?" he asked.

"No," Lydia said. "Nor do we have an answer from God as to what we should attempt."

"Of course it is up to us to figure it out," Joshua joked. "That's why He pays us the big bucks."

The others laughed and a little of the tension fell away. To consider God paying his body to serve him was ludicrous. They lived to serve as did everyone in New Jerusalem. And failure was an option no one wanted to explore.

"Are we headed for a South Sea landing?" Deborah asked.

Joshua gave Deborah a quick nod – one general to another.

"Their ship will either be on the shore of the sea or it will be back in orbit around the planet," Daniel said. "They won't have come all that way to return home to their planet, even if they don't know it is already gone."

Joshua agreed. "We plan for both scenarios then."

"Say it is still at South Sea, perhaps floating by the time we arrive. Floating on the exposed seawater," Deborah postulated.

"Then we will attach our ship and pull off those aboard, if there are survivors," Daniel said.

"That is one possibility," Joshua agreed.

"If they are in orbit, we can contact them," Lydia said. "Tell them to follow us down to a safe landing site. They'll do it because we speak their language. They will think we are Swagians."

"Another possibility," Joshua said.

"We can contact Daco and his group aboard the *Bonanza*," Rahab said. "We can let them carry out the rescue. They will no doubt be overjoyed to learn that some of their brethren from Swage have survived."

"Yes," Joshua said. "Yet another good option."

"Will we be able to land at South Sea?" Jonah asked. "If the ice has already cracked and the sea is rushing out, there will be no place to land."

"There is that to consider," Joshua said.

"How long before we arrive?" Rahab asked.

"I can feel the curve closing," Daniel said. "Uriah knew of several wormholes that could cut time. We may already be close."

The group flocked to the viewing bubble. They looked down on a sea that seemed to be breathing. The icy crust above the sea swelled and heaved. So far it was intact, the dark shape of the huge asteroid still far off but traveling at thousands of kilometers per second.

"We had best set down quickly," Joshua relayed to Uriah. "Leave the engines running. Do you see a spaceship on your view panel?"

"Not yet," Uriah answered. "Hold on, I see something. Look to the eastern shore."

"I see it," Rahab shouted. "A tiny silver oval close to the sea. Are they daft? Don't they see the danger? Why are they still sitting there?"

"Stay calm," Deborah advised. "It's our good fortune that they're still there. We still have time to warn them."

"Get your spacesuits on," Joahua said to Lydia and Deborah. "Try to act like Swagians, only smarter."

Chapter 15

Mona

The Swagian scientists were jubilant. They had made their epic journey purely for the sake of science. Others had come before them to mine minerals but none of them had come to catalog the different species of animals that roamed the planet. A planet very different from the warm jungles of Swage. Already, from the viewing lens of their ship, *Seeker*, they had seen a group of large furry animals huddled together on the shore of the South Sea. The animals had eyes set close together and walked heavily of four feet – both signs of predators. Prey animals tended to be fleet of foot with widely spaced eyes good for spotting predators. They had given the supposed predators the nickname Ice Eaters, as they had not seen them take down any prey on land or sea, yet.

Mona gathered up the supplies she would need for the upcoming onshore excursion: her protective armor suit, her breather, a collection bag, a collapsible scope, her recorder, a tube of water, her waterproof waders, her wrist camera and communicator... What was she forgetting?

"Are you ready?" her exploration partner Soma called from the doorway of her alcove. He was ready to go, already decked out in his spacesuit and waders.

"Just about. I feel like I might be forgetting something," Mona said, looking around her small cot and closet.

"Tranquilizer darts?" Soma asked.

"Yes! Do you have some?"

"I do," Soma said, holding up a tranquilizer gun.

"I have darts as well, though hopefully we won't need them for this overview survey," Mona said, stuffing a few darts into the leather sachel that hung from her waist.

"No, only for protection, should our ice eaters view us as the meals they've been waiting for."

Mona smiled at the thought. Everything about this arrival thrilled her – even the thought of being viewed as a creature's dinner.

"The team is already gathering at the hatch. We'd better hurry," Soma said.

Soma smiled at her partner's eager expression, knowing her own expression must be similar. Other than their shared excitement, they did not look much alike.

Both Swagian, they shared a blue-black skin color. They both had gill slits down their necks, and dark brown eyes. But Soma had the usual tall slender build of a Swagian while Mona was rather short and plump. She did not have the common prominent nose either. Hers was less pronounced. Her most complimented feature was her broad smile. She tried to smile often, but Soma did not seem to take notice.

The large group of biologists would split up into two-person teams once they left the ship to cover more ground quickly. But for safety's sake, never fewer than two: one to signal for help if the other should become incapacitated.

At the hatch, some of the scientists were already going through the airlock, two at a time. It would not do to lose the air they were accustomed to breathing to an atmosphere that may or may not be as compatible. Past records indicated that the air and gravity were similar to that of Swage, although much colder. The gravity was slightly less and Mona giggled to think she would be able to jump higher and run faster here.

"What is funny?" Soma asked.

"Low gravity."

"Low gravity is funny?" Soma said with a straight face. "Glad you told me. I wouldn't have known."

Their turn to pass through the airlock came and they stepped out onto a frozen world. Inside her warm armor, Mona still shivered at the sight. The exhaled air escaping from her breather made a cloud above her.

"This is unbelievable," she cried, jumping up and down to test the gravity. It was true. She was sure she was jumping higher here than she could on Swage. Soma made an impressive jump beside her.

Most of the biologists were going north toward where the ice eaters had been spotted, so she decided to go in the opposite direction.

Soma tilted his headgear to rest on hers so that she could hear his voice through the metal. "Don't you want to go see the ice eaters?" he asked.

"There are too many of us going that way. They'll likely scare them off. Let's see what we find in this direction."

Soma shrugged. He looked out at the heaving sea. "That seems odd," he said.

"What seems odd?" Mona asked, eager to start walking.

"The sea. There are no moons here, so what's causing the tidal movement in the sea?"

Mona stopped. "No seasons either. The planet sits up straight on its axis. That is why the grasslands only grow around the equator." A shiver ran through her body. "Could it be giant predators moving below the ice?"

"I suppose anything is possible on an unexplored planet," Soma allowed.

"If something large enough to cause that swell lives beneath the ice, let's hope it stays in the sea and is not equipped for both the land and sea as we are."

As they turned to resume their journey west, they saw several moving dots in the distance.

"Have your tranquilizer gun at the ready," Mona said, an anxious hitch in her voice. "Those could be ice eaters coming our way, looking for a meal. Do you think we should go back to the protection of a larger group?"

After a moment of watching, Soma said, "I don't think those are ice eaters. They move more like people. Do you suppose the Bando people send hunting parties this far south?"

"There's no indication of that in any of the histories I have read," Mona said.

"Decision time. They are running toward us and they are a fierce people by all accounts. Fight or flight?"

"Look off behind them," Mona said. "Is that a rock formation or a spaceship?"

Soma stared off into the distance, shaking his head. "I don't think it is either one. If it's a spaceship, it's unlike any spaceship we have on Swage."

"Do you think our star system has been invaded by aliens?" Mona asked. "We know the people of Bando don't have the technology to build space ships."

"That could explain why all our communication with Swage has been cut off. I was hoping it was only solar flares that were disturbing transmitter relays – a thing that would soon clear up."

"Surely that hasn't happened. They don't appear to be hostile. I think they're waving at us."

"Maybe waving; maybe winding up to hurl rocks," Soma muttered. "I have my trancs ready."

As the possible alien invaders drew near, they slowed and walked toward them in what seemed a nonthreatening way. However, when the first one spoke, from inside his opaque helmet, the voice sounded angry.

"Don't you see the danger you are in?" the voice asked in the Swagian tongue.

"We see we may be in danger from our own angry countrymen," Soma said. "We didn't know there were others from our planet here on a mission. Are you miners? What new breed of ship is that behind you?"

"No time for explanations," the concealed voice said. "That sea is about to explode into a raging flood killing all of you and a big part of Bando. Run with us, we must gather up the others and get your ship off the ground."

"How can that be?" Mona said, starting to run. "There are no tides on Bando."

"A giant asteroid is on its way here," the male voice shouted. "There's a good chance it will be pulled apart above this sea. Now save your breath for running."

When they caught up with the others, it took a few minutes to convince them of the danger. "Our own countrymen would not try to steer us wrong," Soma said. "We must trust them. They say an asteroid is coming and the sea will soon break out in flood waters. You can see how it heaves beneath the ice already feeling the pull."

"Get aboard your ship and lift off into an orbit around Bando," a woman's voice ordered. "We'll contact you on your communications network once we're both in orbit."

A very loud and ominous cracking noise had everyone looking out to sea as they ran for their ships. The *By Grace* moved forward to pick up her crew.

A few anxious moments passed as the *Seeker* engines came to life and lifted off in a flurry of ice and snow.

Once in the air, both ships opened up communications. "Did you steal that ship from alien invaders?" Mona asked in a tremulous voice.

"No, we did not steal this ship," the deep voice from the alien ship stated. "We will explain everything in time, but for now I suggest you take a moment to view what is happening down below," the voice responded. "You barely made it in time."

Mona looked down to see the ice split and begin to heave up in huge white jagged blocks.

Chapter 16

Daco

Daco was a little surprised to find only a young shepherd boy standing guard when their ship landed at the edge of a sweeping green pasture land bordered by a shelf of rock filled ice to the south and rolling grassland to the north as far as the eye could see.

They waited for a few minutes to see if the Bandos would come in force to attack their ship, but when those minutes were up, Daco's thoughts centered around the danger this idyllic place would soon be facing.

Daco spoke to the shepherd from the open hatch of his ship. "Go and tell your family they are in great danger." Thanks to his translator, he was able to speak to the boy in the language of the herders. "Tell your people to come and talk to me. We can help to save you and your herds if you hurry."

The boy tore off as though being chased by snappers – the wild dogs of Swage.

As Daco waited he realized he should've gone with the boy to save time. The waters of the South Sea might already be rolling north – unstoppable in their power.

Daco's brother Bran came to stand with him. "Do you think they'll believe us?"

"I seriously doubt it," Daco said. "They may not even realize a great sea exists to the south of their world. They have no ships and little reason to explore their planet on foot."

They walked around the pasture and marveled at the great size of the animals grazing there. "Their backs are taller than a man," Daco said, "And that network of twisted horns must weigh as much as a man."

"Here they come," Bran said, pointing to a large group of green-caped people coming toward them. "They aren't stopping to pick up rocks to throw at us."

Daco smiled. "Finally, a bit of good news. Are you wearing a translator?"

"Of course," Bran said.

"Thank you for coming," Daco shouted while the large group was still some distance away.

Hearing their own tongue spoken seemed to give the group pause. They hesitated and looked toward a tall, broad-shouldered man with blond hair covering his head, face and what showed of his arms beneath his fur cape.

The big man came forward, motioning the others to stay back. His skin was very white beneath his hair and long beard. He had no gill slits down his neck and his gait was more of a slog than a walk.

"Who are you?" the man asked. "Did you bring fruit to trade?"

Daco was a little thrown off by the fruit question before realizing the same race of aliens who had visited the miners on their asteroid must have also visited here.

Daco adjusted his stance to look the taller man in his eyes. Daco's face was exposed to the blue-eyed stare of the Bando man before him. There was no need for a breather mask here. "No, I have no fruit but we have other things to trade. Perhaps you would like to trade food for a translator that would enable you to speak and understand the tongues of neighboring clans?"

"Yes, translators for food. But you cannot stay here permanently. That is not allowed."

Daco's heart sunk a little to hear such a thing stated with such finality. Of course they would never know if the miners settled on the shores of the South Sea once the floodwaters receded. He nodded agreeably. "I have come here to warn you that your people and herds are in great danger."

"Danger from you?" the man asked.

These people certainly believed in getting right to the heart of the matter, Daco thought. "No, not from us. There is a flood coming from the south. The waters of the great sea will soon be rushing this way, lifting everything in its path – rocks, ice, animals and people. If you run north now, you may survive. Otherwise your people and animals will be drowned or crushed in the deluge."

The man actually laughed. "Are you perhaps planning to take over our pastures while we all move north?"

"What? No, of course not. What would we want with pastures? We are miners," Daco stated.

"Why would we believe such a fantastic story?" the man asked.

"It is not a story. It is a fact. If you like we can take you up in our ship and you can see for yourself what is on the way here. Though that would be wasting precious time that you will need to move yourselves and your animals north."

The man hesitated at those words. He looked back at his people then turned to face Daco. "I will go with you to see if what you say is true. I am Cray, leader of the Jangle clan. But you must leave two of your own men here as sacrifices should I not return."

Daco opened his mouth to protest, but his brother put his hand on his shoulder. "I will stay." Bran turned to study the group of miners standing near the ship. "Who will stay with me?"

Pheebs stepped forward. "I will stay as well."

Bran gave his brother's shoulder a side-hug "It won't take long to show him the proof of your words. Go quickly – there's no time for argument."

Daco glared at Cray. "Come along then. We have no time to waste."

Cray seemed to be frozen in place. Daco put his arm around the man's shoulders and nudged him forword toward the ship. "We'll return soon," he shouted to the waiting group. While we are gone, pack up whatever you'll need for the journey north."

The Jangles did not move from their spot but watched as their leader boarded the spacecraft with the miners.

As the hatch closed, Daco shouted "Prepare for takeoff. Everyone strap in."

The miners rushed to their cots and Daco led Cray to his brother's cot and showed him how to fasten the harness that would keep him safe as the ship accelerated.

"Ready for takeoff," he shouted to their pilot Socom as he strapped himself to the cot which was welded to the floor of the ship. "Fly south at a low altitude," he ordered.

"Will do," Socom shouted back.

The thrusters came to life with a great roar and the ship began to vibrate.

As soon as they were airborne, Daco released his restraints and moved to a viewing port. The gravity was already lessened but he was not floating as yet. It didn't take long to see what was taking shape below. He went to release Cray from his cot.

Daco pulled the Jangle leader to a viewing portal. "Now watch what is coming from the south. You can see in the distance, the ice atop the sea has already cracked under stress from an approaching asteroid."

"I know what an asteroid is," Cray said in a shaky voice.

Surprised by this information, Daco continued. "Good. That is good that you know. The pull of such a large asteroid is lifting the waters of the sea. As they watched what was happening below, movement caught Daco's eye. A flaming ball shot through the atmosphere and landed in the sea. Water, ice and steams shot up in a huge geyser. "Socom, get us back to Bran", he shouted. Daco turned to Cray, trying to breathe. "A chunk of the ateroid has broken off. We have to get back at once. It will take a few hours for the tsunami to reach your pastureland. Run for the cots and strap in."

Once they were safely strapped in, they could feel the ship's sudden acceleration. "I have seen enough," Cray said. "Take me back to my clan. We will run north with our herds."

"You'll want to warn your neighboring clans as well," Daco said.

"Jangles have no relationship with neighboring clans," Cray said.

"But surely..." Daco began.

"None!" Cray stated. "They will come tonight to kill my cousin. They will find us gone."

Daco didn't know how to respond to that, so he stayed silent for a moment before moving to another subject. "We used up our supply of food coming here to warn you," he said. "If you will give us food or trade for food, we will help you by transporting those of your clan who are too young or too old to travel quickly."

Cray nodded. "You shall have food and our thanks for your help and your warning. But as I said before, you cannot stay here. All our pastureland is already claimed. We have none to share."

"I understand," Daco said. "And as I said before, we are miners. We have no use for pastureland. We might perhaps consider buying land in the permafrost regions once the flood subsides, if anyone actually owns the land and has the right to sell it."

Cray seemed to be caught off guard by Daco's words. He was quiet for a moment before saying, "How would you live?"

"We would grow our own food under domes. And we might trade things like translators from time to time in exchange for skallon meat. You said you are familiar with translators?"

"Yes, I know what translators are," Cray said.

"Good," Daco said. "Perhaps we are making some progress toward becoming friends."

"Jangles have no friends outside their clans," Cray replied.

Their acceleration was quickly followed by a strong deceleration as Socom made a hard landing. "Get your people moving and send food along with your elders and children," Daco ordered Cray.

"Done," Cray shouted as he flung off his straps and ran for the hatch.

Chapter 17

Jhar

Jhar believed the miners. She had left the landing site of the spaceship as soon as they lifted off with her leader to view the coming flood, and returned to her dugout to pack. It took took her only a few minutes to pack everything she owned. Now she was packing for her younger brothers and sisters, but the whole time she was thinking about Dunk. How could she warn him? What good would it do if she was even able to find a way? He would have to convince his clan that they needed to go north. How could he do that without admitting a Jangle girl had warned him? No one in another clan would believe anything a Jangle said.

She thought back to when she had first seen Dunk. They were both so young. Dunk was supposed to be watching his herd of skallon. Instead, he was practicing his rockthrowing. He would put down one stone, then walk a little ways away and try to hit it with a second stone.

If he noticed her watching, he didn't seem to care. In fact, he was probably trying to show off a bit. It worked. She had paused in her dung gathering to watch his game. When one of his skallon crossed the line onto Jangle pastureland, she had pointed to it, thinking he would come and take it back. She realized now he must have been afraid. He had failed in his shepherding responsibility and knew he could be killed if he went onto Jangle land.

Jhar had tried to push the skallon back across onto Sylvan pastureland, but the skallon did not recognize her or her commands. She had finally resorted to pulling a frightened Sylvan boy across the line to get his skallon. A little flurry of words understood only by the actions that accompanied them had started them on their path to learning one another's language.

They had resumed their same jobs the next day and the next, often sharing the names of common objects like rocks, dung and boundary markers.

When Jhar moved up from dung-gathering to mong grass gathering, she still gathered in the same area. They had become friends.

Now they met secretly near the same boundary – just a little farther north at the two rocks. Might he be there now? There would be no reason. Now he was an apprentice tanner. She knew where the tanning grounds were, Dunk had told her they were just past a large squared off boulder that could be seen from the Jangle council dugout. But she had no excuse for going there. To trade for a skallon pelt? Ridiculous. The Jangles had their own pelts.

She could go and tell the truth – that the miners had come to warn them about the flood and to tell them that all of Jangle would soon be moving north. Would they believe her?

No, she needed a better plan. She needed to take a miner with her. Or she needed to convince a miner to go and warn the Sylvans. That plan at least had a chance of working.

She finished up the packing as Sim came into her alcove.

"Jhar going somewhere?" Sim asked his sister, looking at her bulging skin bag.

"Jhar and Sim going north," she said hefting his bag and hers over her shoulder and holding out her hand for his.

Sim took her hand and began a chant. "Sim and Jhar going north, going north."

Sim looked confused when she went south instead. "First we have to speak to some men on a spaceship and then we will go north," she explained.

"Spaceship of fruit givers?" Sim asked.

"No, this is a spaceship of life savers," she said.

The spaceship was dropping down on the pasture when Jhar and Sim joined the crowd of Jangles awaiting Cray's return.

The two miners left behind as prisoners had not been harmed but they still appeared relieved as they watched their spaceship land.

The ship did not settle down gracefully and silently as the fruit givers' ship did. It came down with a great roaring sound amid screeching and clanging as a whirlwind of dust and dirt circled around it.

Jhar moved near one of the prisoners while everyone else's eyes were on the landing spaceship.

She pointed to her ear, hoping the man wore a translator.

The man smiled and showed her the small device that held so much power before putting it back in his ear. He was so strange looking. He had almost no hair on his face or his blue-black skin. He was tall and slender with long slits on either side of his neck. But he was smiling. That seemed to indicate he wanted to be friends.

"You must go and warn the Sylvans about the danger," she whispered.

"Yes, we must do that," he agreed.

We? Did he want her to go with him? Would Cray allow it?

"Our leader will not want to warn them," she said in a soft voice.

"We don't take orders from Cray," he said.

There was that 'we' again. He must know that she took orders from Cray. So the 'we' did not include her. Or did it?

"The fruit givers came before you. They told our neighbors, the Sylvans, that you would be coming. The Sylvans will likely welcome you," Jhar said.

"Thank you for that information," the man said. "That is a big help."

"If you want me to go with you, I will need Cray's permission," she said.

"Don't worry," the miner said. "We will figure it out. Are you ready to move north?"

Jhar set down the two bags she had packed for herself and her brother. "One for me and one for my brother, Sim."

The man winked and smiled at her brother as the hatch on the ship opened and Cray stepped out followed by a few of the miners.

"It is true," Cray said to his clan members. "We must leave at once with our herds. I saw the waters of the sea far to the south rise up in a great column. The water will flow north carrying rocks and great chunks of ice in its grip. Hurry now to pack up and begin driving the herds north. Bring any old, infirm or very young to the spaceship. They will be allowed to fly north. And bring food for them. The miners are out of food."

Everyone seemed rooted to the ground for a moment before Cray shouted, "Go, go now. Move."

Jangles started running for their dugouts.

Jhar stayed behind with Sim to see what the miners planned to do next.

"Did you not hear me, Jhar?" Cray said.

"This miner is going to warn the Sylvans," she said."Maybe I should go with him." She pointed toward the prisoner.

"If they want to warn the Sylvans it is none of our affair. The Sylvans don't need you to go along. I see you are packed. That is good. Now go to help get the skallon moving north."

Jhar nodded with a last look at the miner who had agreed that the Sylvans must be warned. He winked at her and smiled.

"Come along Sim," she said. "Now we go north as I promised."

"Will the man go to warn the Sylvans?" Sim asked.

"Yes, I believe he will," Jhar said.

"Does he know Sylvans are enemies?"

"Yes, he knows they are enemies to the Jangles, but they are not enemies of the miners in the spaceship."

"Will the Sylvan kill the miners?" Sim asked.

Jhar sighed. "No, I don't think so. The miners are no threat to the Sylvans. They have no skallon and therefore no need of pastureland."

"I would like to fly on their spaceship," Sim admitted.

"So would I," Jhar said, smiling. "So would I", she repeated wistfully. "Perhaps they will stay and one day we will have the chance."

"I hope that," Sim said.

"Let's get these skallon moving north," Jhar said.

She took off her green cape and began waving it as she ran toward a small group of skallon. "Run," she shouted. "Run for your lives." As the skallon began to run north, Jhar picked up the two bags, took Sim's hand and began to run with the herd.

Chapter 18

Joshua

Joshua had cut off communication with the Swage biologists after advising them to follow the *By Grace* while they tracked the progress of the flood below.

He asked *By Grace's* pilot, Uriah, to fly north until they reached the pasturelands and then to circle left and right to judge how many clans would be affected by the coming floodwaters.

When he joined his friends on the observation deck, he opened the discussion with the biologist's statement.

"The biologists wanted to know if we stole this ship from alien invaders."

This drew a few chuckles from the assembled group.

"Did you admit to doing so?" Rahab asked in a teasing voice.

Joshua shook his head with a disparaging glance in Rahab's direction. "Where do you suppose they got such an idea?"

"It is simple," Deborah said. "They are sure we are from Swage because we speak their language. Our faces and bodies were covered by our spacesuits. They don't know what we look like. They know there are no ships like the *By Grace* on Swage. They also know communications with Swage were suddenly cut off. So, logically, what would they assume? First, some disturbance on Swage has caused communications to be cut off. Second, we are in possession of a ship not our own. We must have defeated alien invaders and taken their ship. Quite logical. The poor dears have no idea their planet has fallen victim to their own star, and that we are not from Swage. They are scientists and this is the manner in which they form their deductions."

Joshua nodded slowly. "Yes, I see it now. Very astute, Deborah." After a moment of silence, he said, "I don't think we should be the ones to tell them of their planet's demise. It would soften the blow considerably if their own countrymen, the miners, are the ones to tell them. They will find comfort in being with one another."

"Yes," Lydia agreed. "I know the miners were greatly disappointed to learn that we were not from Swage, even though we spoke their language."

"Let's focus on the problem at hand," Joshua said. "Look at the viewing screen. I have positioned the cameras to show the whole of the area which will be affected by the spreading floodwaters. You can see that each clan's pastureland is more or less a square, as wide as it is long, about a day's journey across, walking at a fast pace. I was able to put in boundary lines by noting the color changes in the capes worn by the shepherds when I spun the lens in for close-ups. You can see secondary lines to indicate the final reach of the floodwaters."

The group looked closely at the screen with the calculated flood lines moving relentlessly closer to the green squares. It looked as though four clans would be most severely affected, the Jangle clan taking the brunt of destruction.

"Luckily, the Jangles already seem to be on the move north," Deborah noted. "The miners must have landed and warned them."

"Yes," Joshua agreed. "I see movement there. But I doubt the Jangles will feel inclined to warn their neighbors, the Sylvans."

"Jhar will find a way to warn her friend Dunk," Rahab said.

"Very likely," Daniel agreed. "I believe the miners will find a way as well. It is in their best interest to find ways to befriend these herders. They have nowhere else to go."

"True, but they originally planned to take a piece of the planet by force if necessary," Jonah said.

"I think showing them how to construct translators made all the difference," Lydia noted.

Joshua pointed to the screen. "You see the momentum of the flood. There will not be time to warn all the clans involved. But I have an idea."

"And that is?" Deborah said.

"We can fly low over the herds of skallon. The *By Grace* can go over the clans on one side and the *Seeker* over those on the other side. We can attempt to start a stampede of animals going north. If the shepherds see their herds moving north, they will surely follow."

"Brilliant," Lydia said. "Perhaps we can blast noise from our own spaceships as well."

"Excellent idea," Daniel said. "I know just the recording we can play. A rock band recording from before the second coming."

"Are we all in agreement?" Joshua asked.

Everyone nodded their agreement and enthusiasm for the new plan set everyone in motion.

"I'll watch the screens and direct our attack," Deborah said.

"I'll locate the recording from the archives," Daniel said.

"I'll inform the biologists of our plan," Joshua said.

"Rahab, Jonah and I will pray," Lydia said. "I just know God will help us to save these people."

Joshua opened up the communications link to the *Seeker's* channel.

"This is the commander of *By Grace* speaking. Come in, *Seeker*."

A few seconds later a woman's voice answered. "This is Mona," she said.

"Mona, are you the ship's captain?" Joshua asked.

"We don't actually have a captain. Did you want to speak to the pilot?" Mona asked.

"Yes, I suppose that would work, but who is the leader of your group?"

"That would be our chief biologist, Professor Stern, but he is resting in his cabin. We are afraid he may have suffered a mild heart attack. All the excitement around the flood, you understand. Professor Stern is quite elderly."

"Yes, I see," Joshua said.

"In that case, perhaps I could just speak to you and you could relay my instructions to your pilot?"

"Yes, I guess so," Mona said. "I would maybe have to run it by Professor Stern first."

"Of course," Joshua said as gently as his frustration permitted. "We all, I trust, wish to save those people below from the advancing floodwaters."

"Of course, but how can we when they are hostile to outsiders and we don't even speak their language – or languages – as I understand each clan has its own."

"Yes, quite right. But we might force their herds north by flying low enough over them to start a general movement north – a bit of a stampede – whatever it takes. We believe the clansmen would follow their herds."

"Oh, yes, I see your reasoning. I'm sure Professor Stern would agree to that. I will just pass you through to the pilot, all right?"

"Yes," Joshua said.

"Before you go, could you tell us what happened on Swage? How you came to have an alien ship?" Mona asked.

"Soon, I promise," Joshua said. "I fear there is no time just now. Not if we wish to save the lives of those below."

"Yes, of course," Mona agreed. "Here is our pilot. His name is Santi."

"Santi," Joshua said. "We have a plan to fly low over the pastures that are just coming into view. You see the clansmen to the left are already moving north. But those on either side are not yet aware of the danger and there is no time to inform them. Our ship will take the pastures to the left and you can take the pasture to the right. Fly low enough to spook the herd animals and the herders will follow."

"Sounds like fun," Santi said. "Shall we strafe them a bit to get things started?"

"No, no strafing!" Joshua said. "Just a bit of a nudge."

"Got you," Santi said. "Nice ship by the way. Well done, Swage."
"Ah, yes," Joshua said. "Over and out."

Chapter 19

Daco

Daco walked with Pheebs in the direction of the Sylvan clan. He had left instructions with his brother Bran to lift off when all the very young and very elderly were aboard whether he and Pheebs were back or not, but to make sure the Jangles leader Cray made good on his promise of food. It had been a day since the miners had run out of food and they were hungry.

"According to what the girl, Jhar, told your brother, the Sylvans are expecting us. Maybe even looking forward to our coming," Pheebs said.

"Hard to believe, I know," Daco said. "At least the welcoming part is hard to believe."

"It would be a first," Pheebs agreed.

They had barely stepped past a boundary marker when they were approached by a small group of purple-caped Sylvans.

"This colorcode thing makes it easy to know who you're dealing with," Pheebs said. "Perhaps we should choose a color for ourselves."

Daco laughed. "You don't think our blue-black skin is enough of a clue?"

"Stop right there," a big hairy white-skinned man with bulging muscles commanded.

"We come in peace," Daco said in the Sylvan tongue.

"Are you the miners?" the man asked.

"We are," Daco said, smiling.

"Isn't it customary to bring fruit?" the man asked.

"Ah, the fruit," Daco said. "You speak of our friends, the visitors from another star system. They go on voyages of discovery. No, we are neighbors from…" He stumbled for a moment, unable to speak the name of his lost planet. "We come a short distance – from an asteroid that is bringing havoc to your planet. In fact, that is why we have come. To warn you about the coming flood. A large piece of the asteroid has broken off and has entered your atmosphere. It fell into a sea south of here, and caused the sea to spill out. You must go north quickly or be killed by the fast-moving flood waters."

"I thought you had come to trade," the big man said. "You bring your asteroid to threaten us?"

"The asteroid is huge. It goes where it will. We have no power over it," Daco said. "We do wish to trade, but this asteroid has to be everyone's first priority. It will cover the southern part of your pastureland before nightfall. You must move yourselves and your herds north at once."

The big man laughed. "I see you are coming from Jangle land. They have put you up to this. Tonight we go to either kill their mover of boundary markers or to trade his life for all the fruit the visitors have left behind. Don't let them deceive you. We are within our rights in this matter."

"We know nothing of this person who moves boundary markers," Daco said. "We warned the Jangles just as we have warned you. They did not believe us at first, but we took their leader Cray up in our airship and showed him the advancing waters of the flood. As soon as we landed, he ordered his people to move north. If you go tonight to make a trade, you will find no one there."

"Why should we believe anything a friend of the Jangles says?" the man asked.

"We are not yet friends to anyone," Daco said. "But we don't want to see innocent people and animals die when they could easily save themselves by going north to escapte the flood."

Still the big man seemed unsure. He turned to an older man in his group. "Do you think he speaks the truth?" he asked.

The older man put up his hands – palms out.

The group's attention was drawn to the sky as an airship swooped down over their herds, making terrible screaming noises as it headed toward some grazing skallon.

The skallon first acted instinctively by forming a circle with the young calves inside. Then, as the ship flew closer, they broke ranks and began to run north. The ship veered off and circled around to frighten the next group of skallon into stampeding north.

The big man glared at Daco and Pheebs. "You come here to distract us while you steal our skallon?"

"What? No!" Daco said. "That is not my ship. I don't know who that is, but obviously whoever it is knows the flood is coming and is trying to drive the skallon north."

"None of this is obvious to me," the big man said. "I am Romm, leader of the Sylvan clan, and I believe you are lying. This is certainly your ship. I don't know what you are attempting here, but I will find out." He turned to his men. "Take them to the council dugout and hold them there while we go to see if the Jangles are moving north. Perhaps this is all a ruse to prevent our killing one of their criminals."

"No, there is no time for that," Daco argued. "The floodwaters are already close."

"Then I suppose we will all die here together," Romm said with a sneer.

"Who do you suppose was in that ship?" Pheebs asked as they were led away.

"I believe it was others from Swage," Daco said, happy in spite of their dire situation. "Did you hear of any group other than ours planning to go off planet?"

"Not that I can remember," Pheebs said. "But I agree with you. It looked to be a Swage ship. A little smaller than our own – not so wide at the bottom where cargo is held. Perhaps not miners or traders who would need a large cargo hold."

"I can hardly believe we have friends on this planet," Daco said.

"Not particularly helpful ones," Pheebs noted. "They could have picked a better moment to show up."

"Yes, we almost had Romm convinced," Daco said. "I could read it in his thoughts."

"What will we do now?" Pheebs asked. "It appears we've failed to save either the Sylvans or ourselves."

"I suppose we could escape, but where to? Our ship will leave as soon as the passengers are aboard. The skallon are running north, but for how long? Romm won't make it back in time to save his people or us. We could try to convince our guards to head north but I doubt they would go against their leader's orders. I don't see a path forward and it's difficult to concentrate when I am so hungry. Do you suppose they will feed us?"

"I hope so," Pheebs said.

They walked to the council dugout with four Sylvan men who had very little to say.

Pheebs took one look at the hole dug into the snow and permafrost. "This will fill up with floodwater quickly."

Daco nodded, and tried again to engage with their guards. "This cave has no outlet. When the flood comes it will fill quickly with sea water. Do you all know how to swim?"

"What does 'swim' mean?" One of the guards asked.

"To travel through water," Daco said, making swimming motions with his arms.

The man laughed. "The water here is very cold. You would not want to be in it."

Daco sighed. "Do you have food?" he asked.

"Yes, we have food. You have no fruit?" the man asked.

"No, but I could trade you..." He rifled through his pants pocket for something to trade and came out with a small chisel and a magnifier. "This chisel and magnifier for food." He showed the man how objects appeared larger when viewed through the magnifier and clinched the trade.

The man drew some frozen strips of raw meat up from the permafrost pit and stirred the coals in the fire pit to life. He wrapped the meat in leaves and placed it on the coals.

Daco smiled at Pheebs. "At least we will not die hungry."

"I'll take my meat rare," Pheebs said, "just in case."

Chapter 20

Dunk

Today had not been a good day for Dunk. He had not slept well the night before and could not seem to concentrate on his work. His father had already asked several times if he was feeling well.

As he stretched out a skallon skin to be smoked and dried, his mind wandered back to Jhar. Would she keep her promise to stay away from her cousin's dugout tonight?

So many times he had arrived early for their clandestine meetings just to watch Jhar at work, gathering one thing or another from the grasslands, teaching her younger brothers and sisters so patiently. Many times he had wanted to scoop her up and bring her back to his dugout.

"Watch those hot coals," his father called out.

Dunk snatched up the edge of the skin he had allowed to droop and quickly brought it higher above the smoking fire.

Perhaps he should tell his father he was not feeling well today, before he damaged any of the pelts they were working on. It could even be true. He was certainly not feeling his usual self.

"Will you go tonight to seek out the Jangle who moved the boundary marker?" he asked.

"Yes, I must go," his father said. "Romm has appointed me as one of the reprisal group."

Dunk knew his father was not a man who enjoyed killing. His father was a kind man who loved his son and his clan. Just as Jhar loved her family.

He shook his head in an attempt to clear his thinking. "I heard a rumor that there might be a trade for fruit instead."

"Yes, I have heard that rumor as well," his father said. "Those who have tasted the fruit seem to prefer that solution."

Dunk smiled. "I hope that will be Romm's decision."

Dunk's father smiled as well. "I should like to taste this fruit. It must be quite special to save the life of a boundary mover."

A noise in the sky drew their attention as an airship flew overhead, then circled low to the ground, scaring the skallon, causing them to run north. Some of the new calves were separated from their mothers in the stampede.

"Leave the skins," his father shouted. "We must save our skallon."

Dunk dropped his bone mallet and ran for the nearest calf, left crying out for its mother. He picked up the heavy calf and began running north with it. He saw from the corner of his eye that his father was doing the same.

They would not be able to run far carrying such weight, but as the airship turned, the stampede slowed.

Dunk thought they might be able to unite their two calves with their mothers, but just as they caught up to the greater heard, he could hear the airship circling and coming low again to push the herd further north. He shook his fist at the airship and shouted as it resumed its relentless pursuit of their animals.

"Dunk, go back to the tannery and bring ropes. We can't carry all the calves. We'll have to tie them together and try to lead them north to their herd."

Dunk nodded and ran, thinking as he ran. These must be the miners and their ship – the ones the fruit givers had told them about. They had said the miners would come to trade – to sell them translators, but instead they were trying to destroy their herds. Whatever they were attempting, it wouldn't work. The Sylvans would protect their herds even if it meant outright war. Their skallon were their life.

As Dunk ran about the open ground of the tanning circle collecting ropes, he wondered if the Jangles were being similarly harassed. He wondered if Jhar was running as he was, trying to save their livelihoods.

When Dunk had gathered up as many woven ropes as he could find, he ran north to find his father grouping abandoned calves into bunches.

Dunk began tying ropes around the necks of calves to pull them into small groups. Other Sylvans had joined them, some with ropes and some just pushing the calves north bodily.

The adult skallon were still running, kicking up grass and dust, looking up intermittently at the sky. Sure enough, the airship was circling again for another run at the terrified animals.

Many of his clan were throwing stones and shouting oaths at the ship as it passed overhead. But their stonethrowing was a useless exercise, soon abandoned in favor of gathering the calves together to move them north.

Dunk realized after several hours that he had been moving his calves not only north, but west as well. He desperately wanted to know what was happening in the Jangles' pastures. If he could just catch a glimpse of Jhar and know she was safe, it would be enough.

The sun was already far to the west. It would soon be night. Would Romm still go on his raid? He doubted it. Saving the skallon was much more important. Besides, the Sylvan and Jangles would soon be united in fighting these men in airships.

He heard a new sound coming from the south. It was a different sound from that of the airship turning for another run. This was a bigger sound. A sound that resonated in the ground beneath his feet. A low moaning that rose in volume to a crashing cacophony of movement.

He looked to the south and could hardly believe his eyes.

A great wave was churning north pushing huge chunks of ice and rocks in its path. He had never seen such a thing before. It took only a few seconds of stunned silence before he heard the cries of those around him. "Run, run for your lives."

Dunk looked around frantically for his father. He saw him up ahead, pulling six calves along with him.

As his father turned to find the source of the growing tumult, he saw Dunk.

"Run," Dunk shouted. "Run north."

Dunk soon caught up with his father who had dropped the ropes to run north.

As they reached the greater herd of adult skallon, still running north, Dunk dared to look back at the wall of ice and debris.

"I think it is slowing down," he yelled at his father who ran beside him.

His father hazarded a glance back. "Yes, I think you're right," he said, still running full out.

When they could run no farther and the last rays of their star were fading into night, Dunk, his father and the greater part of the skallon herd finally came to rest.

They looked back at the line of rocks and ice and churned up debris left to mark the boundary of the receding flood.

"Do you suppose the men in the airship knew?" Dunk asked. "Were they trying to save us?"

"I don't know," his father said. "It's also possible they caused this. Certainly such a thing has never happened before in my lifetime."

Dunk noticed that the line of debris went further north as it veered west onto Jangle land. Could Jhar possibly have survived? He could not bear to give up hope.

Chapter 21

Daco

The warmth of the firepit combined with full stomachs had everyone in the Sylvan council dugout nodding off. Daco had removed the translator from his ear so that he could speak to Pheebs without being understood by the guards who were also half asleep.

"When it comes, I will take the two on the right," he whispered.

Pheebs nodded, sizing up the remaining two guards on the left. "They will fight us," he said.

"Yes," Daco agreed, "but even if we warned them and told them what they should do, instinct would take over."

Pheebs fingered one of the stones that surrounded the firepit. "We could knock them unconscious first."

"No," Daco said. "Then they wouldn't be able to hang on to an ice chunk."

Pheebs pursed his lips. "How about we just let nature take its course?"

Daco smiled. "You know we can't do that."

Pheebs sighed and looked again at the two guards on the right that would be his responsibility.

They had settled into a peaceful half asleep when the low roar reached their ears. This was followed by screams and sounds of running.

"There are still a few people who have not run north," Daco said. "Good luck to you, my friend."

"And to you," Pheebs said.

Both men put their translators into their mouths for safekeeping.

The water rushed into the dugout so fast the guards only managed to stand up before they were swamped.

Daco grabbed the capes of the two men on the right and began pulling them toward the entrance. He let them keep their heads above water as long as they could but that only lasted for a few seconds.

The water was not as cold as Daco had expected. An interesting fact that he would ponder later. For now he must somehow pull two struggling men through the dugout to safety.

He settled into the water as his gill slits took over the work of feeding oxygen into his lungs. A small school of fluorescent fish pulled along by the flood helped to guide him.

They reached the entrance to the dugout and Daco pushed his two guards upwards where they were able to breathe. Neither appeared able to swim. He steered both his charges to a large ice chunk where they held on tightly and were swept away.

Pheebs had performed a similar maneuver and sent his guards off on a pile of floating debris.

As they swam and floated on the rushing tide, they snared as many Sylvans as they could and steered them to floating objects they could catch hold of.

When they felt the tide slowing, they grabbed onto large rocks to keep from being pulled back by the retreating waters.

Daco took the translator from his mouth and replaced it in his ear. "Any injuries?" he asked Pheebs.

"I whacked my shoulder on a rock but I don't think it did any real damage. It will hurt tomorrow. How about you?"

"I took a fist in my gut from one of my guards, but other than that I'm all right," Daco said.

"Do you think our guards made it?" Pheebs asked.

Daco shrugged. "I hope so. They gave us food."

"Yes, and I have to say that skallon meat is tasty. Perhaps it won't be so bad living here."

"Did you notice that the water wasn't ice cold?"

"I did," Pheebs said. "Odd that, no?"

"Yes," Daco said. "That south sea needs some looking into."

"It appears no one lives there," Pheebs said. "Therefore no one owns it. And there were fish. Did you see them?"

"I did," Daco said. "Little fluorescent fish. Where there are small fish..."

"Bigger fish follow," Pheebs said, smiling.

"Shall we see what we can do to make friends and influence people?" Daco asked

"Absolutely," Pheebs said.

They saw that most of the Sylvans had followed their herds north and were now in the process of calming the frightened animals. Many dead calves were left in the retreating path of the waters. That would mean a scarcity of meat in the coming days.

Daco asked a tall broad-shouldered man what he could do to help.

"You did not cause this flood?" the man asked.

"No, but we knew it was coming. We saw it from our ship. We tried to warn your leader Romm, but he didn't believe us. He went to see if the Jangles were moving their herds north as we insisted."

One of the guards from the dugout joined them. "You saved my life," he said.

"I'm glad you made it here safely," Daco said. "Did the other guard survive?"

"I don't know," the guard said. "Gerd lost his hold on the ice. I haven't seen him since."

"We will hope for the best," Daco said. "What can we do to help?"

"What do you think, Darp?" The guard asked the broad-shouldered man.

"Start fires," Darp said. "People need to warm up and dry their clothes. The skallon we have managed to save will be all right now."

"Anything to burn other than skallon dung?" Daco asked.

Darp and the guard looked at him as though he had just announced that skallon were only figments of their imagination. "Like what?" Darp asked.

"Never mind," Daco said. "We will begin gathering dung."

"Did Romm return from visiting the Jangles?" Darp asked.

"No," Daco said. "We waited in the council dugout, but he didn't return before the flood hit."

"The council dugout filled with water so fast we were taken by surprise," the guard told Darp. "We would have died there in the dugout if these men hadn't saved us."

"We know how to swim," Daco said. "You would have done the same."

Darp and the guard exchanged a knowing glance. Both men knew that was not true.

"You have our thanks," Darp said.

A younger man came to join them. "Most of the skallon have begun to graze again, father."

"This is my son, Dunk," Darp said. "These two men from off planet tried to warn us of the flood, but Romm didn't believe them."

"Is that why you sent your ship to frighten the skallon into running north?" Dunk asked.

"That wasn't our ship," Daco said. "Our ship is bigger than that ship. We left it on Jangle pastureland where it was to have transported the very young and the very old to safety. I'm sorry there wasn't enough time to do the same for the Sylvans."

"So the Jangles believed you?" Dunk asked.

"Not at first," Daco said. "Their leader Cray went up in our ship with us. We flew south until he was able to see the flood coming this way. I'm sorry there wasn't enough time to do the same for the Sylvans."

"Maybe the ship that stampeded our skallon belonged to the fruit givers?" Darp asked.

"No, their ship is very different. It is composed of a series of revolving wheels. We are as anxious as you are to find out where the smaller ship came from."

"In the meantime let's try to get some fires going," Pheebs said. "It's going to be a very cold night."

Chapter 22

Jhar

Jhar had never been so tired in her life. She and Sim had run with the skallon, urging the calves to keep up. She had dared to put her brother Sim atop a calf when he was too tired to run. A full grown skallon would have rolled over to kill anyone who tried such a thing, but the calf was too young to react so fiercely.

When she had heard the loud roar of the approaching deluge, she found the extra strength needed to run the last distance. The skallon heard the roar as well, and made a last push to safety, shaking now in their fear and exhaustion.

The animals, quivering and twitching, some laying down as though giving themselves over to death, were finally safe. The tide had slowed to the speed of the skallon's pace at the end, running shallow and receding with a sucking gasp.

Jhar didn't notice the spacecraft at first. She lay with her brother Sim, their heads pillowed against the neck of a skallon calf. She thought the calf might be dead but now sensed a faint heartbeat. She sat up to put her fingers on the calf's neck to be sure when she saw the ship sitting a short distance to the north. The long day was ending and the craft was almost in shadow.

"Sim, wake up. I see the ship that carries grandmother. The ship carries my fruit as well. Do you want some fruit?"

Sim opened his eyes. "Fruit?"

"Yes," Jhar said. "We can go aboard the ship and eat fruit."

A smile spread across Sim's face at the possibility of a young child's fantasy coming true. "Yes, I want to go aboard the ship," Sim said.

The pair walked forward as in a dream. The hatch of the ship was open and a group of people had gathered around it. She didn't see her grandmother, but she recognized the man her leader had held captive while Cray himself flew south to view the south sea flooding. Bran was the name of the hostage. He had spoken kindly to her and winked at her brother.

She and Sim walked up to the dark-skinned man. He smiled at them.

"You are Jhar, if I am not mistaken. You are the owner of our fruit cargo," he said.

Jhar managed a tired smile. "Yes, my brother Sim is very tired. I have promised him a piece of fruit and a peek inside your ship. I hope I have not promised too much."

"Not at all," Bran said. "Come aboard. I believe your grandmother will be very pleased to see you both."

Jhar saw her grandmother sitting beside a huge wooden structure on a thing made of a brown material. Her grandmother was picking at a piece of skallon wrapped in a mong leaf. The baskets of fruit were piled next to the wooden structure.

Grandmother's face lit up when she saw Jhar and Sim. "My little ones. Come to me." She held out her open arms and Jhar and Sim rushed into them.

"I made sure no one touched your fruit," Grandmother told Jhar. "No one tried anyway. Cray sent enough food to the ship for everyone."

Jhar squirmed out of her grandmother's tight hug and got pieces of fruit for the three of them. As they sat on the brown things grandmother called chairs, eating their fruit, grandmother brought them up to date on events aboard the ship. "Many have already left to open up their northern dugouts," Grandmother said.

Jhar knew the Jangles had dugouts all along the route the skallon migrated from one patch of grass to another as each was depleted in turn. She nodded as her grandmother continued to speak. "Your mother has gone to open up our dugout. I stayed here because I knew you would come for your fruit. We had Romm, the Sylvan leader, on board with us. The fool came to see if the miners who warned him of the flood had been telling the truth. I guess he found out."

Grandmother frowned. "Romm saw the fruit and demanded all of it in exchange for Grum's life. Cray told him he would be allowed to ride with us on the space ship to save his own life. No fruit. It's up to you to decide what is fair."

Jhar nodded. "This is very good news, Grandmother. What do you think is fair?"

Grandmother thought for a moment. "Give him one basket of fruit and the saving of his life in exchange for Grum's. I think that would avoid bloodshed. Though Romm is a fool and spites himself with his bluster. He may not accept what is fair."

"We were able to save most of the skallon," Jhar said. "Only the weak were unable to run to the end."

Grandmother nodded. "I would have perished along with the weak skallon if not for the miners," she said.

"No, you would not have fallen. You are too stubborn," Jhar teased. She saw her brother chewing up the last of his fruit before beginning an exploration of the ship.

"Best not to touch anything, Sim. We don't know how things work aboard the spaceship."

Bran took a chair and joined them at the table. "Would you both like a tour of the ship?" he asked.

Tired as she was, Jhar found herself nodding her assent.

"This is our dining area," Bran said. "We all eat together every evening and talk about the ore we have mined during the day. We also assemble our translators here. Onri is in charge of that. We hope to trade them for skallon meat in the future."

"I would make such a trade," Jhar assured him.

"Excellent. Come with me. I will show you the heart of our ship."

Jhar and Sim went with him down a ladder to another level of the ship. "This is our fusion reactor. It is the engine that generates the power we need to take off and to slow down."

Sim looked carefully at the reactor. Jhar could see he longed to touch it, but refrained from doing so.

"Here we have our cargo hold," Bran said. "This is where we store our ore for sale."

"We have copper here on Cold Land," Jhar said. "We use it to make our green dye."

"Good to know," Bran said. "Perhaps there are other precious ores on Bando as well."

"What is Bando?" Jhar asked.

Bran looked embarrassed. "Of course I meant to say Cold Land. Bando is the name of a planet we have visited."

"There are other planets?' Sim asked.

"Yes, so many," Bran said. "But most are too distant for us to reach, even with our flying ship."

"I would like to visit another planet," Sim said.

"It may happen in your lifetime," Bran said. "I have a nephew. He is older than you, but you might like to meet him and learn more about other planets. His name is Aldo."

"I would like that," Sim said.

Bran turned to an open chamber beside the cargo hold. "This is our air lock," he told them. "We use it when we visit asteroids to mine their ore. The asteroids have no air that is breathable. We have to store our own air in canisters. We don't want the air on our ship to escape when we go outside, so we put on our spacesuits and our breathers before we go into the airlock. One door closes to keep the air in, then another door opens to allow us to step outside."

"Are the asteroids like planets?" Sim asked.

"No, they are smaller. Often we must set them spinning so that when we step outside onto an asteroid we don't float away for lack of gravity."

"Float like the ice floats on the water?" Sim asked.

"A little like that," Bran said. "Only without the water."

"I wish I could live on this ship," Sim said.

Bran laughed. "I don't think your mother would like that. In fact we had best go and find her in your new dugout. We can take some baskets of fruit along with us."

Chapter 23

Mona

"Where to now, folks?" Santi called out from the pilot's chair of the *Seeker*.

The biologists aboard were huddled around viewing ports. They had been watching the success of their mission to keep the skallon and their herders moving north ahead of the tidal surge. They cheered and clapped intermittently as they watched those running for their lives below.

"We need to find that alien ship and learn what has happened back in Swage," Mona said to her fellow scientists.

"Didn't they say they would call us on our comm system?" Soma asked.

"Yes, but they haven't," Mona said.

"How is Professor Stern doing?" a student named Caro asked.

"We should go see," Mona said.

"All of us?" Soma asked.

"I'll go," Mona said. "For now, maybe we should just go back into orbit around Bando?"

"Santi, go into orbit around Bando," Soma spoke into his comm link.

"Will do," Santi replied.

They felt their ship make the sharp turn toward space and dashed for their harnesses before they began losing gravity.

"I didn't mean right this second," Soma muttered to himself.

Mona rushed to a handhold on her way out of the observation deck. "I'll just make sure Professor Stern is harnessed in."

Mona opened the door to Professor Stern's cabin slowly, hoping she would not startle him. Even with so many biologists on board no one seemed to know what to do for someone who may have had a mild heart attack. They had followed the procedures outlined in their first aid manuels and given him blood thinners and advised bed rest.

"Are you awake, Professor Stern?" she asked in a soft voice

"Yes," Professor Stern said. "Hard to sleep with everyone celebrating up above."

"Oh, I'm sorry. We were trying to save the lives of the skallon and their herders," Mona said. She thought Professor Stern looked much better. His skin no longer had a gray cast and his eyes were clear of red veins.

"And that involved a lot of sky dives and trick flying?"

"Er, yes," Mona said. "Santi was trying to fly low enough to scare the skallon into running north."

"I see," Professor Stern said. "Who decided we should put aside our own mission to do this?"

"Actually it was the Swagians in the alien ship that ordered us to do it," Mona said.

"Isn't it our mandate to have as little interaction with the local inhabitants as possible?" Professor Stern demanded.

"Yes," Mona admitted, "though this was an unusual circumstance – I mean with the lives of the inhabitants at stake. That ship full of Swage visitors saved our lives as well. We didn't realize there was an asteroid coming near enough to cause a huge tidal surge."

"True," Professor Stern admitted reluctantly. "Did you find out how our Swage bretheren came to have that alien ship?"

"No, and believe me, I tried. We are wondering, what with our communications with Swage suddenly cut off, if maybe there was an alien invasion of our planet and they took that ship after subduing the attack."

"I suppose that would explain it," Professor Stern said, the previous grumpiness beginning to leave his voice. "They said nothing to explain their possession of the ship? You asked that specific question?"

"I did, and their answer was to save lives first and talk later."

"This is later," Professor Stern said.

"Yes, our comm link is open. They are not responding."

"Perhaps we should call a meeting," the professor said, preparing to sit up.

Mona put her hand on his shoulder to restrain him, then pulled his harness into place. "Actually, we are trying to find them. Santi is taking us back into orbit around the planet. I should go and strap myself in as well."

Professor Stern frowned. "Our mission is to study predators and we have already found some likely candidates at the south sea. If we haven't made contact with this alien ship after two orbits around Bando, I believe we should return to the south sea and resume our mission."

"Yes, of course we must do exactly that," Mona agreed. "How are you feeling now, Professor?"

"Much better. Thank you for asking. I believe I just over-exerted myself, running back to the ship as we did. Likely no need for it. Those Swagians in the alien ship were most likely miners, here to steal minerals. We can't let them make choices that involve our cooperation. We are on an educational mission. We have very different priorities from those on a commercial hunt for trade items."

"Yes, of course," Mona agreed. She felt her body weight falling away as they neared orbital altitude.

"Two orbits – no more. Either we see them or we don't," the professor ordered.

"Yes, I will tell the others," she said, grabbing hold of the door frame as she glided back toward the ladder that would take her to the shared quarters.

"How is the professor?" Soma asked his team partner as she anchored herself in a cot beside him.

"He seems much better. Good enough to be upset about our taking orders from traders. He says we must take no more than two orbits around the planet before we return to our work at the south sea. Of course he is correct. As biologists here to observe, we are mandated not to interfere with the locals."

"It was an extreme circumstance and we saved many lives," Soma replied.

"Yes, I'm glad we did as we did," Mona said. "But what do you make of the other ship's silence? The ship's captain promised to tell us what was happening in Swage as soon as the crisis was over. Their unusual ship seems much superior to ours. I'm sure their comm system must be working. Why aren't they responding to our calls? For that matter, why isn't Swage responding to our calls? Do you suppose the aliens won the battle? Maybe only these few escaped with a stolen ship? Do you think it possible our planet is now under the rule of aliens who have cut off all contact with the outside universe?"

"I can't imagine a worse scenario," Soma said. "We really must find that ship and learn the truth. How can we concentrate on predators when our own planet may be in danger?"

"Obviously, we can't, despite Professor Stern's orders. We must find that ship. Where do you suppose they would go if we are correct in our assumptions?"

"I suppose they would go back to the south sea to find us," Soma said. "Surely they would be planning some sort of strategy to win back our planet."

"Perhaps these aliens who have taken over are so far above us in their technology that we have no chance of victory. In that case, the Swagian visitors may be thinking of staying here on Bando permanently," Mona said as the thought popped into her head

"That would make sense. Saving the lives of the Bandos would also make sense, By saving them, they are sure to win their good will. But it doesn't explain their silence."

"No, it doesn't," Mona agreed. "There is something we are missing."

"We will find them or they will find us," Soma said. "We need one another."

Chapter 24

Daco

After an uncomfortable night spent around dung fires, Daco and Pheebs woke up to a lot of activity on the northern Sylvan pastureland. It took a moment for Daco to remember he had survived the flood and was now a guest of the Sylvan clan. He was uncomfortably close to a group of enormous skallon who stood sniffing the air while looking in his direction.

The guard Daco had saved came by with some skallon meat.

"Much appreciated," Daco said, continuing to stare at the skallon. "Do I need to be afraid of those skallon?"

The guard sat down by the coals of the fire and Daco wondered if they had reverted back to prisoner status once again. "No, the worst thing you can do is appear afraid of them. If they smell fear they will stomp you to death. They won't attack while I am here. They recognize me and my purple cape."

"Perhaps you have a couple purple capes we could borrow?" Daco asked.

"Yes," the guard said, stirring the coals with a stick and tossing in more meat wrapped in mong leaves.

Daco ate a piece of the cooked skallon meat the guard pulled from the fire.

"People are opening up their northern dugouts," the guard said, nodding in the direction of Sylvans running to and fro.

"Of course," Daco said. "What does that chore involve?"

"Mainly tossing out squatters," the guard said. "Ripcons like to make their homes there. You are familiar with the ripcons?"

"No, we've not had the pleasure," Daco said.

"No pleasure. Fierce little animals – try to tear off your arms."

Daco noticed that several people carried torches made of dried mong leaves woven together into ropes and clumps.

"Are we free to go now?" Pheebs asked, "Or are we still to wait for your leader Romm to return?"

The guard massaged his chin with his hand. "It looks like you were telling the truth about the flood coming," the guard said in a sardonic tone of voice. "No argument there. Also, Romm may be dead. So I guess you are both free to go where you will. Though I have no authority to give you pastureland or even a place to stay. I'm sorry about that."

"No problem," Daco said. "We'll just go across to Jangle land and hope our ship is there."

The guard nodded slowly. "I suppose I should go with you – and Darp should come as well. There is still the problem of the boundary marker mover to be dealt with and both Darp and I were chosen to go with Romm to kill the offender."

"Wasn't there the option of some kind of trade?" Daco asked.

The guard stared at Daco for a moment. "You people seem averse to killing."

Daco thought about his original plan of taking Bando land by force if necessary. "Killing is always an option, but sometimes there are better solutions."

The guard grunted as though other solutions required too much thinking.

"I will find Darp," the guard said. "Best to gather up some rocks. Many ripcons running around angry at being evicted."

Daco and Pheebs filled their pockets with rocks while they waited.

A few minutes later the guard returned with Darp and Darp's son, Dunk. They all carried the bleached-out leg bones of skallons. He handed Daco and Pheebs purple capes.

"Do you have rocks?" Darp asked.

Daco and Pheebs pulled a few palm-sized rocks from their pockets to show the man.

"Good," Darp said. "We have brought meat for our journey. The Jangles will give us nothing but a fight. We go to settle accounts."

Darp's son Dunk looked very uncomfortable with his father's harsh words, but said nothing. Daco assumed this would be the first time the young man had been involved in such a final carriage of justice.

They hadn't gone far before the promised attack came at them in the form of three very angry animals who seemed to be ninety percent jaws and teeth with the remaining ten percent comprised of bristling fur. They walked on four legs, their round bodies about a meter in height, brown with white muzzles and necks. When they opened their jaws, several rows of sharp white teeth protruded.

Daco barely had time to get the stones from his pocket before one of the creatures lunged for his arm. He swung around to avoid the gaping jaws and tried to kick it with his boot. This put him off-balance and he struggled to remain upright while the three Sylvan men hammered the beast with clubs made of skallon bones.

Undeterred, the ripcon leapt at the guard while his two ripcon companions tried to run around and attack from the rear.

Pheebs was slinging rocks as fast and accurately as he could and one of the ripcons went down in a mound of thrown rocks.

Dunk used his skallon leg bone to beat the second animal into submission.

The third ripcon thought better of his plan and ran off to where a few skallon were grazing.

This seemed to infuriate the three Sylvan men more than the attack on themselves. They all tore out after the animal, pelting it with rocks and beating it with leg bones until the animal went down.

"They attack the calves," Dunk said, still angry when he returned to join Daco and Pheebs.

"Nasty little brutes, aren't they?" Pheebs agreed.

"Not anymore," Dunk said with a smile.

They continued on through the morning until Darp called a halt. He pointed to a large stone, half buried in the grass and dirt. "Boundary marker," he said. "We are on Jangle land now."

"Will they try to kill us for coming onto their land?" Pheebs asked.

"No," Darp said. "That is allowed for trade. They will know why we come today. Revenge is also allowed, but they will fight us anyway."

"Won't they outnumber you?" Daco asked the obvious question.

"Yes," Darp said, but they will not kill us, because then more Sylvan would come. We are in the right here. The boundary marker mover must die. They know this."

"So they will only protect him up to a point, but they won't prevent you from killing him eventually?"

"Yes," Darp said, rewarding the correct answer with a smile.

"You may need this," Daco said, handing his translator to Darp. "Put it in your ear and you will be understood by the Jangles."

"I have heard of these," he said, putting the small object in his ear.

They came to a herd of skallon and Darp spoke to the young herder who watched over them.

"Where is your council dugout?" Darp asked, a curious look coming over his face as he heard his voice speaking Jangle.

The young herder pointed to the northwest with his fingers held up against his view of their star. "About two fingers away," he said. "Your leader Romm is there." He held his two fingers pressed together to locate the position their sun would be in by the time they arrived there.

Darp looked surprised. "Romm didn't die in the flood?"

"No, he flew up in the airship with the old people and the babies." A bit of scorn crept into the young herder's voice and it was not lost on Darp.

"Was he injured?" Darp asked.

"Not as far as I could tell," the boy said with a shrug. "How do you speak our language?"

A heavy frown settled over Darp's face. "Thank you for the information," he said. He took the translator from his ear and showed it to the boy.

The boy answered with a nod. "I have heard of these translators. Watch out for ripcons. They are on a rampage."

"We will," Darp said. He picked up more stones as he trudged along in a silent state of agitation.

"Is your leader in trouble for flying with the elderly?" Pheebs whispered to Dunk.

"It certainly appears so," Dunk said. "My father does not look kindly on men who don't pull their own weight."

Pheebs nodded. "That is true in our thinking as well."

"Father may ask that we call for a vote when we return to Sylvan land. We have no use for a leader who does not lead."

"A good philosophy, I think," Pheebs said.

Chapter 25

Daco

Daco spotted his ship soon after they stepped onto Jangle pastureland. The grasslands were flat for the most part making long unobstructed views possible. His heart beat a little faster knowing he would soon see his son Aldo, his brother Bran and all his friends.

"That is your airship?" Darp asked.

"Yes, you can see it is bigger than the ship which was frightening your skallon. I was hoping to find both ships here so I could find out who the other ship belongs to."

"It isn't the fruit givers' ship?" Dunk asked.

"No," Daco said. "Theirs is very different. It's larger, and made up of a series of moving wheels. We only caught a glimpse of it in the sky above our asteroid, but I understand one of the Jangle girls actually went onboard the ship."

"Do you know which Jangle girl?" Dunk asked.

"I believe her name is Jhar," Daco said as he watched Dunk's father give his son an inquisitive glance.

Dunk only shrugged in response to his father's curious expression.

They passed a few battles between herders and rampaging ripcons along the way. The herders seemed to have the situations covered so they offered only a few stones thrown with great accuracy on the part of the Sylvans and so-so accuracy on the part of Daco and Pheebs.

As they neared the entrance to the counsel dugout, Daco and Pheebs stopped short.

"We'll part company here and go on to our ship," Daco said. "Your business here doesn't concern us."

Darp nodded his agreement. "The Sylvans thank you for your help. We will trade skallon meat for translators at your convenience," he said as he handed his translator back to Daco.

It dawned on Daco suddenly that without a translator, the Sylvans would be unable to understand any offers the Jangles might present in hopes of saving their clan member's life.

"Keep it," Daco said. "I will trade you this translator now. We will collect our meat later."

Darp replaced it in his ear. "Thank you," he said. "We will bring the skallon meat to your ship."

Daco was continually amazed at the intricacy of the Sylvan tongue. It involved various resonances other than spoken words – humming, clicks and whistles among other sounds. He doubted a foreigner would be able to master it.

Daco and Pheebs turned toward their ship and saw Aldo already running in their direction

Daco rushed forward and scooped up his son, holding him tightly in his arms.

"I was afraid the flood might have injured you," Aldo said. "There were rocks and big chunks of ice moving along with the water."

"I was afraid for you too," Daco said. "Did the Jangles treat you well? Did they give you food as they promised?"

"Yes, they brought food for all of us. I made some friends with the Jangle children," Aldo said, "but most of them were younger then me."

"I'm glad to hear it," Daco said. He held his son at arm's length. "Just seeing you restores my soul."

"Why didn't you come back?" Aldo asked.

"The Sylvans were holding us as prisoners until their leader Romm could verify our warnings about a coming flood."

Aldo frowned. "I saw their leader Romm. He just strutted about like a proud bird showing off his plumage."

"I don't think he will be leader of the Sylvans much longer."

"The Jangle leader is much nicer," Aldo said. "He told us we would be fine and he would see us further north. He left the food and then went to run with his skallon to escape the flood."

Daco nodded. "Where is your Uncle Bran?"

"He went with Jhar and her grandmother to their dugout. He carried one of her baskets of fruit. Jhar and her grandmother each carried one, but there are six baskets left. No one ate any because Jhar's grandmother said they might need the fruit to save someone's life."

"Perhaps we should take some of the baskets to her," Daco said. "Do you know where her dugout is?"

"No, but I know children now that I can ask," Aldo said.

Daco entered his ship and was relieved to find it as he had left it. He greeted other miners and promised that he and Pheebs would give a full account of their time with the Sylvans around the table that evening at dinner.

Tull and his son, Onri, stopped him and insisted he at least tell them if there were scores to settle with the Sylvans.

"No," Daco said. "Their leader is lacking in leadership skills, but I believe he will soon be replaced."

Onri pulled four new translators from his pocket and handed them to Daco. "We have managed to assemble these in your absence. We thought you might need something to barter with. We only hoped it would not be a trade for your life."

Daco hugged Onri. "Thank you. As it turns out, the Sylvans are now in our debt. We saved at least two of their guards from drowning in the flood."

"Good news," Tull said. "Where are you off to now?"

"We are taking some of the fruit to Jhar's dugout. It turns out she was actually aboard the fruit givers' ship. I have a few questions I would like to ask her."

"Yes, I have a few questions myself," Tull said. "I would love to know what powers their ship."

"I doubt Jhar would be able to answer that," Daco said, "but you are welcome to come along."

"Thank you, but no," Tull said. "I think my time would be better spent here, manufacturing more translators. So far it is all we have to trade for food."

"We could perhaps offer scenic tours in our ship," Daco said.

Tull smiled. "I hope it does not come to that, but desperate times call for desperate measures as we all well know."

"Yes, and I suppose this situation would qualify as desperate times. Have you any information on the second ship from Swage?"

"What?" Tull asked. "What are you talking about? There is a second ship from Swage here?"

"It would appear so. A ship very like our own was flying low over the Sylvan skallon herds, causing them to run north. Their actions saved Sylvan lives by forcing them to run north following their herds."

"That would explain some of their leader, Romm's, insane questions," Tull said.

"What questions?" Daco asked.

"How many ships we had. If we were planning a massive invasion. If we were paying people to move boundary markers."

Daco shook his head. "Once we finish our business here, we will make it our first priority to find that ship."

Chapter 26

Jhar

Jhar felt comforted to be back with her family in their northern dugout. Her mother, father and older brother Mutt had rid their dwelling of ripcons and dangerous insects and her grandmother already had meat roasting in mong leaves atop a dung fire.

Jhar helped her younger brother, Sim, get into clean clothes and listened to his excited chatter.

"I could go to other planets on the miners' ship," he said. "Maybe I could be a miner and visit astroids."

"Asteroids," Jhar corrected. "But what of the skallon that depend on us?"

Sim considered his sister's question. "I could look after them when I wasn't on other planets," he said.

"Like right now," Jhar said.

Sim smiled. "Yes, but after we eat."

"Yes, and where do we look for the food we eat?"

"To the skallon we protect," Sim answered rotely, the oft repeated words coming unbidden to his lips.

"Good," Jhar said. "I am happy to see you have not forgotten you are Jangle with your new life as a planet traveler."

"Can we go back to the ship with Bran?" Sim asked.

"Perhaps, if they are allowed to stay here. Right now he is talking to father. He may be offering to trade a translator for skallon meat."

"Do you think father will do it?" Sim asked.

"Yes," Jhar said. "I know father hopes to save Grum's life. Grum is his sister's child. And even if Grum is an idiot, we don't want him to be killed. If father has a translator it will allow him to speak to the Sylvans when they come to kill Grum."

"Will you give them all your fruit to save his life?" Sim asked.

"I suppose I will if it comes to that. We will have to see what kind of a trade the leaders can arrange."

"Why do you think Grum did it?" Sim asked. "He knew it was forbidden to move a boundary marker even if he was doing it for the skallon."

"That is a good question, but one I don't have an answer for. He says he thought no one would see him, but that is not a reason to do something wrong."

"No," Sim agreed.

"Shall we go to see if mother needs help?" Jhar asked.

Sim pulled on his last boot and stood up. "I want to hear what father and Bran are saying," Sim said.

"So do I," Jhar admitted. "Maybe if we are quiet we could do some mong leaf braiding close enough to listen."

"Yes," Sim clapped his hands together.

"If they notice us listening, we may be asked to leave," Jhar warned.

"I will be quiet as a gilmeet," Sim promised, speaking of the small creatures that waited under rocks to ambush bugs.

Jhar gathered up some mong leaves and sat down with Sim below the soft light of a braided torch to begin sorting the leaves by length. They were against the wall of the dugout in partial shadow, but within listening distance of the fire pit where Jhar's mother, father, and brother Mutt sat talking to Bran.

"Jhar," Bran called out as soon as he saw her. "Come and join us. We are just talking about possibilities that involve your fruit."

Jhar and Sim moved close to the fire pit and the smell of roasting meat made her realize how hungry she was.

"As I was telling your father, Romm has already expressed a desire to trade all your fruit for Grum's life. He saw that you still had some baskets stacked up in the dining area of the ship. We think he will take fewer and still make the trade, but it will be up to you in the end."

"Grandmother thinks we owe him nothing since his own life was saved by giving him passage north on your ship. Even though it was you who offered him ship's passage, she believes because it was on Jangle land we can take credit for the rescue."

"Yes," Bran said with a hint of a smile. "And I suppose there is some logic in that argument. But what do you think?"

Jhar was silent for a moment, thinking. "Romm is a reckless, posturing man. He thinks the more he demands, the better it makes him look as a leader. He will not try to consider what is fair."

"Yes, that is the same impression I have of the man," Bran said. "And if I find he has harmed my brother either by intention or by recklessness, I will seek my own vengeance."

Jhar took a moment to imagine what that vengeance might look like. She chewed thoughtfully on a bit of skallon meat before speaking. "What do you see as fair?" Jhar asked.

"I would hold Grum responsible for his actions. I would order him to work for the Sylvans for a period of time to pay his debt, but I know that is not how things work here," Bran said. "There is no interaction between Sylvans and Jangles."

Jhar's father spoke up. "I like the idea of holding Grum responsible," he said. "The boy makes bad decisions. For my sister's sake I would like to find a way to change that. Grum does not seem to think rules apply to him. My sister was so happy to have a son. Perhaps she coddled him too much."

"Is he apprenticed for any work?" Bran asked.

"Only shepherding duties so far," Jhar's father said. "I could perhaps take him on as an apprentice for making scrapers and punches from skallon bones."

"And the scrapers and punches he makes over a period of time could go to the Sylvans as partial payment," Bran suggested.

"I can suggest it," her father said, "but it will be up to Romm and our leader Cray to hammer out an agreement."

Jhar nodded thoughtfully. "I like these ideas. Perhaps cousin Grum can be saved from himself. I am willing to offer up as much of my fruit as is needed to complete whatever agreement Cray can bring about."

"Should we go to the council dugout after we eat and tell Cray what we have decided?' Jhar asked.

Bran shook his head. "I will leave you to it. I need to return to my ship and wait for my brother. As I said before, any agreement you come to with the Sylvans is separate from my own reckoning on behalf of my brother and Pheebs. If they don't return soon, I will fly to Sylvan's northern pastures and find out the reason why."

As grandmother began passing out pieces of mong-wrapped skallon meat to the group, a voice echoed through the dugout.

"Hello the Jangle dugout. Three men of Swage ask permission to enter."

Bran stood up. He did not even notice the hot meat he held was burning his fingers. "Daco," he called out. "Is that you?"

"Enter, men of Swage," Jhar's father responded. "You come in time for food."

As Bran took turns hugging his brother, his nephew and his friend Pheebs, the others made room around the fire pit.

Daco and Pheebs both singed their mouths in their haste to eat the delicious hot food.

"Tell us what happened with the Sylvans," Bran said. "We were very worried when we had to fly north without you."

"Romm refused to believe our story about a coming flood," Daco said. "He left us at the Sylvan council dugout under guard. We managed to save ourselves and our guards when the dugout flooded. I know at least two of the men we saved were able to hang on to debris and ride north with the flood. I don't know if the other two guards are still alive."

Bran frowned. "Romm has much to answer for."

Chapter 27

Grum

Grum lay on his cot of skallon rugs and tried to snuggle down into the hairy depths so that he wouldn't hear his mother's weeping.

It seemed she was the only one who cared that he would soon be killed. His father was so angry he barely spoke to his son. His sisters just stayed away.

Why couldn't everyone see that he was only trying to help? The young skallon calves needed more milk. And that meant their mothers needed more grass. The Sylvan skallon weren't clustering in that corner of their pastureland. What was the harm in giving the Jangle skallon a chance to eat that grass? They wanted it. He had to keep chasing his herd back away from the border.

Grum sighed and stared at the ceiling of the dugout. The Sylvans had come for him. He had heard his sisters talking. Suddenly his morose thoughts turned to anger. Why make it easy for his killers? Let them catch him if they wanted to kill him.

He threw off his covers and put on his heavy boots. Suddenly he was full of energy. He would go north – into the ice and snow.

He grabbed a skin bag and filled it with scraps of skallon meat he pulled from the fire pit. He took a small juke gourd that had been hollowed out and filled it with water. Wrapping himself in his green cape, he left the dugout.

He headed for the western border that divided the Jangles from the blue-wearing Brites. The Sylvans would hesitate to cross over into Brite pastureland. They had no right to be there. No Brite had been stupid enough to move a boundary marker.

As he made his way north he began to question his actions. When he left the northern tip of Jangle's pastureland he would be walking into snow and ice. He would be in the land ruled by the great beasts called horids. They had fur as white as snow and preyed on anything smaller than themselves. That would include Grum. A full-grown horid was massive in size. It stood as tall as a man but walked on four feet like a skallon. Its claws and teeth were long and sharp. They ate the gray skirts that lived in tarns and streams but slithered onto the ice to bear their young.

Grum knew a horid would make quick work of him, but it would also make quick work of those that dared to pursue him. He realized suddenly that he had no hope of surviving. It had been stupid to run away. There had been talk of a trade for his life. As he trudged north he wondered why he always seemed to make the worst possible choices. Was he truly stupid or did he have some sort of wish to die?

He stumbled on through great banks of ice as snow fell around him. Not light fluffy flakes as fell on the borders of the pasturelands, but wind driven clouds of snow and sleet. He could no longer see what was right in front of him and that is why he walked right into it.

His head took the brunt of the blow as he had been leaning forward, fighting the wind that howled around him.

He couldn't make out what it was he had collided with. Some sort of metallic structure. He thumped it with his gloved hand. Definitely metallic. It sounded hollow and it was tall. He looked up to see how far it reached above him, but was immediately blinded by falling snow.

He heard something creaking open off to his left. Then a hand reached out and pulled him off his feet and inside. "What are you doing out there?" A very deep voice growled.

Grum attempted several answers – running away, looking for horids, trying to escape, trying to kill himself. He finally settled on the closest thing to the truth. "I don't know."

A woman with a kind face walked toward them. "What have we here, Uriah?"

"Hard to say," Uriah replied. I saw him in the viewer. He walked right into the ship and set off the cloaking alarm."

"Come with me," the woman said. "We will get you some fruit and something warm to drink. My name is Lydia."

"I am called Grum." He tried to smile but thought his face might be frozen.

Lydia took his hand and led him to a platform which rose of its own volition. She stepped up onto it as it moved and pulled Grum along with her.

They rose to the level of a tunnel that led to a room furnished with white soft looking structures facing out to look through an invisible wall. He could barely hear the storm blowing outside. In fact it was not even cold inside.

She handed him an orange thing the size of his fist. He recognized it as the fruit he had eaten when he had been trying to burn down this ship alongside other members of his clan. These were the people who had given Jhar the fruit. The fruit that Jhar had offered up to save him. He bit into it and nearly swooned from the pleasure. He believed such food might purchase a life. Perhaps even his life.

"Come and sit with me, Grum. I believe I have heard mention of your name." She looked at him with soft brown eyes. Her skin was a light brown color and her long hair was dark, woven into a complex network of curves.

"I am the mover of a boundary marker. My life is forfeit," he said.

"Yes, of course, the boundary marker mover. Have you escaped then?"

"There is no escape," Grum said. "I don't know why I thought it was a good idea to run away. But at least now I have been aboard a spaceship and eaten more fruit."

"I heard there was a chance your life would be traded for the fruit we left with Jhar."

Grum nodded. "Yes. I have heard that rumor as well. If she does offer it up then she will hate me, too. Everyone knows the only way to set things right is for me to die."

"Yes, I see the quandary you are facing. Many of us have felt our destinies lay in our own hands. Laws must be followed. Works must be accomplished. Then we heard the truth and it set us free. We were saved by the grace of the One who created us."

"Our parents?" Grum asked. "I believe even my father hates me."

"Look back in your father's lineage. Someone fathered him and someone fathered his father. Go back to the very first man that ever lived. Who created him? And why?"

"I don't know," Grum said. "There have always been Jangles."

"Have there?" Lydia asked. She smiled again. "Have you seen the miners' ship?"

"Yes," Grum said. "They are still there on Jangle land. No one knows what to make of their coming. And now they don't seem to want to leave. They have begun to trade translators for skallon meat. Some think they are good people who will help us to trade with our neighbors. Others think they are spies or invaders who have come to steal our pastureland. Sides are forming for and against them. I think there may be war eventually."

"Don't be so sure," Lydia said. "Sometimes a gift is truly a gift. We can either accept it or reject it." She stood up. "Now I will make us some tea and then I will call on my friends to decide what should be done to reunite you with your clan."

"My clan no longer wants me," Grum said. "But it is no longer a matter of concern. I am ready to die."

Chapter 28

Jhar

Jhar sat uncomfortably in the Jangle council dugout listening to the men around her. She had been as surprised to see her friend Dunk there as he had been surprised to see her. She hoped she had been better at disguising her emotions than Dunk had been. His jaw had dropped and his eyes opened wide. A smile followed which he quickly turned into a frown.

Since her brother, Mutt, chose to sit in the large opening beside their father, she had no choice but to sit between her brother and Dunk.

Dunk immediately whispered out the side of his mouth while looking straight ahead, "What are you doing here?" He spoke in the Jangle tongue.

Jhar tried to calm her breathing but was unsuccessful. *Didn't he realize he was speaking Jangle?* She chanced a look at her brother, but his focus was concentrated on their leader, Cray.

Cray was telling those assembled that the Jangles had saved the Sylvan leader's life by asking their friends, the alien miners, to take the Sylvan leader aboard their ship along with the Jangle elders and babies to fly north before the flood killed them. Those Sylvan men who had come along to kill Grum seemed embarrassed by their leader's acceptance of such an offer.

Jhar decided it was safe to risk an answer to Dunk's question since everyone's attention now seemed riveted on the Sylvan leader.

"I am the owner of the fruit. I have to be here," she whispered back in the Sylvan tongue.

"We must meet," Dunk said, shielding his mouth with his hand.

Jhar's mind went blank with fear. She tried to think of a place in this northern section that would be familiar to Dunk but isolated from everyone else. It could mean their own deaths if anyone saw them. No good place came to mind.

Dunk continued to look straight ahead as he scratched his nose. "At the boundary marker. After the meeting."

Jhar nodded and then realized Dunk was not looking at her. "Yes," she whispered.

As the meeting continued, most was lost on Jhar. She was too busy thinking about what Dunk might want to talk about. Perhaps he just wanted to see her as she also wanted to see him. It looked as though the Sylvans were leaning towards a trade for Grum's transgressions rather than a bloodletting. She began to relax and listen.

"The life of your leader for the transgressions of a boy barely in his teens seems more than fair," Cray concluded.

"You knew my terms before this meeting even started," Romm growled out in response. "All the fruit those aliens left here in exchange for the life of a boundary marker mover. And in return for a brief ride on your so-called friends' ship, we will not go to war with the Jangles for aiding aliens."

"Those aliens warned us of the flood," Cray said. "Otherwise we would all have died along with the skallon we depend on for life."

Romm stood up as though to leave. "My offer stands."

The other Sylvans should have stood along with their leader in a show of solidarity, but they did not.

Jhar thought the purple-caped man man on the other side of Dunk must be Dunk's father. That man stayed seated as did the Sylvan man next to him.

Romm stared at his clan members in disbelief before sitting back down.

"To save time," Cray said, "we will counter with one basket of fruit if the owner of the fruit agrees."

Jhar nodded her agreement and her father spoke to those assembled. "We are sorry for my nephew's transgression and believe he needs to make amends. I plan to take him under my instruction to teach him to craft the scrapers and punches from bones which we use in the making of capes from skallon hides. We offer to give a hundred days worth of Grum's work product to the Sylvans in addition to the basket of fruit."

The Sylvan men with the exception of Romm nodded their approval of the offer.

It appeared to Jhar as though a trade was about to be reached when Grum's father ran into the dugout, breathing hard.

"My son, Grum, has gone north. I followed his tracks to the northern border where a great storm is blowing. There I lost his tracks in the falling snow. I fear he may already have fallen prey to horids."

Romm stood once again. "We will go and see the truth of these words. This father could be lying to save his son."

Everyone stood up, some to follow Romm's order and some to save Grum from death at the jaws of a horid.

As all rushed from the dugout, Dunk pulled Jhar aside. "At dark by the boundary marker."

Jhar nodded and followed the others out of the dugout.

They picked up the tracks made by Grum and those made by his father outside Grum's dugout. They began to follow the three sets of tracks, Grum's and his father's. Only one track showed someone returning.

They had gone a short distance before Jhar's father pulled her aside. "This search is no place for women. Go back and wait at our dugout or at Grum's dugout."

Jhar didn't argue. She knew she would be sent back. She gave a fleeting glance at Dunk who was watching her before he turned to follow the others north.

As she passed the entrance to Grum's family dugout she stopped. Grum's mother and sisters were surely frantic with worry. She stepped inside and called out, "Hello, it's Jhar come from the council meeting to bring you news."

Grum's mother, Rind, came out from her alcove to meet her.

"What has the council decided?" Rind asked. Her face mirrored her anxiety.

Jhar realized at once that Grum's mother didn't know Grum was missing. His father must have come directly from his failed attempt to find Grum to the council dugout. For a moment she was struck dumb. She wouldn't be the one to kill Rind's hopes.

"The council is very close to making an agreement. They asked that the Sylvan leader's flight to safety be part of the bargain and the Sylvans who came on Romm's orders seemed to agree. In addition, we offered a basket of fruit and my father offered to teach Grum to make punches and scrapers from bones, and to give Grum's work product for a hundred days to the Sylvans."

Rind clapped her hands together and smiled. "I must tell Grum at once."

Jhar held Rind's arm to stop her. "Something else has happened," she said gently.

"What?" Rind asked

Jhar was stopped from answering by shouts outside the dugout. Grum's father rushed inside.

"The fruitgivers' ship has just landed beside the miners' ship. No one will go to look for Grum until they find out why this ship has returned."

"What do you mean, look for Grum?" Rind asked. "Isn't he here in his alcove?"

Jhar began to back out of the dugout. "I will just go and see if they have another message for us." She turned and ran from the dugout.

Chapter 29

Mona

Mona sat with Professor Stern on the observation deck of the *Seeker* looking out at the thick clouds that blanketed the planet below. The professor was finally well enough to leave his couch but Mona wasn't sure his recovery had improved his mood. He scowled as he looked at her. Although he was completely bald now and his skin sagged beneath his chin, his dark eyes still held a firm intelligence.

"Have we completed two orbits of the planet?" he demanded.

"Yes," Mona replied, "but so far we've not encountered the stolen alien ship."

"What makes you so sure it's stolen?" the professor asked.

"How else would you explain a Swage-speaking crew aboard an alien ship?"

"Perhaps they purchased it," Professor Stern said. "It could be some aliens came to Swage to establish a trading partnership and some of our more affluent citizens decided to purchase one of their ships."

Mona had the grace to be embarrassed. "Yes, that would certainly explain it. Do you think that could somehow explain our cut-off communications as well?"

"It could that be our high command has also purchased a superior communications satellite from these aliens and is now in the process of transitioning," the professor speculated.

"Of course. How could we have jumped to such a nefarious conclusion? We are supposed to be scientists. We test every theory."

"No harm done," the professor said. "But I think it is time we return to our original mission. Don't you agree?"

"I agree completely," Mona said. "I'm sure our Swagian friends will join us there at the south sea as soon as they finish their work of saving the Bando clans."

Professor Stern spoke into his comm bracelet. "Santi, take us down to the south sea please."

"Will do," Santi said. "Brace for re-entry," he announced.

Everyone pushed off from wherever they had been floating and made for their stationary cots to be secured for landing.

Mona settled in next to her exploration partner, Soma. "We have been so shortsighted," she said. She explained Professor Stern's theory of the alien ship and Soma agreed with her assessment of shortsightedness.

"Yes, we should have considered more explanations than we did," Soma agreed. "And there could even be some other explanation. Professor Stern's theory may also be incorrect."

"Agreed," Mona said. "We must use scientific thinking."

"And my scientific thinking has a hunch," Soma said.

Mona laughed. "What is your scientific hunch?"

"My hunch is that once we stop looking for them, the alien ship will find us."

Mona nodded and felt the pressure of deceleration as the ship entered Bando's field of gravity.

The *Seeker* settled in an open space a little to the south of their previous landing site as the shorelines of the sea were still littered with debris from the flood. Among that debris were thousands of dead sea animals – a bonanza for biologists.

The *Seeker* had barely landed before the biologists were ready and waiting beside the airlock.

"I can hardly wait to see an ice eater up close," Mona said.

"I assume you are speaking of a dead one," Soma said.

"Yes, of course, though we will have our tranquilizer guns waiting and ready. Live ice eaters may be feeding on the corpses of their preferred food."

Soma grimaced. "We should have brought nose plugs."

Soma's words rang true the moment they stepped outside the ship. Even though the carcasses were frozen solid, the aura of death in the form of rotting flesh was all around them.

"Look at all these fish. I had no idea so much life was swimming below the ice," Mona said.

"For that matter, how is it possible at these temperatures that the sea isn't frozen solid?"

Mona agreed it was a mystery. She walked to the edge of the sea, which was now a longer walk. Some of the sea's water had been left behind in the flood zone.

She put her hand in the water and a smile grew across her face. "It isn't ice cold. Not warm exactly, but certainly not freezing as we expected. You know what that means?"

"I would guess a source of heat from below," Soma said smiling. "Magma perhaps? Steam vents?"

"This is very exciting," Mona gushed. "And it explains the wealth of sea life we see strewn about."

"Yes, a small fish feeds a large fish, a large fish feeds a very large fish or sea mammals."

"And predators that are likely at home on land or sea," Mona finished.

"Shall we begin cataloguing?" Soma said, smiling voraciously.

"I'm ready with my recorder," Mona said, matching his smile.

For the remainder of the day, the biologists were in their element, taking samples of the dead animals that littered the beach and noting a few living animals that were taking advantage of this unexpected windfall.

The ice eaters were still alive for the most part, and so fixated on their feast of large gray finned sea animals that they barely noticed the hovering biologists.

The living ice eaters evidently did not view the biologists as food and only showed aggression if they ventured too close to the meal in progress. Some of the younger ice eaters romped and played or slept beside their mothers. They were actually very cute little balls of white fur.

"I've used up all of the free space on my recorder," Mona complained.

"Here, use mine," Soma said, unlatching the clasp at his wrist.

As Soma read off descriptions of the corpses along with measurements of size, Mona took pictures and recorded her partner's observations.

Bando's star, always low in the sky this far south, dipped even lower and the biologists headed back to their ship, too elated to rest, but too exhausted to continue in the fading light.

"I have never had such a gratifying day," Mona said with a weary grin.

"Nor I," Soma agreed. "This day's research will keep a fleet of biologists working for years to come."

"If only we could broadcast our findings to our whole world," Mona said. "We will be heroes on Swage. Everyone will be thrilled to hear of these new life forms."

"Most are unique because of the cold climate, but some seem to have evolved with similar adaptations to our own Swage fauna depending on their position in the food chain," Soma noted.

"Yes, I have noticed that," Mona said. "Many of these are similar to our own fish, though we haven't yet tested their DNA. It could be something other than carbon-based."

"So much work and so little time," Soma said. "We have food and fuel enough to stay sixty of our Swage days on this planet."

"If the fish here are edible, I don't see why we couldn't extend our stay," Mona pointed out.

"We'll have to catch a live one to try it," Soma said. "We wouldn't dare to eat the flesh of something that smells like these."

"No," Mona agreed, "but we could venture out into the sea with spears after a meal and some sleep. What do you think?"

"I think we could run the idea past Professor Stern," Soma said. "I would be up for a fresh fish meal."

Mona laughed. "My life is perfect. I could never have even dreamed of a day such as this."

Soma grimaced. "I have learned to be suspicious of too much happiness. I don't wish to tempt fate."

Chapter 30

Daco

Daco's reunion with his son and brother had been happy and emotional. So emotional he hesitated to bring up the next subject, that being another emotional grenade. He took a deep breath before saying, "There was a space ship flying over the Sylvan pastureland. It flew low purposely, scaring the skallon to make them run north."

Bran nodded. "The visitors who gave us the translators?"

"No," Daco said. "This ship looked a lot like our ship. I'm sure it was a Swagian ship."

Luckily Bran was already seated. He looked as though he might faint otherwise. His voice shook as he tried to speak. "There are survivors from our planet?"

"I believe so," Daco said. "The ship is a little smaller than ours. Less cargo area but definitely of Swagian design."

"We always knew we weren't alone in the universe. First the Bandos and then the translator makers. You're sure it was a Swagian ship?"

"Yes, I'm sure." Daco was quiet for a moment. "Probably not a trading ship with the small cargo area."

"We have to find it," Bran said.

"Of course we do," Daco agreed, "but we have to be smart about it. We'll need to refresh our fuel supply soon. We have to conserve the few resources we have left."

Bran nodded. "We need to call a meeting of all the miners."

"They're likely already hearing about this Swagian ship from Pheebs," Daco said.

A loud banging at the side of the ship interrupted their conversation.

Bran looked out a viewing portal and said, "It looks like Jhar, and some others behind her."

"Best we go out rather than inviting them in," Daco said. "We don't want to appear to be taking sides in their ongoing disputes."

They found several miners gathering around the airlock, ready to open the outside hatch and Daco put up his hand to stop them.

"Bran and I will go out to see what the disturbance is."

"Do you want to take a blaster?" Tull asked.

"No, we know the girl," Daco said, "and it looks like her father and brother with her. I'll give a signal if we need reinforcements."

The inner hatch went up and the two brothers stepped into the lock. They didn't need the transition from inside air to outside air here as Cold Planet air was breathable, but they kept the hatches closed as a precaution against unpredictable neighbors.

When the outside hatch opened, Jhar stepped forward. "Thank you for seeing us," she said. "Grum has run away."

"I'm sorry to hear it," Daco said. "Especially when it looked as though you were close to putting together a trade to save his life."

Jhar nodded. "Also, the fruit givers have returned."

"What?" Daco had assumed the fruit givers had returned to their planet in another galaxy. He flashed back to their leaving. Their last gift to the miners had been the mysterious talking book. Daco hadn't had a chance to listen to it as yet.

"Have you spoken to them?" he asked.

"No, not this time," Jhar said. "But they told us you would be coming and then you did come. They seemed to know you, so we thought we should tell you."

"We really appreciate that," Daco said. "Where is their ship?"

Jhar pointed off to the east. "It looks as though they landed close to our border with the Sylvans."

"Shall we all go together to welcome them?" Bran asked.

Jhar nodded. "We thought you might both use your ships to help us find Grum if it's not too late."

"You think Grum may be in danger?" Bran asked.

"We are sure of it," Jhar said. "He ran north into the jaws of the horids."

"Just give me a minute to tell my crew what is happening and we will go with you to speak to the fruit givers," Daco said.

Daco was only gone for a few moments and then returned with Tull, Onri and Aldo at his side.

"Let us go and see what has brought our friends from another galaxy back to Cold Land. The irony of including the Jangles in his pronoun, *us,* was not lost on Daco. Were they really becoming his friends? His countrymen? It seemed he was more of a friend to the Jangles than their close neighbors, the Sylvans were. Did their coming to him in an emergency mean they trusted the miners? Perhaps. Then again – any port in a storm. It could be they thought a friendship with the miners might be useful in dealing with the fruit givers. He would withhold both judgment and hope for the time being.

The unique wheeled ship of the fruit givers was not far off. A crowd of Jangles and a few Sylvans were already gathered around it. The colors of their capes made it easy to differentiate one from another.

Daco approached with a smile that was not feigned. "Hello the ship," he called out. "May we come aboard?"

The hatch opened and an adolescent boy stepped out.

"Grum," Jhar shouted.

A green-caped man stepped forward to hug the boy. "Why did you run away, son?" the man asked.

Grum shrugged as though he had no answer for that question.

"Our leaders have reached an agreement to spare your life," the man said.

Grum shrugged again. "I am already dead to my clan," he said.

Lydia stepped down from the hatch and put her arm around Grum. "He wishes to make amends for his actions," she said. "He is ready to face whatever punishment you deem fair."

Cray looked at Grum. "You gave us a scare and we're glad to see you alive. We thank the fruit givers for returning you. You will learn to make scrapers and punches and give one hundred days of your work product to the Sylvans. Your life is spared."

A tiny ray of hope shown from Grum's eyes and Lydia smiled down at him. "Remember all we have told you. Your beliefs rule your actions. Search for the truth."

Lydia looked up and met Daco's eyes. "Joshua would like to speak to you and your associates. Have you time to come aboard for a chat?"

"Certainly," Daco said, making his way through the gathering crowd. He turned back to call out to Jhar – "wait here if you want. I won't be gone long."

Jhar nodded.

Daco, Bran, Tull, Onri and Aldo went aboard the alien ship for the first time. They all tried to take in as much information as possible. A fleeting glimpse of the engine area told them it was not the fusion reactor they were familiar with. In fact it didn't appear to be a fusion reactor at all. Some sort of electromagnetic set up perhaps?

The ship's hull was also foreign. Not the microfoam filaments of their Swagian ships. Unbelievably, the turning wheels appeared to be made of crystalline peridot.

They stepped aboard the ascending platform as Lydia demonstrated and were on their way up several levels to meet with Joshua.

Chapter 31

Jhar

Jhar waited outside the fruit givers' ship with many others. As their red star dipped below the horizon, turning the sky first red, then violet, people began to drift away. Grum left with his father. Cray told the Sylvan men they were welcome to stay in the council dugout for the night, then left for his own dugout.

Dunk's father Darp spoke to his son. "We can learn more in the morning," he said. "We need to sleep."

"I know where the council dugout is," Dunk said. "I want to stay a few more minutes in case they bring out more fruit."

His father nodded. "Don't stay too long."

Jhar could hardly believe what was happening. She was to be left alone with Dunk? She took a deep breath when they were finally all alone in the gathering shadows.

"I was so worried about you," Dunk said.

"And I was worried for you, too. How did you escape the flood?" Jhar asked.

"We were forced to run north. A ship flew over our pastures low enough to stampede our skallon. We had no choice but to follow them."

Jhar knew the miners' ship had been here at Jangle land, carrying the old and very young to safety. "The fruit givers' ship?" she asked.

"No, it must have been the miners' ship," Dunk said.

"It couldn't have been," Jhar said. "The miners were here with us. They carried your leader Romm to safety."

Dunk nodded. "Yes, my father and Cray lost respect for Romm because of it. There must be a third ship. Do you think we're being invaded?"

Jhar smiled at her friend. "It's so good to see you here. I'm glad our leaders were able to spare my cousin Grum."

"I thought I might die of grief if I lost you to the flood," Dunk said.

"Yet here we both are alive and most of our skallon alive as well." Jhar raised her hands palm up in a gesture of amazement.

"It's not enough," Dunk said. "Things are changing. My father has hinted that I should think of digging my own dugout and start a family now that my tanning apprenticeship is coming to an end. Who could I bring into my dugout when I only want to be with you?"

"Such thinking is dangerous," Jhar cautioned.

"I no longer care about danger. Even as I faced danger with my father, my thoughts were all of you. You bring joy and meaning to my life."

"But it is forbidden," Jhar said. "What you hope for can never be."

"Then my life is over," Dunk said.

"Can't we still meet as friends?" Jhar asked.

"You are wealthy now, with fruit to trade for whatever you want. Some Jangle man will ask you to share his dugout. You will have children. Our friendship will wither like uprooted grass."

Jhar knew he spoke the truth and she began to feel the loss of her friend like a pain in her heart. "But what else can we do? Can you dig a dugout on the border where we each go our separate ways every morning?"

Dunk smiled. "I am willing to try it."

"Even if our clans were willing to allow it, which is of course ridiculous, what of our children? Would they be Jangles? Sylvans? Accepted by both clans or neither?"

"I'm willing to become a Jangle," Dunk said. "I'm a tanner now. You must value tanners here in Jangle."

"Yes, your skills would be welcome here," Jhar said. "But what of your father? He depends on you, doesn't he?"

"I believe if I left he would take another woman into his dugout. I think he has only waited this long for my sake. I have no brothers or sisters."

Jhar knew Dunk's mother had died when he was very young. He barely remembered her. "We could ask Cray's permission, but I don't think we have thought of all the ramifications. What if my family doesn't accept you? We could be cut off from them as well."

Dunk smiled. "You think they could resist my lovely tanned hides and my funny jokes?"

Jhar laughed. "Probably not. Also, as you say, I'm wealthy now. Perhaps my fruit could sway people toward acceptance."

Dunk gathered Jhar into his strong arms and sunk a hand into her hair to bring her closer. "Thank you Jhar. You have saved my life by agreeing to try. If all else fails perhaps we can stowaway together on one of these invading ships."

Jhar smiled. "Do you think we might bring a few skallon with us? It appears to me the miners have no source of food. The fruit givers might be the better choice."

"I feel as though this might actually work," Dunk said. "Since Cray has accepted the miners as friends even though they have no pastureland and no skallon, what a small jump it would be to accept a Sylvan with valuable skills."

"Yes, these miners and fruit givers have opened the Jangles up to new ways of thinking. The translators they offer in trade have made communication between clans possible. We are not so different as we once believed."

"Only our colors divide us now," Dunk said. "I have always liked the color green."

Jhar had a moment of indecision. Were they being foolish, thinking such a thing might be possible? Might they both be killed for even suggesting such an outrageous proposition? "Are we making a terrible mistake that could cost us both our lives?" she asked.

"Let me be the one to test it," Dunk said. "I will speak first to my father and then to Romm. If I am killed for it, this ends with me."

"But how could I then live knowing I was the reason you died? And Romm is unyielding. He would like nothing better than to use you as an example of his authority."

"Yes, you're right about Romm," he said. "I believe he will soon be replaced as leader. When we return to Sylvan pastures my father plans to call for a vote. I'm sure of this."

"Then do us this favor," Jhar said. "Will you wait until Romm is replaced as leader before you present our case? We might have a better chance of success with a new leader."

"I'll do as you ask," Dunk said. "I trust your observations. But you have to make a promise to me as well."

"And what is this promise? I have to know before I can agree."

"If you see any young Jangle man digging a new dugout you will stay far away from him. You will not smile at him or allow him into your father's dugout to sit around your fire pit."

Jhar laughed. "You really do have a good sense of humor. I will do as you say. No smiles. No guests at our fire pit. If I don't see you again before your journey home, take care and stay safe."

Dunk held her close in his arms before finally turning away to find the council dugout in the dark.

Chapter 32

Daco

Daco was very happy to see Joshua again. Without the translators these alien visitors had provided, he didn't know how he and his fellow miners would have survived. The translators had given him something valuable to trade for food and made the communication needed for trade possible.

"Joshua, my friend," Daco said. "We thought you might have returned to your home in another galaxy. This is indeed a welcome surprise."

"It's good to see you as well," Joshua said. "It appears you and your miners have been accepted here."

"Not entirely," Daco said, "but so far we have been able to trade translators for skallon meat and that has kept us fed. We have as yet no land to call our own."

"And your family has come with you," Joshua said, smiling at Aldo, Bran, Tull and Onri.

"Yes, we are reunited after a near catastrophe. You were here to witness the flood?" Bran asked.

Joshua nodded. "We flew low over two squares off to the west to scare the skallon into running north."

"You flew to the west," Daco said, "but a ship similar to our *Bonanza* flew over the Sylvan square to the east where I was being held prisoner."

"Yes," Joshua said. "That ship you saw over Sylvan land is what I wished to speak with you about. I didn't know you were being held prisoner."

"It was a misunderstanding that has been resolved. I am now friends with the Sylvans. And I'm relieved to hear you know of the second Swagian ship. I was beginning to wonder if I imagined it since no one else seemed to know of it," Daco said.

Joshua laughed. "The ship carries biologists from your destroyed planet Swage."

"Biologists!" Daco and his brother said it at the same time.

"They have come here to study cold climate predators," Joshua said. He paused and closed his eyes for a moment. "They don't know they have no planet to return to."

Daco looked at his brother and saw his own sad face reflected in his brother's countenance. "I see."

"We thought it best they hear the news from you," Joshua said.

"So you have met these biologists?" Tull asked.

Joshua nodded. "They were out of their ship looking for predators on the shore of a southern sea as the asteroid flew closer. They had no idea they were in danger from the sea itself," Joshua said.

"Did you have time to speak with them?" Onri asked.

"Only enough time to order them back to their ship to save their lives," Joshua said.

"But how did they know to fly over the Sylvan square of pasture?" Daco asked.

"I ordered that as well," Joshua said. "Once we were both airborne, I was able to establish communication with them."

"Biologists," Bran murmured. "They have no idea Swage is ruined?"

"They know something is wrong," Joshua said. "Communications with Swage were suddenly cut off. When they heard us, people who spoke their language, they assumed we were from Swage. We wore spacesuits so they could not see our faces."

"But your ship," Aldo said.

Joshua looked at Aldo. "Yes, the ship gave them some concern. One of the biologists, Mona, decided Swage must have been invaded by aliens. She believes we must have captured this foreign ship during a battle."

Daco nodded slowly. "Yes, it is unthinkable to imagine the truth."

"It must be a comfort to know a few more of your countrymen survived," Joshua said.

"Only my empathy for what they will feel on hearing the truth dampens my excitement," Daco said. "Do you know where they are now? We should go at once to welcome them."

"My guess would be that they have returned to their investigations at the southern sea," Joshua said.

Daco looked around at his friends and family. "We could leave at dawn tomorrow?"

Bran shrugged. "We still have no guarantees of acceptance here, but we can at least make the biologists part of our future strategy."

"You might take a closer look at the southern sea area," Joshua said. "It appears no one owns it as yet."

Daco nodded slowly. "The floodwaters were not as freezing cold as we expected."

Joshua smiled. "You noticed."

Daco returned his smile. "Is there any chance you and your crew might join us at the south sea? We know your technology is advanced far beyond our own. Your presence would be a gift to us all."

"We left once and were forced to return by news of the *Seeker's* arrival. Perhaps this time we will delay a bit to be sure our work here is finished."

"The *Seeker*?" Tull asked.

"The name of the biologists' ship," Joshua said.

"Please visit us at the southern sea," Daco said, sensing this visit was coming to a close. "We would welcome any advice."

Joshua stood up. "We will if conditions here allow it," he said.

The miners took this to be a sign that their visit was over and stood as well. Daco led his family and friends though the tunnel which connected to the center shaft where the escalade was in motion.

As the miners stepped onto the descending platform, Joshua called out to them. "Lydia has some fruit for you for your journey south."

"You have our deepest thanks," Daco said.

As Joshua had promised, Lydia stood beside the lowest hatch surrounded by five baskets of fruit, one for each of them.

"This fruit is especially welcome just now," Daco told Lydia. "We need to make more translators to trade for skallon meat."

Lydia nodded. "Give our thanks to the biologists for flying over the Sylvan pasturelands."

"I certainly will," Daco said. "Their flight saved many lives, perhaps my own among them."

They stepped out into a dark night. Luckily three had their shiners with them. When Daco turned his light on, he was surprised to see Jhar still waiting in the dark.

"Jhar, you should not have stayed so long. You must be freezing out here."

"It is always this cold at night," Jhar said, as though she supposed they might not know that.

Daco gave a short laugh. "Yes, your planet is very predictable. Let us walk you home at least."

"Grum and his father went home together," Jhar said. "Thank you, Bran, for your suggestion of making Grum responsible for a portion of his debt. That argument helped to save his life."

"I'm glad it helped," Bran said. "The fruit givers have solved the question of the second ship. The one which flew over Sylvan land and sent everyone running north. It is a ship from our home planet Swage."

"You didn't know they were here?" Jhar asked.

"No," Daco said. "We plan to leave tomorrow at dawn to find them."

"Oh," Jhar said, looking down at her feet. "What are those glowing sticks you have to light our way?"

"We call them shiners," Daco said. "Would you like to have one?"

"I would," Jhar said. "I could trade you fruit for one but I see you already have fruit from the aliens."

"Why don't I give you one now and when we return again to trade you can give us some skallon meat."

Jhar smiled. "I'm glad you aren't leaving for good. My people may not be welcoming but I want you to stay."

"We like the idea of staying as well," Daco said, setting down his basket of fruit to give her the shiner he had placed atop the basket.

"Should I suggest to our leader Cray that we might offer a small section of land in trade?" Jhar asked.

"No, say nothing as yet," Daco said. "We have to discuss our future plans with these biologists from our homeland before we make a final decision about our future."

"But you promise to return for your skallon meat?" Jhar said, flashing her new shiner about in all directions.

"Yes," Daco said as they reached the entrance to her family dugout. "And you promise to stay safe until we return."

"I will try," Jhar said, in a voice that indicated there might be some doubt.

Chapter 33

Jhar

The next morning Jhar awoke to a quiet dugout. She had slept late. Her family had already left for the pastures. She checked for her baskets of fruit and her new shiner. Still there in the alcove by the firepit. She had planned to take meat to the miners' ship if they hadn't left yet to pay for her shiner but decided she needed to speak to Rahab instead.

The alien would understand her muddle over Jangle's rules and her feelings for a man in an enemy clan. Rahab had helped the men who came to spy on her city. She would know how Jhar felt. Going against the rules of her clan was no small thing. Although anything had seemed possible while she was with Dunk, she knew she was acting like Grum. Making poor decisions that were not lawful. Her own family would be right to disown her.

Mornings this close to the northern border of the pastues were freezing cold. Snow was falling as she left the dugout. The skallon gathered into close-knit groups to survive. Ice still clung to blades of grass making a crunching noise as she walked. The fruit givers' ship was close to the northeast marker of her clan's pastureland.

As Jhar reached the alien ship, she slowed. Four strangers waited outside the spaceship – two in red capes and two in blue capes. She knew the clan to the west of the Jangles wore blue. They were called Brites. She didn't know who the red capes were.

Putting the translator Bran had given her in her ear, she walked forward. "Good morning," she said. "You gentlemen are from the Brite clan?" The two men were so surprised they almost dropped the objects they had been holding.

"How do you speak our language?" one of the blue-caped men asked.

"No, she is speaking our language," one of the red-caped men said. "It is not possible. She must be a demon," the red-caped man said, backing away.

Jhar removed the translator from her ear and showed it to the men before replacing it in her ear. "I will let you try wearing this to see what it does, but only if you promise not to harm it or me."

The man who had called her a demon shook his head and moved further away, but one of the blue-caped men nodded and reached out for it.

He put it in his ear and spoke. "Are you understanding me?" he asked.

Everyone nodded.

The Brite clansman handed the device to his fellow clansman who put it in his ear and said, "I am called Chi."

The second red-caped man took the translator and put it in his ear, even though his hand shook a little as he did it. "I am of the red-caped clan Flag and I am called Stan."

Stan's fellow clansman backed away still farther as though Stan had now become a demon, too.

"The men in this ship wear these as well." Jhar told them after reinserting the translator. "If you come bearing trade items perhaps they will give you one in trade."

Chi put his hand out to reclaim the translator. "We come bearing gifts and I assume the Flags do as well."

Stan nodded in agreement.

"This ship flew low over our pastureland, moving our skallon north just before the flood waters came. It saved our lives and the lives of our skallon."

Jhar nodded. "These are good people aboard the ship. They have a different way of thinking. I have come today seeking advice."

"Will they see us?" Chi asked. "Should we just leave our gifts and go?"

"I don't know," Jhar said. "I only hope they will allow me to go aboard."

The second red-caped man took a few steps back toward the group but still seemed ready to flee at any sign of suspicious activity.

Stan showed Jhar the copper ring they had brought as a gift.

"But this is beautiful," Jhar said. "How did you craft such a thing?"

"It is a new process we have perfected," Stan said. "It takes a very hot fire to soften the metal."

"Don't give away our secrets," the second Flagman hissed.

"It's all right," Jhar said. "I don't need to know."

The hatch of the fruit givers' ship opened and Rahab stepped out. "Jhar, what a nice surprise. Have you come for a visit?"

"I hoped to speak to you," Jhar said. "It would mean a great deal to me if you could spare me some time."

"Of course," Rahab said. She looked at the other four men. "Someone will be coming soon to invite you four aboard."

As Jhar entered the ship she heard the hatch close behind her.

Jhar followed Rahab as she stepped on the ascending platform, and again as Rahab stepped off at the fourth level.

They sat around a small table laden with fruit and cups of hot tea.

"What did you wish to talk about?" Rahab asked, inviting Jhar to eat and drink with a wave of her hand.

Jhar took a small sip of tea before beginning. It tasted a little like mong leaf tea.

"My friend Dunk wants to become a Jangle so that we can share a dugout and raise a family together," she said.

"How lovely," Rahab said. "And is that what you want as well?"

"Yes," Jhar said. "But it is not allowed. We could both be killed for daring to present such an idea."

"Are you sure that it is not allowed?" Rahab asked.

"Yes," Jhar said. "The Sylvans are enemies of the Jangles. We don't associate with them except to trade. I am sure of that."

"Who makes these rules?" Rahab asked.

Jhar shrugged. "Our ancestors, I suppose. It has always been that way."

"And you think by even asking your leader Cray if Dunk could become a Jangle and share a dugout with you, you could both be killed?"

"Yes," Jhar said eagerly, thankful that Rahab saw the problem so quickly.

"It seems both the Jangles and the Sylvans are on the verge of accepting the miners as trading partners and even as friends," Rahab observed.

"Yes, that is true," Jhar allowed.

"This is likely because the miners have something valuable to offer to both clans," she continued.

"Yes," Jhar agreed.

"In my past, as I told you, I offered something of value to those who came to conquer our city."

Jhar remembered what Rahab had told her. "You hid the spies from your people."

"Yes. And for that they protected me and my family when they came to conquer our city," Rahab said.

"So if I had something of value to offer my clan, they might allow Dunk to become a Jangle and dig a dugout for us here on Jangle pastureland?"

"It is possible," Rahab said. "What has Dunk to offer?"

"He is a full-fledged tanner now," Jhar said.

"And what have you to offer?" Rahab asked.

"I have the fruit you gave me," Jhar said.

"Then when the time comes, you might lead with those benefits which you offer the Jangles in exchange for allowing a departure from the usual customs."

"So, best not to argue on the basis of feelings or fairness?"

Rahab shrugged. "That has been my experience in my past. Now, however, I have a Spirit which dwells within me. Things like fairness, justice, love for my fellow man and concern for those in need take a higher priority."

"What is this Spirit which dwells within you?" Jhar asked.

"It is a gift from our God. You can learn more about Him in a book we gave to the miners."

"I'm friends with Bran and his brother Daco now. I think they would allow me to see this book."

"You would not regret doing so," Rahab said. "But enough of strategy. Please, have some fruit and tell me more about your young man, Dunk."

Jhar smiled. "He is my best friend," she began.

Chapter 34

Mona

Mona and her exploration partner Soma left their ship clothed in pink rubber suits for warmth, carrying extenders for their feet, goggles to protect their eyes and spears for bagging fish.

A thin layer of ice had already settled atop the waters of the withdrawn receded south sea, but that could be easily broken to gain entry.

"What if something very large decides to attack us?" Mona asked.

"Unless it's colorblind it should not confuse us with the blue and gray and brown fish we have seen stranded on shore as the tsumi surge drew back," Soma said. "And we have our spears."

"We will only spear a few small fish, right?" Mona was not feeling as brave this morning as she had yesterday. This morning the sky was overcast and it appeared snow was imminent. They knew little of the creatures that inhabited this sea. They did know that ice eaters lived here and very likely went into the sea to stalk their prey.

"Yes," Soma said. "But if something with teeth or claws appears threatening, best to retreat."

"Right," Mona said. "Retreating is always a good option."

Soma stomped on the thin ice at the edge of the sea and it broke easily. He sat at the graveled edge to put on his feet extenders and swim glasses.

Mona did the same as she looked out over the flat black water with its glassy ice surface. No waves or ripples broke the surface of the ice. Yet it still possessed an underlying power. And she was sure it held secrets in its depths.

They dove in as the first flakes of snow whipped around them.

Visibility was not good. Mona could see only about the length of a foot in front of her. Her gills took over the job of pulling oxygen into her lungs and she began to relax. The water was cold but not freezing cold.

As they moved forward the sea floor dropped. They descended with it and found the water warmed as they dropped.

Soma pointed to something below with his spear.

Mona swam foreword until she was beside him. Then she saw it. Bubbles coming up from beneath the floor of the sea. Escaping gases from a vent. And around the vent, a cluster of shells.

Soma was already loosening a few shelled life forms from around the vent with the tip of his spear.

Mona dove down to collect them into the net bag that hung from her belt. They were curved bivalves. A promising source of food. A large shape moved closer in the water and she was suddenly peering into the many eyes of a many-legged sea creature. The creature was a deep purple color and its arms or legs or whatever the many appendages were, snaked out around it.

No teeth or claws presented but those arms looked capable of hugging a person to death or perhaps just holding on to a person while it feasted. She backed away.

The creature continued to study her, appearing more curious than threatening before gathering its appendages up into a bundle to propel itself away into the darkness.

Mona gathered the bivalves Soma had freed from one another as her partner signaled a move forward, deeper into the blackness.

Ominous shapes moved by in the dark water following schools of small glowing fish. Soma lunged at something Mona could not make out. He pulled back on his spear and there was a medium-sized fish attached, about the length of Mona's forearm.

The fish was too large for Mona's specimen bag, so she nodded and pointed to the surface.

The two explorers broke through the ice at the surface and breathed air once again.

Soma held up his fish, still hanging from his spear. "This one looks highly edible to me. What do you think?"

"I think we have gathered a wealth of discoveries in a very short time. Those warm water vents are incredible. I wish we had a geologist with us."

"Do you want to spear a fish or are you ready to do some lab work?" Soma asked.

"Lab work, by all means," Mona said, hoping she didn't sound too relieved. "And next time we should wear headlamps. I could barely see my hand in front of my face."

Soma flashed a smile. "This is going to be a lot to explore, but I am more than ready."

"Yes, me too," Mona lied. She was more than ready to get back to the safety of their ship.

They swam back to shore. Mona had no trouble keeping up since Soma was encumbered by the weight of the fish on his spear.

They stood up when the water grew shallow and walked the short distance to shore. Far down the rocky beach Mona spotted a small family of ice eaters – a mother and two cubs – wading into the water. Yes, they could definitely swim and hunt in the sea.

"See that?" Mona said, pointing down the beach.

"Ice eaters," Soma said. "Looks like a family picnic in the works."

"Yes," Mona agreed. "I'm glad we aren't on the morning's menu."

Soma laughed, then hesitated. "We could wait here a while to see if they eat while in the water or drag their food on shore. That would also give us a chance to see what it is they hunt."

Mona sighed inwardly. They were so close to being warm and safe in their ship. But they were biologists. This is what biologists did. They studied animals and their habits. "Of course we must take advantage of this opportunity," she agreed.

They moved a little closer to the ice eaters. In their bright pink rubber wetsuits they were very visible against the falling snow and the gray overcast.

The mother ice eater was a little smaller than a skallon. She and her cubs were covered in white fur with the close set eyes of predators. Their snouts drooped down in funnel shaped masses of whiskers. The mother took note of their presence by sniffing the air and watching them intently. Then she moved closer to her cubs and waded into the sea. Soon they disappeared beneath the layer of ice.

Mona and Soma sat down on the gravel beach to examine their collected bounty while they waited. The bivalves were oval in shape, a medium gray color with hard shells. The shells were tightly closed, but Soma used his spear point to pry one open. Inside, the meat was a pinkish color with the consistency of a tongue.

"This looks edible to me," Mona said. "Perhaps a bit tough, but the meat could be ground up."

Soma nodded. "And this fine fellow appears to be a gourmet item. It looks a little like a skipper," he said. The mention of a fish from their planet, Swage, brought a wave of homesickness to Mona but she tried to switch her thinking to the excitement these new discoveries deserved.

"Yes," she said. "And I loved the taste of skippers. Wouldn't it be a marvel if these are similar?"

"I'd be happy to learn that even some of the sea life here is edible," Soma said. "This place is a wonderland just waiting to be explored. I can't fathom why the people who live here haven't explored these polar regions of their planets."

"They seem to be devoted to their livestock," Mona said. "When the skallon began to run beneath our ship, the shepherds didn't hesitate to run after them."

"Yes," Soma agreed, deep in thought, "but all of this..." He looked out at the dark sea and swung his hand around to encompass it. "All of this just waiting to be discovered."

Mona stood up when she saw movement at the edge of the sea. "It's the mother ice eater," she said. "And she's dragging a very big fish ashore." Mona turned back, smiling, only to find Soma looking in the opposite direction. She followed his gaze to see a ship very like their own ship, *Seeker,* landing close by.

Chapter 35

Dunk

When the contingent sent to kill the boundary marker mover returned to Sylvan land they assembled at the council dugout to make their report to the council. Darp asked his son to come along as he had witnessed the agreement made at the Jangles' council dugout.

Dunk hoped that Romm would be deposed as Sylvan leader but it was not his place to suggest such a bold idea. The dugout had not as yet been cleared of ripcon squatters and Dunk could hear them moving around in the dark recesses of the dugout.

Romm stood in a circle of torch light close to the large firepit to lead the discussion of recent events. He began by putting his own actions in the most favorable light. "It would have been easy enough to kill the boy who moved the marker. He was a coward who tried to run away to avoid death. But since he was no real threat, I decided to put Sylvans first by accepting a trade of one year's work product of scrapers and punches along with this basket of fruit which we can all share."

Romm began tossing out pieces of fruit to the various council members assembled around the fire pit.

Gerd, one of the guards that had been tasked with guarding the alien prisoners, stood up to speak. "I have spoken to two others who were tasked with guarding the aliens who came to warn us of the coming flood," he said. "One of us, Mund, died in the water. We three were saved by the prisoners we were left to guard. I question our leader's decision to leave Sylvan land and go to Jangle at such a crucial time."

The guard who had accompanied Darp and Dunk to Jangle stood up next. "We learned at the Jangle council dugout that our leader chose to fly north in the alien spaceship along with the Jangles' elderly and children, saving himself from the flood waters. I question that decision."

At that point many discussions broke out among the council members for and against their leader.

Romm stood up and glared at his accusers. "I had no way of knowing whether those aliens spoke the truth. It could have been a ruse to make us all run north while they took over our southern pastures. And when I arrived in Jangle and learned the truth there was no time to return to Sylvan land. Would you have had me running north saving the skallon of our enemies?"

More arguing among the council members followed before Gerd stood up. "I call for a vote."

At this, everyone quieted. A call for a vote could not be argued. There would be a vote and a majority would decide whether Romm continued as leader or a new leader was appointed.

"All who want a new leader stand up," Gerd said, as he looked at those seated around the pit.

One by one those seated began to stand until the decision was obvious. Very few remained seated and a furious Romm walked out of the dugout saying, "You will all regret this. Mark my words."

The remainder of the council looked at one another critically. Who would they trust with the powerful position of Sylvan leader?

"I nominate Darp," Gerd said. "He is a steady man and didn't flinch when Romm asked him to go along to wield justice on the boundary marker mover. All in favor of Darp as our new leader please stand up."

Everyone around the fire pit nodded as they stood to acknowledge their new leader.

Dunk could see the surprise in his father's face as he stood to accept this high position. "I shall try to always make decisions in the best interest of Sylvans as long as I am leader," he said in his usual sincere manner.

Dunk congratulated his father on this high office, wondering as he hugged his father how this would affect his decision to become a Jangle. Surely it wouldn't be good for his father's standing as leader if his son wished to leave his clan. But he had already told Jhar this was what he would do. He had no choice now but to go ahead with the plan.

Before leaving the dugout, Darp asked Gerd to form a group to clear the place of ripcons and other pests. "Take some of the fruit home to your families as payment," he said.

Gerd smiled and nodded.

As he walked from the dugout with his father, he said, "I am sure you will be a good leader, father. You always make good decisions."

"Thank you Dunk," his father said. "Your good opinion of me is the one that matters most."

"I fear I have made a poor decision – one that will make me less of a son in your eyes." Dunk said.

His father looked at him with concern. "And what is this poor decision you have made?"

"I have a secret friendship with a Jangle girl. We have been meeting secretly for years since we were very young. I have strong feelings for her and now she is of age to start a family. I want to be the one to share her dugout."

"Yes, I know of these secret meetings," his father said.

"You do?"

"Of course. What kind of father would I be if I did not keep track of my only child? The meetings seemed harmless to me and I knew you were lonely after your mother died."

"Then you know this girl is Jhar, the girl who owns the fruit," Dunk said.

"Yes," his father said.

"I told her how I feel. She feels the same. But she has a large family. It would be harder for her to leave. I have only you. I don't want to leave you, but I don't think I could bear to see Jhar start a family with someone else. I offered to become a Jangle because I saw no other solution. Can you ever forgive me?"

"There is no forgiveness required. You will always be my son whether you are a Jangle or a Sylvan. But you know there is a risk with such a decision. The Jangle may not accept you. They may come in the night to kill you."

"Yes, I know this. Jhar knows it as well. They may kill us both." Dunk looked at his father hopefully. "Do you see another way?"

His father was quiet while he considered his son's question. "You could ask rather than demand. You could make your case for becoming a Jangle in order to share a dugout with a Jangle girl, but then you would be required to abide by the Jangle council's decision. Are you both willing to do that?"

"Jhar may be willing but I am not," Dunk said. "I would throw in with the aliens before I would give up Jhar."

Darp nodded. "I had similar feelings for your mother, so I understand."

"It means so much to me that you do, father. I realize that I am putting your new leadership role at risk with my selfish desires and I wish I could be a better son."

Darp laughed. "You remind me of myself. If you have such failings you no doubt inherited them from me."

"If I could convince Jhar to become a Sylvan instead, would you, as our leader, accept her into our clan?"

"I would, of course. She is a wealthy woman now with her fruit and her translator. She has much to offer us."

"That is the biggest problem. With her new wealth I am afraid she will have the interest of many Jangle men."

Darp nodded. "Yes, I see the problem calls for swift action."

"I plan to meet her tonight at the boundary marker. I will see what she thinks of your suggestion – asking the permission of the

Jangle council before I begin to dig a dugout on Jangle land. But I must also tell her I am not prepared to abide by their decision should it go against us."

Darp smiled. "I hope you will tell me how she receives your proposals."

"I will surely do so. Yours is always the voice of reason," Dunk said. "And please watch your own back as well. I don't believe Romm intends to take his loss without repercussions. He's likely plotting a rebellion as we speak."

"Yes, of that I have no doubt," Darp replied.

Chapter 36

Daniel

Daniel and Jonah looked out at the four men standing beside their spaceship: two in red capes, two in blue capes. "These four are not mentioned in our mission statement," Jonah said. "We could ask Uriah to accept their gifts and send them on their way."

"Yes, but we made them part of our mission when we flew over their pasturelands," Daniel pointed out. "Are you willing to share your experience of dealing with your enemies?"

"Yes, I suppose so, that could be why I was sent," Jonah said. "It's hard to remember how tightly I held my views so long ago."

"Yes," Daniel agreed. "We didn't have God's word written on our hearts back then. Our hatreds ran deep."

"And so it is with the shepherds," Jonah said. "Let's welcome them aboard and give them fruit."

The two men took the revolving platform down the central shaft and opened the hatch at ground level.

"Welcome, men of Cold Land," Daniel said. "Will you come aboard and visit with us?"

All four men heard the invitation in their own language. Chi thanked them and stepped aboard holding out his offering of smoked skallon meat.

"Ah, the meat of your animals," Daniel said. "Yes, a most appropriate gift."

"I am Chi of the Brites," the blue-caped man said. "We are grateful to your ship for flying above our herds to move them north. Some think you may have caused the flood, but I don't agree with that thinking. Why would you cause the flood to kill us and then try to save us?"

"We are grateful for your reasoned thinking," Jonah said. "A mind open to reason is a powerful thing."

"This is my brother and leader of our clan, Chai," Chi said.

"We are pleased to meet you, leader Chai," Daniel said. "I am called Daniel and this is my friend, Jonah."

The Brite man nodded and smiled.

Stan stepped forward and handed over the copper ring. "I regret we brought only one ring when there are two of you," Stan said. "This is a new process for us, but we would be pleased to make a second ring. We are very grateful for your intervention. It saved our herds from the flood waters. I am Stan, leader of the Flag clan and this is my cousin Swarm."

"Welcome aboard, men of the Flag clan," Daniel said. "Your gift is a thing of beauty."

"Your ship is a thing of beauty," Stan said. "I cannot fathom how such a structure came to be."

"Perhaps not," Daniel said, "but I dare say your grandchildren will be able to. Please follow us and we will rise to a level where we can chat a bit."

The Cold Land men followed them, stepping onto the revolving platform. They stepped off at a high level where they could see far into the distance – perhaps all the way to Brite pastureland.

The four visitors grouped around the large viewing portal to look out at familiar landmarks from a new perspective.

"There's the boundary marker between the Jangles and Brites," Chi said to his brother.

Chai nodded, turning to face his hosts. "Did you come to Cold Land just to save us from the flood?" he asked with a hint of suspicion.

"We will not be sure why we came until we are ready to leave," Daniel said. "Only God knows that."

"You follow orders from your God?" Chai asked.

"It is our honor and privilege to accept the missions God offers us," Daniel said. "This one involved meeting with the miners who have come to trade with your people and doing what we felt appropriate armed with our knowledge of the coming flood. We saw flying low over your herds as a way to save some. We are always pleased to be able to help save lives."

Chai nodded. "Some seem more pleased to end lives. Our enemies abound."

"Sometimes enemies are made due to a lack of understanding," Jonah cautioned.

"I believe we understand our enemies very well," Swarm said. "They are people who would like to have our pastureland. And how are we to know you are not among them?"

"Swarm," Stan said. "We aren't here to accuse these people of wanting our land. We are here to thank them for saving our skallon, and ourselves as well."

Swarm frowned and turned away to look out at the surrounding grasslands.

"Please have a seat and eat some fruit," Daniel offered in his most affable manner. "Jonah here has a most interesting story about dealing with enemies that you might like to hear."

The four men looked at the couches situated with views out the portal. They appeared unable to decide what to do with them.

Daniel took a seat and the four followed suit, sitting awkwardly until they gradually relaxed into the comfort of these new structures.

Daniel took a piece of fruit and offered more to the men now seated.

Chi took a fruit and bit into it as Daniel had. His lips spread wide as a smile claimed his face. "Chai, you must try this."

Chai leaned in to take a bite of his brother's fruit, but Chi swung it out of reach. "Take one for yourself," he said, grinning.

Soon they were all eating fruit and beginning to enjoy the camaraderie.

"This God who sent you," Chi said. "He lives on your planet?"

"Yes," Daniel said. "But he is not only our God. He created the whole universe."

"Including Cold Land?" Chai asked.

"Yes," Daniel said.

"Why have we not heard of him?" Chai asked.

Daniel shrugged. "Only God knows the answer to that," he said. "But if the miners stay on Cold Land, you should know they were given a book that tells about the relationship our people had with God in their long history. My story and Jonah's story are in this book. Perhaps they will allow you to read it."

"They will not be allowed to stay on Cold Land," Swarm said. "No one will sell them pastureland. Not even our enemies."

"God sent me once long ago to save my enemies from God's own hand of death," Jonah began.

"Did you refuse?" Swarm asked.

"Yes, as a matter of fact, I did," Jonah said. "I set off on a ship in the opposite direction."

This admission caught everyone's attention. "And how did your God react to that?" Chi asked.

"He sent dangerous weather to the ship I was on. A great storm. I was bringing disaster on the crew with my disobedience and was thrown overboard where I was swallowed up by a great sea creature. I spent three days in the belly of that creature. I prayed for God to rescue me."

"Then what happened?" Stan asked.

"The whale spit me out onto dry land," Jonah said.

All was quiet as the men contemplated this.

"What did you do then?" Chai asked.

"I went to tell my enemies that if they did not repent of their evil ways, God would destroy them. I told them this was the only warning they would get."

"And did they listen?" Swarm asked.

"They did," Jonah said. "I saved the lives of my enemies with my warning and decided to die of anger and shame in the desert."

"Was God grateful?" Swarm asked.

"He asked me if it was right for me to be so angry."

"And how did you reply?" Swarm asked.

"I did not reply. I went into the desert and built a dwelling there. How could I return to my people after saving our enemies? God gave me a bush to shade my dwelling. And then he took it away. I was very angry about this as well. Then God asked again if it was right to be so angry over the loss of my plant. This time I answered him. I said it was right and I was so angry I wanted to die."

"What did God say to this?" Stan asked.

"God told me I had neither planted nor tended the bush so it was not my concern. Then he said he had compassion for the people who had repented and changed their ways."

All were quiet for a moment, considering Jonah's story.

"A strange story, but one to contemplate," Chai said. "This God of yours, is he often difficult to decipher?"

Jonah smiled. "Inscrutable," he affirmed.

Chapter 37

Jhar

Jhar had her young brother dressed and ready to go out to the pastures. She found an empty basket to hold the mong leaves she planned to gather and grabbed two pieces of fruit for their breakfast.

"Are you ready to find lots of mong leaves today?" she asked Sim.

Sim nodded, holding out his hand for the fruit.

Jhar smiled and gave it to him. She wondered about the fact that the fruit stayed fresh even though it was now several days old. Mong leaves began to shrivel after a few days and dried to husks over time.

Jhar took Sim's free hand in her own and they walked out of their dugout into a cold bright morning.

Just outside their dugout her father had already started Grum's apprenticeship. They were sorting through dried skallon bones, pulling out the ones that could be turned into scrapers and punches.

"Sim and I are off to pick mong leaves," she told her father.

Her father looked up from his sorting. "Leader Cray's nephew Scar was here a few minutes ago wanting to talk to you. I thought you were already out in the pastures."

"Yes, I slept in a bit. I had a late night," Jhar said.

Her father nodded. "He will catch up to you eventually."

"Did Scar say what he wanted to talk to me about?"

"No. Most likely he wanted to trade for some fruit. Do you mind if Grum and I help ourselves to some for a midday meal?"

"No, I don't mind," Jhar said. "I thought we should eat it before it went bad, but it doesn't seem to be withering."

"I can't imagine what kind of place these aliens must come from," her father said. "Fruit that does not rot?"

"None of us can imagine," Jhar said. "But those aliens who are miners seem a little more believable. They at least are concerned about food and are willing to trade translators for skallon meat."

"Thank you for offering up a basket of your fruit for my life," Grum said.

"You are family," Jhar replied, as though that explained everything.

"I plan to pay everyone back for helping me," Grum said.

"Are you really my cousin Grum?" Jhar asked, pretending to be suspicious.

Grum laughed and held up a bone for his uncle's inspection.

Her father tested the sharpness of the bone's edge with his thumb before setting it to one side. He looked out at the pastures and appeared to be thinking. "Cold Land used to be so predictable. Now we have aliens and floods. What next?"

People changing clans, Jhar thought to herself, but she wasn't quite ready to broach the subject out loud. "We had best be off if we hope to accomplish any work today," Jhar said, pulling Sim along with her.

Jhar saw her grandmother stirring something in a large pit dug into the ground. Most likely dyeing skins to use for capes. She was talking to someone as she stirred the water with a long pole.

As she and Sim got closer, Jhar recognized Cray's nephew, Scar.

"There you are, sleepy heads," her grandmother sang out. "Have you come to help?"

Jhar smiled. "We will help if you need us," she said. "I had thought to gather some mong leaves to dry for torches. We used most of what we had evicting ripcons from our dugouts."

Jhar looked at Scar. "My father said you wanted to talk to me?"

Scar nodded. "Can you walk with me? I wanted to show you something."

Jhar nodded and turned to face her grandmother. "Can I leave Sim here with you for a while?"

"Of course. Sim is just what I need. A big strong man to stir this pole around."

Sim giggled and reached out for the pole.

"Here, let's stir it together," Grandmother said.

Scar led Jhar back the way she had come. "I was thinking I might dig a dugout here close to your family dugout," he said. "It's time I started my own family. I wondered if you might like to share my dugout and start a family with me."

Jhar stopped walking. "That is a very kind offer, but someone has already asked me to share a dugout and I have said I would."

"Who?" Scar asked.

"I can't say yet because I haven't told my family of the offer. I want to have their agreement before any excavation takes place."

"I see," Scar said. "If your family does not approve of your choice might you still consider my offer?"

"Yes, of course," Jhar said.

"I suppose there is nothing more to say then," Scar said.

Jhar nodded. "I thank you for your offer."

Scar gave a backhanded wave as he walked away.

Jhar walked back to where grandmother and Sim were inspecting a dyed pelt hanging on the end of their pole.

"What do you think?" Grandmother asked. "Should we go for a deeper green?"

"Yes, I think a little more time in the dye would make a stronger color," Jhar said.

"It's good I have my helper to keep stirring," Grandmother said.

Sam giggled and attempted to stir the long pole against the sodden skin.

"What did Scar want?" Grandmother asked.

Jhar took a deep breath. "To dig a dugout for me where we could start a family."

Grandmother's face lit up with a smile. "And what did you answer?"

"I told him someone else had already asked and I had accepted," Jhar said.

Grandmother's smile fell away. "You don't care for Scar?"

"It's not that," Jhar said. "I told him the truth. I have already accepted another offer."

"Who?" Grandmother asked. "Why have I not heard of this?"

"Because the person who made the offer is a Sylvan," Jhar said.

Grandmother either sat down or fell down. It was hard to tell. "I knew all these aliens coming in would change things. But a Sylvan? How does a Sylvan even know you?"

"Actually, I've known him for most of my life. We met as children and grew up learning one another's language. He is my best friend."

"Was I not living with you the whole time?" Grandmother said. "How is it no one knows of this best friend?"

"We would meet secretly near the boundaries between our pasturelands. Often close to dusk."

"You always were our wanderer," Grandmother recollected. "But you know such meetings are unlawful."

"Yes, we both know," Jhar admitted.

"Why not just accept Scar's offer and tell your friend you must stop meeting with him?"

Jhar shook her head. "My feelings for him run too deep."

Grandmother shook her head. "You have not told your mother or your father?"

"No, but I see now I can't wait any longer. Dunk warned me that others would come soon asking me to share a dugout."

"Dunk? This is the name of your young man?"

"Yes," Jhar said. "He's a tanner, finished with his apprenticeship. I'm hoping that skill might be something in his favor."

"Certainly we need more tanners," Grandmother allowed. "But what of your children? Where would you live?"

Dunk has offered to become a Jangle," Jhar said.

Grandmother stood up and took her pole in hand to begin stirring. "I suppose such a thing might be possible now that so many of our laws are being challenged. We can talk to our neighboring clans now with these translators. The Sylvans agreed to let a boundary marker mover stay alive. Everyone seems anxious to trade with the aliens."

"Yes," Jhar said, feeling hopeful. "Perhaps our request won't seem so unimaginable as it once would have been."

"You know I will always take your side," Grandmother said. "But I still see trouble ahead for you and this Sylvan, Dunk."

Chapter 38

Daco

The miners' ship, *Bonanza,* landed on the shore of the South Sea close to the *Seeker* – the Swagian ship that had carried the biologists to Cold Land.

Daco thought about how he might soften the terrible news of their planet's demise and decided there really was no way. Best to gather all the scientists together so that he only had to tell the story one time and they would all be together to comfort one another.

Bran and Aldo were looking out a portal that offered a view of the biologists' ship when Daco joined them.

"I think it best we invite them all here to sit around our table and share some skallon meat before we tell them what has happened," Daco said. "Joshua told me there are twenty-four of them so they will all have a place to sit and around a dozen of us can join them at the table."

"Yes, that sounds like a good plan," Bran said. "I'll let the others know."

"Thank you," Daco said, shaking his head. "This won't be easy for any of us."

"Shall I go to their ship to issue the invitation?" Bran asked.

"I would appreciate it," Daco said. "I could see a few people scattered along the beach as we landed. I'll go to invite them aboard."

"Might as well get started," Bran said, heading for the airlock. "Shall we say dinner in an hour?"

"Yes, that should give us time to make sure they all get the invitation," Daco said. "Will you come with me, Aldo?"

Aldo nodded. "Do you think they might already know somehow?"

"Joshua said they did not. He thought the news would be better given by other survivors from their planet and in that I suppose he was right," Daco said.

"They will be very sad," Aldo said.

"Yes, there is no help for that," Daco agreed.

Daco and Aldo walked along the dark waters of the South Sea in the direction of two people who had come up out of the water and were carrying spears and a bag.

"Hello Swage brethren," Daco called out.

The woman dropped the bag she was carrying and ran toward them. The man with her soon followed.

"Finally, we have someone to ask," the woman said.

Daco could see that she was quite young – a student perhaps?

"I am Mona," she said, catching her breath. "And this is my exploration partner, Soma. Tell us, have aliens invaded Swage? Are you still in contact with anyone there? All our communications with Swage were cut off suddenly." She appeared to stop speaking only because she had run out of breath.

As she took several deep breaths, Daco spoke quickly. "We do have some news but we thought it best to tell everyone at the same time. Can you come to our ship in an hour? We will have a meal of skallon meat ready for you."

"Skallon meat?" Soma said.

"A local delicacy," Daco said. "Excuse me, but I must extend the invitation to others who are out exploring. And you will want to change into dry clothes. We look forward to hearing what you have found in your exploration of the sea so far."

Daco began to walk away but Mona grabbed his arm. "But you have told us nothing!"

"All will be told in an hour. Be sure everyone on your ship comes. It is important," Daco said.

Daco pulled Aldo along with him in an attempt to distance himself from Mona's questions.

Soma called out to them, "Steer clear of the ice eaters. They can be aggressive if someone comes near their food."

"Ice eaters?" Daco said, turning back.

Soma pointed further down the beach to where a large furry white animal and two smaller versions were feasting on what appeared to be a grey sea animal.

"Yes, I see them. Thank you for the warning," Daco called out. "See you in an hour."

Daco headed for another small group that appeared to be collecting dead sea life left stranded by the flood. One seemed to be an older man – perhaps the group's leader?

"Hello fellow Swagians," Daco said. "We come to invite you aboard our ship for a meal and an exchange of news."

The older man looked up from his work. "What a nice surprise," he said. "Yet another ship of Swagians."

"Another?" Daco said.

"Yes, although the other ship was definitely not built in Swage. The one with seven stacked rings? Have you seen it?"

Daco smiled. "Yes, the fruit giver's ship. We know it well."

"What is the story behind its acquisition?" the man said.

"I forget my manners," Daco said. "I am Daco, leader of a mining crew and this is my son Aldo. We have news to share but we prefer to tell everyone at the same time. Can you come to our ship in an hour?"

"Of course," the man said. "I am Professor Stern and these others are my students. We are here for thirty days or so to study cold climate predators."

"Yes, a rare coincidence that we should be here at the same time," Daco said.

"Even more rare that a third ship should be here," Professor Stern said. "And especially rare that we should all be here to witness the flood."

"Yes, we look forward to seeing you all in an hour," Daco said turning to walk back to his ship. To Aldo he said, "I think we have told enough people now that everyone will hear the invitation. Let's go back to the ship and make sure we have enough food to go around."

"It looks as though there are fish in this sea," Aldo said pointing to a cluster of carcasses heaped in a gully "Perhaps they are edible."

"That is my fervent hope," Daco said.

The table was laid out in its most inviting fashion with copper plates and shiny steel eating utensils. The portions would be small but hopefully colorful napkins would make up for the scantiness of the meal.

Pheebs, Onri, Tull and his wife, Dray, welcomed the biologists aboard and showed them to the dining table.

"I don't know when I have seen such a large table," Professor Stern remarked. "We have several small tables on board the *Seeker* which also serve as lab tables."

When all were seated, Daco said, "Please eat. I apologize for the meager offering but the important thing is we are all together. I will have several announcements to make at the end of the meal."

Everyone tucked into their meal and many complimented the food and asked questions about the source of the skallon meat.

It didn't take long to finish eating. Everyone looked up in anticipation as Daco stood.

"You all are wondering why your communication with Swage was suddenly cut off. We know the answer to that question. At the time it happened we were on our ship heading for an asteroid we hoped to wrap and mine. But our planet Swage was still in sight behind us. There came a violent solar storm from our star and a giant solar flare reached out to envelop our beloved planet in flames. I am sorry to have to tell you this but our planet is now a burned-out ruin. We have no home to return to."

No one spoke for a moment as disbelief turned into quiet sobbing and then into wails of pain, fear and anguish.

Daco sat back down and began to cry himself, reliving the horror of what he had seen.

Chapter 39

Mona

Mona thought she could not cry anymore but a memory of her youngest sister crawling into bed with her saying dream monsters were jumping on her mattress brought a fresh round of tears. She had lost her mother, her father, her grandmother and her two younger sisters without even being aware of it. How was that even possible? They had been so proud of her. So in awe that she was flying to another planet to do research. Another round of deep sobs sent her from her bed to wash her face.

As she poured water onto a washcloth she decided the best solution to these unending tears was work. They needed to survive somehow and that meant finding an ongoing source of food. She needed to run tests on the fish Soma had speared – tests for toxicity. If that fish was edible, likely more of the South Sea's inhabitants were edible as well.

She pulled on yesterday's clothes and stumbled out of her sleeping alcove and into the galley/lab of the ship. Someone was already there. "Soma," she said. "You couldn't sleep either?"

"Sleep?" he growled. "Sheena is gone. My fiancé. My life. My future. What have I to dream about now? And my family. They were planning our wedding while I was gone."

Soma was usually so good-natured. Mona had never seen him so angry before. So diminished. His eyes, normally full of fun and mischief, seemed flat and menacing. "I guess we both decided work was the best option," she said.

Soma just shrugged as he slammed a scalpel down on the counter. "We will have to eat. I decided to just cook this fish and eat it. If I die we will know it is toxic. Saves a lot of time and without food we will all die anyway."

"Makes sense," she said backing away from the scalpel. "For the sake of science I thought I might just run a few tests – perhaps discover a new toxin before I starve."

"I'm sorry," Soma said. "Go ahead and run your tests." He pushed the scalpel in her direction. "I'm going for a walk."

As Soma left the galley, Mona took a deep breath. "People grieve differently," she said aloud to herself. "People grieve differently," she repeated, finding it a good mantra to keep repeating as she sliced a tiny piece of fish on to a glass square to slide it under their powerful microscope.

At the highest power of the microscope she found the fish's DNA to be quite similar to fish in the waters of her old planet Swage. Likely Soma could have eaten the fish and lived. She wondered if he would have been disappointed to continue living.

After several more tests, she declared the fish toxin free and carved off a large filet, deciding to poach it.

The fish had turned a delicate tan color after a few minutes in boiling water. She removed it to a plate and doused it with her favorite fish sauce before sitting down to eat it.

Soma came into the galley. When he looked at Mona about to take a bite of the fish, he swept the plate away from her. "What are you doing?" he shouted.

"It's all right," she said. "I've done all the tests. This fish is toxin free. I was about to have a late night snack."

Soma's rigid body seemed to turn into an old man's slumping posture. He returned the plate to her. "Of course you have done the tests. I seem to have lost my mind. Please forgive me."

"Nothing to forgive," she said. "Everyone grieves differently. Would you like to share this fish? You were the one who speared it after all."

"Yes," he said, breathing heavily and sinking down into a chair. "I would like that very much."

They each took a bite at the same time and shared a surprised expression. "This is delicious," Mona said.

"It really is," Soma agreed. "We'll have to catch a few more and invite the miners over." He gave Mona a grateful smile. "I have never had a sister, only two brothers and my fiancé. Would you agree to be my sister? My new family?"

"It would be my honor. And I have never had a brother – only two sisters. You are my new family. This is a thing to celebrate."

"It is," Soma agreed. "I noticed that most of the miners are men. They will all come a'courting now that their families are gone as well. As your brother I will guard you from any I deem unworthy."

Mona laughed and was amazed that she still had the ability to laugh. "Shall we put on headlamps and go fishing?" she asked. "I imagine I would be a big hit with the miners if they saw I could provide food as well as a pretty face."

Soma laughed and seemed surprised at his outburst as well. "Let's try to find more like this fish. I think since we're the first to catch and cook it, we should have the honor of naming it."

"I agree," Mona said. "That will require some serious thought."

Mona and Soma were not the only ones to decide night fishing would be a good idea. Several miners wearing wet suits and goggles were walking along the shore with nets, looking for a shallow place to enter the sea.

Soma walked closer to them and they stopped to talk.

"Night fishing?" Soma asked.

"Our need for food has become critical," one of the men said. "I only hope these fish are safe to eat."

Mona realized the man speaking was Daco, leader of the mining group and the one who had told them the awful truth.

Soma continued tallking. "Mona has done toxicity tests on a fish I speared. It was not only edible – it was delicious. We thought if we caught more like it we could invite all of your miners over for breakfast."

As Mona listened, Soma went on to describe the fish he had speared and its similar appearance to a favorite fish on Swage.

Mona had a brother now. And one she could be proud of. She could hardly believe the change in her partner. He seemed full of energy to meet this new challenge of keeping everyone fed – no longer a man looking for a way to die.

While she was also intent on surviving, she knew her own grief would not give way so quickly. Her family and their pride in her achievements had always been her greatest strength. She needed to know her accomplishments mattered to someone other than herself. *Would one of these miners truly come a'courting as Soma had predicted?*

Mona was not really a pretty girl in her own mind. She wore glasses most of the time as she found vision inserts uncomfortable. The hair on her head was sparse and lank, barely covering her scalp. She was short and a little on the plump side, although she thought she may have slimmed down a bit while aboard ship. The food prepared by other students was not nearly as tempting as her mother's delicious meals.

She put these thoughts aside as she waded into the water holding tightly to her spear. Now she was the provider. She knew what Soma's fish looked like and she was sure she had the strength within her to spear one just like it if it should appear in the glow of her headlamp. At least she hoped she had the strength within her.

As they walked deeper into the water she felt someone staying close to her as if protecting her from potential harm. It was not Soma. He was in front, leading this expedition. She tried to make out the shadowy presence. She was not sure but she thought it might be Daco.

Chapter 40

Jhar

Jhar suspected her grandmother had told her mother about Dunk, but she asked to speak to both her mother and father in a rather formal way, regardless of what they might already know.

"What is this about?" her father asked as they sat around their fire pit, eating fruit and skallon meat.

"I have turned down Scar's offer to share a dugout because I have already agreed to share one with a Sylvan man. You have seen him with his father, Darp. His name is Dunk and he is a tanner."

She took a breath and felt a great relief having finally said what needed to be said.

"How do you propose to do that since it is against the law?" her mother asked.

Jhar looked down at her hands, folded together in her lap. "Grum is still alive. Sometimes exceptions to the law are made."

"Why does it have to be this Sylvan man?" her father asked.

"I have known him since we were children, playing together in the pastures."

"When you were old enough to know the law you should have stopped seeing him," her father said.

"Of course you are right, but I didn't. I know we will have to go before the council with this request, but I hoped to have your support. Would you like to meet Dunk?"

"Perhaps we should wait until the council agrees before we meet him," her mother said. "It would not do to welcome him into our home if this will not go forward."

Jhar shrugged. "Whatever you think is best."

"What will you do if the council does not agree to your request?" her father asked.

"I suppose we will try to find another way to be together," Jhar said.

"Cray would be within his rights as our leader to order your death if you proceed without permission," her father warned.

"Yes, we both know this," Jhar said.

"And you will defy the law?" he asked.

Jhar raised her hands in surrender. "I don't know. I would need to speak to Dunk. We must decide together how far we are willing to take this. But I think asking the council's permission is the first step we must take. Perhaps they will agree."

"If the council agrees we will meet your young tanner," her mother said. "I am sure if you think him a good person, we will think him one as well."

"Shall I ask leader Cray for a hearing?" Jhar said.

"Do you know if Dunk's family is in agreement?" her father asked.

"I could find out," Jhar said.

"Yes, I think that is wise. If his family will not hear of this, it is futile to put your request before the council," her father said.

"All right," Jhar said. "That is what I will do."

Her mother put her arm around her daughter's shoulder. "This is a dangerous undertaking, but we will support any decision that does not lead to your death."

Jhar hugged her mother. "Thank you," she said.

That evening, Jhar waited by the boundary marker hoping Dunk would show up. She heard a familiar whistle and saw a shadow moving toward her. "Dunk?" she whispered.

"Who else?" he asked.

Jhar smiled. "Hard to say these days."

Dunk reached out to touch her face and she felt tears overflowing her eyes.

"Your news is that bad?" Dunk asked gently.

"Not really. I have told my family and they are afraid their full support could seal my death. They don't want to meet you until the council agrees to let me share a dugout with a Sylvan man."

"I see," Dunk said.

"What of your family?" Jhar asked.

"It turns out my father has known about us all along. He has only me to watch over. He will support whatever decision we make."

"Then I suppose we must take the next step and make a request for a council hearing," Jhar said.

"Yes. Let the formal request be that a Sylvan tanner requests to become a Jangle."

"Your father agreed to that?" Jhar asked.

"He did. And since we last talked, my father has become leader of the Sylvan clan, so his agreement carries some weight."

"What happened to Romm?" Jhar asked.

"He was voted out. Our clan didn't approve of several of the decisions he has made lately. Especially his decision to fly north with the children and elderly."

"I'm glad to hear that," Jhar said. "I admit I thought the man pompous and arrogant."

"Yes, we all did," Dunk said, "and predictably he has vowed revenge on those who voted him out."

"This could mean trouble for us. The law would be on his side if he opposes us."

"But we will not be involving the Sylvan council. Our fate lies with the Jangle council, unless you would consider becoming a Sylvan."

"I don't want to do anything to further upset my family if I can help it," Jhar said. "I think I should ask to be heard at the next Jangle council meeting."

"I suppose that is the next step," Dunk said. "Should I attend the meeting?"

"I would think so, but perhaps not. I'll need to ask leader Cray if you should be present. He may not know himself. I don't think anyone has asked to become a Jangle before."

"Not a popular choice? I can't imagine why," Dunk teased.

"I suppose people are lining up to become Sylvans," Jhar retorted.

"I will have to put that question to my father. It looked for a while as though we might have aliens making such requests."

"Perhaps if we had a spaceship to fly people around in and translators to sell we would have a better chance at the council meeting," Jhar said.

"Are your aliens still here?" Dunk asked.

"Only the fruit givers are still here. They have received visits from the blue Brites and another tribe – the red-caped Flags. Perhaps the fruit givers are planning to stay."

"Do they trade fruit for skallon meat?" Dunk asked.

"No, they never seem to need anything. They appear to have an unlimited supply of fruit."

"Lucky them," Dunk said. "How is your supply of fruit?"

"I have five baskets left. I have been giving it away to everyone, thinking it will go bad if it is not eaten. But it never seems to rot."

"Really!" Dunk said. "That is most curious."

"Yes," Jhar agreed. "And I went back to speak to Rahab. I thought she could advise me on how to go about dealing with the council since she once went against her own people and hid spies from her leader."

"And she lived to tell of it?" Dunk said.

"Evidently. The invaders protected her and her family because she protected their spies."

"Perhaps our invaders will protect us. They have already given you fruit because you were helpful to them."

"Yes," Jhar said. "They might. Although I think the fruit givers plan to go back to their home. The miners, though, trade for skallon meat and seem more interested in making friends among the Jangles. They flew away this morning, but said they would return to trade."

"We could certainly use all the friends we can make just now," Dunk said.

"Yes, we do," Jhar said. "Bran and his brother seemed eager to help us. Bran made the suggestion that saved Grum's life."

"Let's hope for their return and support before the council meeting," Dunk said.

Jhar nodded and realized she could barely see Dunk in the gathering darkness. "I must go now. Tomorrow night?"

"A herd of ripcons and two horids could not keep me away. Tomorrow night. Same place," Dunk said. He laid his hand against her face, now dried of tears before he turned away.

Chapter 41

Daco

Daco's instincts had always been those of a protector. He tried to protect his band of miners, especially when they were using explosives. Mining was, by its very nature, a dangerous profession and he supposed all of them, if they were honest, were drawn in a little by the dangerous aspect of the work. But in his core, he was first a protector, especially of women and children.

When he saw Mona trudging into the sea alongside the men, he felt obliged to watch over her. None of them knew what dangers these waters might be concealing.

He tried to stay close to the young biologist, a difficult chore in dark waters with only his headlamp to provide light. Luckily, for some unknown reason, she and her partner wore pink dive suits which fairly glowed in their pinkness.

He noticed bubbles rising from a shallow depth in the seafloor and tapped Mona on the shoulder. He pointed down toward the bubbles.

The girl seemed to know he wanted to have a closer look and began heading toward the vent.

Daco kept his hand out, testing the heat of the fissure as they drew close. When the escaping gases grew sufficiently warm, he held up his hand in a stop motion. He stuck the point of his spear close to the exit point of escaping gases and then felt the tip of the spear with his hand. Hot.

He swung his hand in an upward motion hoping Mona would realize he wanted to swim up to the surface.

She started up at once, holding her spear between her legs to enable her to use both arms to move upward.

As they broke the thin surface ice, Daco was excited, needing to talk to someone about the vent. He wished he had brought a floater so that he could have marked the position with the buoy on the surface.

"Did you see other vents like the one we saw just now when you were fishing this morning?" he asked.

Mona nodded. "Yes, there seem to be a lot of them. I believe that is why the sea water is not as cold as one would expect. It would be good if we had a geologist among us."

Daco and most of the miners were geologists but he supposed now was not the time to bring out his resume. "These vents could be very useful to us," Daco said.

"Yes," Mona agreed. "They attract a lot of sea life, especially bivalves. And if these bivalves are edible, as I now suspect, they could be a valuable food source."

"Luckily some of my men brought nets, so I am sure they will recover a few for you to test."

Mona nodded and paused for a second before asking, "Are you staying close to protect me?"

Caught, Daco thought to himself, and wondered if that protection would be welcomed or abhorred. "I suppose I might be – just a little. We don't know what predators may be lurking in wait down there. I hope I have not offended you."

"Not at all," Mona said. "Having just lost my entire family, your protection makes me feel – ah – less alone, I guess. It is a comforting feeling."

Daco smiled. "Good. Then I will continue to be your protector in the sea. I suppose we should concentrate on spearing a fish now, but I may be drawn away if I see another warm water vent. I hope you don't mind."

"Not at all," Mona said. "I'm a biologist here to explore, after all."

"Let's get to exploring then," Daco said.

They descended again and moved into deeper water, aware of fish darting around them in small schools – some iridescent in their coloring, beautiful against the dark water.

Up ahead they could see men wielding spears. A few already had large fish dangling from the tips. Moving forward Daco saw a shape similar to a Swage skipper fish and drew back his arm, ready. As the fish drew closer Daco was sure it was the same one Soma had described. It was light grey in color, with eyes atop its head and a mouth that drooped down with a hanging bottom lip. He thrust his spear foreword and impaled it.

Mona shook a fist to salute his success and moved towards her own prey, a smaller version of the one he had just speared.

She thrust her spear foreword but the spear did not go in far enough to hold. As the fish struggled to break free, Mona shoved the handle of her spear over to Daco. He pushed the spear further into the fish, while still holding onto his own prize in his left hand.

Mona nodded her thanks and took over the transport of her captured fish.

All the fishermen were heading for shore now. Many had speared fish and a few had nets full of bivalves.

Soma came over to congratulate Mona holding his own big fish under his arm. "Good job, sister," he said.

"Daco helped me," she said.

"Thank you," Soma said, looking over at Daco. "I should have been watching out for her myself."

"You are brother and sister?" Daco asked, noting they looked nothing alike. Soma was tall and slender with a large nose, while Mona was short and plump with a round childish face and a bit of an upturned nose.

"We are now," Soma said. "We are each other's new family now."

"I believe we are all of us family now," Daco said. "Out of necessity if nothing else."

"Yes," Soma said gleefully. "And now we are a family with a food source."

Daco's brother Bran waded over to where they stood talking in the shallow water. He had his own fish trailing along on his spear behind him.

Soma studied their catches. "Yes, these are all the same as the one we have caught and tested. These are safe to eat."

"Excellent," Bran said. "It couldn't have happened at a more opportune time. We aboard the *Bonanza* were officially out of food."

"We aboard the *Seeker* still have plenty of food, which we will of course, share," Soma said. "We will eventually run out of starches and dried fruit but at least we now have plenty of protein."

Daco nodded and smiled, then looked at his brother. "Did you notice the warm water vent?"

Bran's face broke into a wide grin. "I certainly did. Vents, in the plural. Are you thinking what I'm thinking?"

"If you are thinking steam to rotate a turbine which activates a generator to produce electricity, then yes, I am thinking what you are thinking."

"Electricity?" Soma asked. "Are you saying we can now produce electricity in this frozen wasteland?"

Daco looked around. "Plenty of stones to build shelters. We have pipes. We can fashion a structure above water to hold a turbine and pipe up steam from the vents, then run a line to shore to connect with a generator. Yes, we can certainly have houses with electricity."

"And heat?" Mona asked hopefully.

"And heat," Daco said. "As far as we know, no one owns this land. It is ours for the taking."

Mona clapped her hands together. We are going to have a life after all. And one with heat!"

"Let's get these fish on board and cooking," Bran said. "We have a lot of work to do and hungry stomachs to fill."

"Your ship or ours?" Soma asked, grinning.

"Our ship is bigger. Let's assemble there," Daco said, "but if you can bring some of that starch you are hoarding with you, it will be very much appreciated."

Chapter 42

Daco

As morning dawned cold and gray with little warmth from a distant red star, activity around the north shore of the South Sea increased. Several miners were out in the sea taking measurements, laying pipes across the thin layer of ice and marking the location of undersea vents with flags stuck into the ice.

The biologists were inside their ship doing tests on numerous sea creatures, checking for toxins and taste. Daco had come to the *Seeker* to find out the results of the bivalve tests before putting bivalves on the day's menu.

He saw Mona in the ship's lab/kitchen and took note of the wonderful smell of baking bread.

"Is that really bread I smell?" he asked.

Mona laughed. "It is. We still have ground grains and yeast available."

Daco could feel his mouth watering and hoped he wasn't drooling. "The smell alone is making me want to cry for happiness," he admitted.

"We have fifty-eight people to feed. That takes a lot of loaves of bread," Mona said. "Our good news is the bivalves have passed all of our toxin tests. We will be bringing a few cooked ones and feel free to cook yours as well."

"Good news all around," Daco said. "We have men out marking vent locations and others making rock piles to begin construction of shelters."

"This is amazing," Mona said, offering Daco a piece of dried fruit brought from Swage. "We have actually found a new home here on Bando."

"I'm afraid we will have to give up calling it Bando," Daco said. "The herders call it Cold Land and they were here first."

"What are they like – the herders?" Mona asked, "We only flew over their pastures to scare the skallon. We haven't actually seen any of them close up."

"Much more intelligent than we previously thought," Daco said. "Their whole culture is intertwined with the skallon they shepherd. The animals provide for all their needs and their strict rules seem to keep everything in balance. We have traded some translators with them and that has already had a profound effect on the interaction between clans."

"Translators?" Mona said. "What are translators?"

"I will tell everyone about them today at our communal meal. They will be important in our dealings with the inhabitants. We should have all our fish cleaned and cooked in an hour or two. Will your bread be ready by then?"

"Yes," Mona said. "We plan to bring a few other treats from our stores as well."

"Come whenever you are ready. We'll have to eat in our cargo hold. That's the only place large enough to hold everyone."

"We will be there," Mona promised.

Daco went over his mental list of discussion topics as he walked back to the *Bonanza*. He felt as though he had so many balls in the air at the same time he was sure to drop one.

Bran was waving to him from an ice hole cut into shallow water.

"How goes the marking?" Daco called out.

We have too many choices," Bran shouted back. "Shall we go first with a shallow one or farther out with a hotter one? There are vents everywhere. We may very well be sitting at the edge of a tectonic plate."

"I will add it to my list of discussion topics," Daco said, moving closer. "We will be gathering for a meal in an hour or two. And there will be bread."

"Bread? Seriously? I will have to tell the others."

Daco waved and continued walking toward the *Bonanza*. One topic loomed large in his thinking. How much interaction did they want to have with the herding clans? It appeared they could stay completely isolated – perhaps fly up once a year for skallon meat and pelts that they could exchange for translators, but was isolation the best strategy? The fruit givers had suggested they offer a school to slowly bring the herders into a knowledge of advanced technology. The fruit givers were so far advanced in their own technology that Daco saw no chance of ever reaching their level – especially now that the Swage survivors would have to begin again on a new planet. It was a decision that would have to be made communally.

He walked through the open hatch of his ship and found Tull and Dray directing cooking operations.

"Will we be ready in an hour?" he asked.

"Ready enough," Dray said. "I have laid out mattresses for people to sit on in the cargo hold. Our dining table will hold all the food. People can load their plates up here and then bring the food down to the hold to eat."

"Good," Daco said. "I had hoped we could all be together. We have a lot of decisions to make – or at least think about."

"It looks like the South Sea will be our permanent home then?" Dray asked.

"Yes, it's beginning to look that way," Daco said. "It's not really as though we have another option."

Two hours later, everyone was settled in the cargo hold with plates of fish, bread and helpings from five large platters of Swagian deserts – dried fruit baked in sweet dough.

Everyone was busy evaluating the tastiness of the new fish or in ecstasy over the starches so long denied them.

Daco sat next to Professor Stern. "I thought I would bring up some matters we need to discuss at the end of the meal," he said. "As leader of your group of biologists have you any topics you would like to discuss?"

"I don't really know," Professor Stern said. "We came here to study cold climate predators. With all the survival matters we have before us, I think we should set that research aside. We are testing each new fish caught for toxins and have found only one to avoid: the many-armed cephalopod. It is highly poisonous and should not even be touched. Setting all that aside, do you really see us surviving long-term in this freezing climate?"

"I do," Daco said. "We can trade with the clans for pelts that are surprisingly warm. That will do for our clothing. We have fish to eat and rocks to build shelters. And I think we will have steam to bring warmth into our stone houses before long. In the meantime we have our ships and the means to make more fuel."

Professor Stern smiled. "You are more optimistic than I, but I hope you are right. I feel responsible for these young biologists who are barely old enough to leave their homes, let alone their planet."

"Yes," Daco said. He looked over the crowded cargo hold and saw a situation he had not considered. Many of the miners, most of whom had no wives or families to return to, were choosing to sit beside the female biologists. Some of the male biologists seemed to be annoyed by this development.

"I suppose I had best begin my announcements now, before the goodwill of good food wears off," he said.

Daco stood up and clapped to get everyone's attention.

"Let us have all the miners on the port side of the cargo hold and all the biologists on the starboard side. We will need to divide up some of the chores to be undertaken and we need to speak to everyone's strengths."

A great deal of shifting around commenced and finally everyone was reseated.

"We need volunteers to pile rocks for building shelters. Let me see a show of hands from either group for that activity."

Some of the miners were slow to raise their hands, wanting to see first who in the biologist group was volunteering.

This is not going to be easy, Daco thought to himself as he counted raised hands. "We need a second group to become familiar with the production of translators." The same reluctance to commit on the part of the miners was evident. "All those who have not yet volunteered, send your names to my diary. I will try to match your new short-time duties to your strengths. I know we all want to do our part in these new and challenging times." He sat back down and hoped the evening would end without confrontations breaking out.

Chapter 43

Jhar

Jhar found leader Cray at the council dugout. The representatives from the Brite and Flag clans were with him. They had evidently traded the fruit givers for translators because everyone was hearing their own language as they spoke.

"We would see these miners who are your friends," the Brite man named Chai said.

"They are not here just now," Cray said. "I'm not sure I would call them our friends either. We think they want to stay here and that is, of course, not possible. No one would sell pastureland to aliens. We would never value profit above our skallon who need the pastures for sustenance."

Leader Stan of the Flag clan stood to speak. "The fruit givers told us stories from their past that seem to carry important messages. We are told these miners have in their possession a book that holds these stories. We should like to know more of this thing called a book."

"I know nothing of a book," Cray said. "The miners did not mention it to me."

Jhar's presence had not yet been acknowledged by any of the men present but she spoke anyway. "I have also heard stories from the fruit givers' past," she said.

Everyone's attention turned to Jhar.

"What have you heard?" Cray asked.

"I heard the story of Rahab's betrayal of her own people in favor of the God who holds back the waters," Jhar said.

Everyone present sucked back a big breath at the words "betrayed their own people," and Jhar thought that did not bode well for her own petition.

"Do you know when the miners might return?" Cray asked.

"No, I have come today on my own account," Jhar said. "I wish to call for a council meet to make my case for an exemption."

Cray looked at her as though she had just grown a second head. "An exemption?"

"I have a Sylvan friend who wishes to become a Jangle and share a dugout with me," she said.

Cray tilted his head as he looked at her. "But you know such a thing is forbidden."

"That is why I seek an exemption from that rule," she said.

Cray shrugged. "You are within your rights to call for a council meet but I can tell you now what the result would be."

"Perhaps not," Jhar said. "The young man is a tanner by trade and I have fruit to offer the council for my part. We need more tanners here and an exemption was made in the case of Grum who committed an even more serious offense."

Cray considered her words for a moment. "You make good arguments," Cray said. "I will call a council meet for two days hence. Does your young man wish to be present?"

"He can be if you think it wise," Jhar hedged.

"What I think would be wise is your abandoning this idea which will only lead to sorrow. Didn't my nephew Scar make you an offer?"

"He did," Jhar said, "but I had already accepted an offer from the Sylvan man."

"Surely the Sylvan man would prefer life over the death such an action would bring," Cray stated.

Jhar could see the men from Brite and Flag nodding their agreement. "Perhaps that particular law has run its course and needs to be amended now that we have translators and can better understand our neighboring clans," Jhar suggested.

"These are arguments you may bring up at your hearing," Cray said. "But I hope you will be willing to abide by the council's decision in the matter."

Jhar nodded but whether in agreement or in acknowledgment of his words was not clear.

That night Jhar sat at the boundary marker between Jangle and Sylvan pastures waiting for Dunk. She heard his familiar whistle and said, "Over here."

Dunk plopped down beside her and took her hand. "Any progress?"

"We have our council date – two days from today. Cray says it is your choice whether or not you attend."

"I will most certainly attend," Dunk said. "And I will bring gifts of undyed pelts with me."

Jhar squeezed his hand. "That can only help our case."

"Why are you so sad then?" Dunk asked.

"What makes you think I am sad?" Jhar thought she had been hiding her sorrow at Cray's prediction well.

"Please," Dunk said. "Give me some credit for knowing you. Your sadness has the smell of dry mong leaves."

Jhar smiled at the ridiculousness of Dunk's words. "Perhaps I am a little sad. Cray's opinion of our request was not encouraging."

"What was his opinion?" Dunk asked.

"That you would do better to accept the council's verdict than be dead of your own refusal," Jhar said.

"He was that certain of a negative outcome?"

"He seemed to be, though he allowed that Grum had lived in spite of his transgression."

Dunk was quiet, thinking, for a moment. "Perhaps we should discuss an alternative plan."

"You have an alternative?" Jhar asked.

"What would you think about living with the miners? They have things they could teach us. Perhaps we could learn to make translators for trade."

"The miners have ships that fly through the air. That seems quite a bridge to cross between their knowledge and ours," Jhar said.

"But they don't know how to survive here on Cold Land. We do. We have knowledge to exchange," Dunk pointed out.

"Yes, maybe," Jhar said. "Today when I spoke to Cray there were four outsiders present. Two from Brite and two from Flag. I met them earlier waiting to give gifts to the fruit givers. They said the fruit givers had saved their skallon and their clans by driving the skallon north with their spacecraft to outrun the flood."

"That is why they were bringing gifts?" Dunk asked.

"Yes, and one of them had made a ring out of copper by some new method. It was shiny and very beautiful. The method by which it was crafted was a secret they wouldn't share."

"And does this somehow help our case?" Dunk asked.

"It shows that things can change. We can learn new things," Jhar said. "And there was something else."

Dunk pulled her hand close to his mouth and blew on it to warm it. "What else?"

They asked when the miners would return. They said the fruit givers had told them the miners had in their possession a book of stories that they wish to see. Just as Rahab told her story to me, some of the fruit givers must have shared stories with them. They thought these stories had importance for their lives. They want to know more of this book."

"Did Rahab speak to you of the book?" Dunk asked.

"Yes, she said the miners had it. She told me I should ask to see it and find her story there."

"This is very mysterious," Dunk said, "and it may be important. The fruit givers seem to live in a world apart. They have no need of us. They hold secrets we will never root out."

"I hope the miners return soon," Jhar said. "Perhaps this book they have will show us a way out of our impasse."

"Yes, I hope so, too" Dunk said, pulling her closer. "We must find a way."

Chapter 44

Daco

Daco sat at the big miners' table where Onri and his team were turning out translators as fast as they could. Onri's mother, Dray, and his sister, Mica, were both part of the team. Onri's father, Tull brought in scrapings from the vent pipes that were rich in the rare metals solidified out of the black smoke from the boiling hot vent steam. They suddenly had all the gold, platinum, copper, manganese and zinc they needed to craft the small earbuds.

Daco was surprised to see Onri had acquired a new team member from the biologist group – Soma, Mona's newly minted brother. He sat next to Mica and appeared to be entertaining her with a vast store of jokes.

Daco tried to tune them out and concentrate on the lists he was making. Those men working long hours out on the ice needed warmer clothes. He hoped to trade translators for warm skallon pelts. They could also use some of the long skallon bone scrapers for scraping the insides of their vent pipes for the metals brought up in the heavy sulfides escaping the vents. And they needed punches. Punches made from skallon bones would make sewing the pelts into clothes much easier.

Daco scrolled through his wrist diary as he considered his list. He added the words 'mong leaves.' It seemed the Cold Land clans survived on skallon meat and mong leaves. He guessed that mong leaves must supply a variety of vitamins and minerals that were surely lacking in a diet rich in protein. He thought there might be a few leaves left from the food Cray had brought to the ship to feed the young and elderly on their trip North to escape the flood waters.

"Soma," he said. "Could your group do a study of what the mong leaves have to offer in the way of essential nutrients?"

"Mong leaves?" Soma asked. "What are those?"

"Let me check our cargo hold and see if I can find some," Daco said. "Outside of skallon meat, mong leaves seem to be the only other things the Cold Land clans eat."

He walked down to the dark cargo hold wearing his headlamp. The hold was now home to bins of frozen fish and the many varieties of crustaceans that gathered around vents to eat the smaller forms of life that thrived on the bacteria nurtured by the rich sulfides smoke. A circle of life and minerals that were, taken together, a little microcosm of life in general.

He found what he sought at the bottom of an empty bin. A mong leaf, frozen, but hopefully still able to reveal its nutrients under a microscope.

Daco returned to the table of translator manufacture with his pathetic prize. "This is a mong leaf – a little worse for wear, but hopefully still able to share its secrets."

"You should take it to Mona," Soma said. "She could give you a list of nutrients within the hour."

Daco noted that Soma seemed reluctant to perform the work himself and guessed that he didn't want to give up his seat next to the lovely Mica.

"Yes," Daco said. "That is what I should do. It looks like we'll be making a trip North very soon to trade translators for pelts, scrapers and skallon meat. Some of you biologists may wish to come along and meet the inhabitants of Cold Land."

"I certainly want to accompany you," Soma said, turning to Mica. "Will you be going?"

"Yes," Mica said. "I know they use mong leaves for making torches and baskets and ropes as well as eating them. I would like to speak to Jhar about all the things she does with them."

"Who is Jhar?" Soma asked.

"She is a Jangle girl. One of the friendlier inhabitants of Cold Land. And she seems to be a special friend of the fruit givers as well," Mica said.

"Yes, they made her a wealthy woman with all the fruit they gave her," Daco said. "Delicious stuff – that fruit. It's likely all gone by now."

"The fruit givers saved us from the flood as well," Soma said. "We thought they were Swagians because they spoke our language. They told us to get out of here fast and then ordered us to fly over the skallon to stampede them. Mona was having fits because they refused to tell us how they came to have an alien ship."

Daco nodded. "They wanted us to be the ones to tell you what had happened to Swage."

Everyone was quiet for a moment remembering the impact of that terrible news.

Daco shook it off mentally. "Well, I shall take my poor sample leaf over to the *Seeker* and see if it is the magic we need to supply all that we will be missing with a fish diet."

"Yes, and if you do see Mona, tell her to arrange to come along on your trip North. She'll want to gather bits of everything growing on the pasture."

"Certainly," Daco said, with a backward glance at Soma and Mica. Mica was already smiling, anticipating Soma's next joke, perhaps.

As Daco walked along the shore the short distance between the two Swagian ships, he could see the miners beginning work on the platform that would hold the turbine.

Tomorrow, he thought. They would fly out tomorrow. His men needed warmer clothes. Many of them, himself included, had lost weight and muscle mass. They needed more food and he would have to find a way to get those nutrients they were lacking.

"Hello the *Seeker*," Daco called out as he stepped through the open hatch. Most of the biologists were out in the sea, gathering new specimens or fishing. A few had volunteered for rock piling and some new structures were beginning to take shape.

He walked to the lab which was also the kitchen and found Mona there looking through the lens of a large microscope.

"Mona?" he said. "Sorry to disrupt your work."

Mona's head snapped up. "Daco?" She smiled. "How goes the work outside?"

"All good," Daco said. "We do have a problem though. We are all losing weight and we need nutrients our friends who live in the sea cannot provide. I am hoping this little leaf I hold may be the solution. It is called a mong leaf and besides skallon meat, it is about all the Cold Land clans eat."

Mona took the small frozen leaf he held out to her. "Mong leaf, you say."

"Yes, I plan to fly the *Bonanza* north tomorrow to trade with the clans for things we need. If these mong leaves can provide what we are missing in our diets, I will trade translators for as many mong leaves as I can."

Mona removed the small glass plate that held a scraping of something unknown from under her scope and replaced it with a bit of the mong leaf. She spread a drop of iodine over the leaf on its little glass square. "Let's see what we have here," she said.

Mona nodded as she peered into the scope. "A C3 grass. A monocot, webbed structure. I see some vascular bundling and the Swagian cross. Good stomata pores." She looked up. "Do you want to take a look?"

"Sure," Daco said, "though I am certain it won't mean much to me."

He looked through the scope to see a beautiful webbed pattern of dark blue balloon-like structures. "Would these leaves give us the nutrients we are lacking in a fish diet?" he asked.

"Yes," Mona said. "I would have to do more tests but it is likely packed with lutein, beta-carotene, starches, sugars and vitamins."

"Could you come with us tomorrow when we fly north to Jangle and look at what grows in the pastures there?"

A wide smile took shape in Mona's face. "Absolutely," she said.

Chapter 45

Daco

The morning of their flight back to Jangle, Daco was out giving final instructions to his crew of miners. "If in doubt, wait," Daco said. "We only have one generator and we want to get it all right the first time if possible. We will try to get our trading done in two or three days at most. In the meantime there will be plenty of room for you on the *Seeker*. Twenty of the biologists are coming with us and only ten of the miners. And don't be shy about eating their food. We will be feeding their twenty biologists aboard the *Bonanza* and all food is owned in common now."

Daco stopped to think for a moment. Had he forgotten anything? Any crucial piece of information?

Pheebs laughed. "I am sure we will all be here when you get back, Mother Hen," he said.

Daco affected an offended expression before it changed to amusement. "Yes, I am aware you all know your craft as well as I do. Just be careful. We are too few to lose anyone."

He turned back toward the *Bonanza* and most of his miners followed to see their ship off. Everyone except Daco was aboard and ready to leave.

Daco gave a final wave before boarding and those who had followed were waving back as the hatch closed.

Once inside, Daco noted the chaos as the nine miners aboard welcomed their twenty guests. They pointed out the available cots and enclosures where the newcomers could stow their gear.

Mona and Soma had brought their large microscope aboard. It took up one end of the dining table and was tied down with straps. There was still room for everyone to crowd around the remaining open space of the large dining table.

"Everyone, find a secure place to strap into," Daco shouted. "Some of you may have to double up."

Even the *Seeker's* pilot, Santi, had come along. He would be strapping in next to Socom, the *Bonanza's* pilot, to learn both the route and the *Bonanza's* control panel in case he was ever called on to fly the *Bonanza* in place of Socom.

As they lifted off, Daco realized he was already beginning to think of the South Sea as home. And these days, having a home was a precious thing. He could see his fellow miners already back at work on the new platform, welding the pipline into place. The need for warmth was second only to the need for food.

When the ship left Cold Land's gravity field, Daco drifted free of his restraints and looked around to make sure all potential flying objects had been secured. It seemed the biologists were seasoned enough at spaceflight to have made sure of that.

Daco drifted among the students, most of whom were still strapped in, asking what their specific area of study and research was. He needed to know their individual talents to put them to use. It looked as though Professor Stern no longer saw himself as leader now that their original mission had become very secondary to survival. The loss of his homeland had hit him particularly hard. He had lost not only his biological family but his colleagues and his science lab as well. There was no one to receive his research findings.

Perhaps they should hold an election for leader of the South Sea group. Daco smiled. He knew his miners, who outnumbered the students, would elect him anyway. He may as well try to take the young scholars under his wing now.

Aldo was having fun pushing off and floating through the air at an alarming rate of speed.

"Hold up there son," Daco said, grabbing on to Aldo's pant leg as he zoomed by. "No need to raise havoc by turning yourself into a projectile."

Aldo laughed. "I was being careful not to hit anyone."

"I know, but these students are young and impressionable. We don't want to give them any ideas," Daco said with a grin.

Aldo laughed. "I think they already have ideas."

Daco followed his son's line of sight and saw that several of the male biologists were bouncing off one another. He moved in their direction.

"Settle down, gentlemen. There will be time enough for games once we land. We will be landing in green pastures where big furry four-legged skallon with sharp horns rule. If they smell fear on you they will stomp you to death. And the skallon are plagued by smaller furry animals, ripcons, which have huge jaws and quick tempers. You will want to avoid them. They will attempt to pull your arms off if given the chance."

The biologists were suddenly quite calm, listening closely.

"Should we carry laser guns?" one asked.

"Probably not necessary," Daco replied. "The Jangle shepherds keep their herds and the ripcons under control. But some rocks and clubs made of skallon long bones would not be a bad idea."

Daco moved on to speak to various groups until they heard Socom make the announcement. "Prepare for descent."

Daco moved back to his anchored cot, viewing his list to begin prioritizing his various tasks. Aldo snuggled next to him, sharing his restraints.

"Anything in particular you want to trade for in Jangle?" he asked his son.

"Fruit," Aldo said, without thinking the question over.

"I doubt there is any left," Daco said, "but we will ask Jhar."

"Good," Aldo said. "And maybe I could get a warmer coat."

"Yes," that is on my list. Number one priority."

"Did you bring fish to trade?" Aldo asked.

Daco was embarrassed to admit he had not even considered the idea. "I should have. It is just that they are so resistant to change and they only seem to think of skallon meat and and mong leaves as food. We have fish aboard. Perhaps we should offer their leader some fish to eat to see if they might consider fish as a trade item for our next trip."

"It couldn't hurt to try," Aldo said with his child's wisdom.

"No, it could not," Daco said. Or could it, he thought to himself.

They landed close to the alien ship. Daco was surprised to see the fruit givers' ship was still here. He suspected their home planet must be some sort of paradise they were eager to return to, and was eager to ask what had delayed their departure.

He was even more surprised to see four men standing beside the alien ship in new cape colors – blue and red.

As soon as the ship landed, everyone aboard was quickly out of their restraints. Daco realized he should have thought ahead to issue instructions about leaving and returning to the ship. He rushed to the exit hatch to correct that error.

"I would like everyone to stay aboard while I find out who these new people in red and blue capes are and what their business here is. The Jangle all wear green capes and they are the ones we have come to visit and trade with."

"I will go with you," his brother Bran said, pocketing a laser gun.

"This should only take a few minutes," Daco said, inserting a translator into his ear.

The two brothers exited the airlock and the four men started walking toward them. They did not seem threatening. They actually smiled at the brothers.

"Are you two of the miners?" A man in blue asked.

"We are," Daco said. "What brings you to Jangle land?"

"We have come to see you," the man answered.

"Why?" Daco's surprise was evident.

"We would like to see the book the fruit givers say you have. We want to hear the story of Jonah."

Daco knew at once what book the man referred to. He realized they had all been too busy, too focused on surviving, to have given the amazing talking book any notice.

"Well, that can certainly be arranged," Daco said. "As we are crowded inside and have students eager to begin exploring, we should perhaps schedule a time later in the day? Perhaps you could come and share a dinner of a new type of food later? You could bring some of your skallon meat in case our food does not agree with you. After our meal we could look at the book together."

The men nodded.

"I am Chai, leader of the Brites," one of the blue-caped men said.

"And I am Stan, leader of the Flag clan," one of the red-caped men said. "Will there be fruit at the meal?"

Daco shook his head, putting on a sad expression. "Unfortunately, we are all out of fruit."

Chapter 46

Daco

Daco returned to his ship to find the biologists grouped around portals, staring out at the Jangle pasturelands.

He called them together and gave some last-minute guidelines. "Think of yourselves as observers. You should not interfere in any way with the skallon or their shepherds. You may wear translators, but don't lose them as we will be trading them later for things we need to survive."

He stopped to try to imagine any danger he might warn against and decided there were too many to list. These were adults after all.

"Try to take a sample – a small one – of anything that appears edible. And be back in five hours. We are going to have local guests for dinner."

With these warnings, the students surged from the ship, only to stand in clumps of three or four outside, deciding which direction to go.

Daco looked at the remaining miners. His friends and family. "I'm going to the Jangle council dugout to ask leader Cray for permission to trade here. Then I'll try to visit the fruit givers if they will open their hatch to me."

"I'll go with you," Bran said.

"Me too," Aldo said.

"Have we anything we might trade with the fruit givers for more fruit?" Dray asked.

"They don't appear to need anything," Daco said. "But I'll invite them for tonight's meal as well."

"Good," Dray said. "They might accept that. And they could show us more about the talking book."

"Yes," Daco said. "I'll mention that if given the opportunity."

Daco moved to the hatch opening. "We are off then. The rest of you, try to stay out of trouble," he said, smiling.

Daco, Bran and Aldo walked over to the council dugout and found Cray inside speaking to a few councilmembers.

"Hello, Jangle council," he called out. "Have we come at a bad time?"

Cray turned around and invited them in with a swinging motion of his arm. "Not at all. Please join us. We're discussing our agenda for tomorrow's meeting."

"I'm hoping we can add our names to your agenda. We'd like to propose some sort of permanent trade guidelines between ourselves and the Jangles. We've brought translators to trade."

"Yes, we can add that to tomorrow's agenda," Cray said. "I don't think our main business will take long as we've already reached agreement on the first item."

"I see," Daco said, though he had no idea what Cray was talking about. "Shall we bring our translators with us then?"

"You can if you like," Cray said. "I will trade skallon meat for one right now if you have one with you."

"Yes, I do," Daco said, "and I am never one to pass up a good trade. As it happens we have invited four men from the Brite and Flag clans to eat with us tonight and they may not approve of the food we plan to serve – fish from the South Sea."

"Fish?" Cray said. "Is that something you grow aboard your ship?" A little shiver went through Cray's body and Daco suspected that someone had told him about the edible moss and fungi they had seen while aboard escaping the flood.

"No," Daco said. "Fish are creatures that live in the sea. You may have noticed a few of them carried along in the floodwaters. There is a range of size from the size of a finger to as large as a skallon."

"I would like to taste the meat of such a creature," Cray said. "If you want to leave a translator now, I'll bring the skallon meat tonight when I come for dinner."

"Good," Daco said. "I plan to visit the fruit givers' ship and invite them as well, but I don't know if they will accept or even open their hatch to let me in. I was surprised to see their ship is still here."

"I am surprised by that as well," Cray said. "They rarely come out and seem not to need anything from anyone. They did invite representatives from Flag and Brite aboard though, and since then the four men have stayed here, asking when you might return to trade."

"Yes," Daco said. "The fruit givers gave us a talking book. The men from Brite and Flag went to see it."

"This talking book is some kind of animal who speaks?" Cray asked.

"No, a book is a thing made up of thin pages – like leaves. The pages have written characters on them that represent words. Books contain stories but they don't generally speak aloud. Just how this particular book does so remains a mystery to all of us."

"I would like to see this book," Cray said.

"We will expect you tonight," Daco said.

"Will you sit with us now for a small meal?" Cray asked. "We have skallon meat roasting in the fire pit."

"I would never turn down skallon meat," Daco said. "Thank you."

As they settled around the fire pit, Cray asked, "Where are you and your miners staying now if it's not a secret?"

"No, it's not a secret," Daco said. "We've decided to settle down at the South Sea. It seems no one owns that land as yet and we have the fish to sustain us."

"It's too cold there to survive," Cray said. He frowned."I'm sorry we can't offer you pastureland."

"We believe we'll be able to survive there, though as you say, it's very cold. One of the things we will want to trade for is skallon pelts. They are warm and will help with survival."

"All the clans will likely trade pelts for translators," Cray predicted.

"Yes, we hope so," Daco said. "What do you know of the Flags and the Brites?"

"They are better neighbors than the Sylvans," Cray said. "Less hostile. Though now there is a new leader of the Sylvan clan. His name is Darp and he is a tanner by trade. He is not so hostile as their old leader Romm, though his son Dunk has become a problem."

"What's the problem?" Bran asked.

"He wants to become a Jangle," Cray said. "That isn't allowed."

"Why would he want to become a Jangle?" Bran asked. "Especially now that his father is leader of the Sylvans?"

"He wants to share a dugout with Jhar, who owns the fruit."

"We know Jhar," Bran said. "Does she want this as well?"

"Evidently she does," Cray said. "Though it makes no sense. If they don't abide by the council's ruling they will both be killed."

"Jhar is a good person," Aldo said. "You shouldn't kill her."

Cray smiled at Aldo. "You are too young to understand," he said. "We must all live by our rules. Otherwise there would be no order to our society. The rules are known by all. We all know that if we disobey the rules, we must suffer the punishments. Does that make sense to you?"

Aldo nodded. "Yes, but killing Jhar makes no sense."

Cray raked through the fire pit with a skallon bone and pulled out a bit of meat wrapped in a mong leaf. He handed it to Aldo. "Some day you may be a leader like your father. Then it will all make sense."

Chapter 47

Daco

Daco sent his son and brother back to the *Bonanza* for lunch. He stood alone outside the door of the fruit givers' ship, knocking three times on the door of the hatch.

The hatch opened and Joshua stood smiling before him. "Daco! What a nice surprise. Won't you come in for a visit?"

"Thank you," Daco said, walking into the warmer air of the ship.

"How are you and all of your people?" Joshua asked.

They stepped aboard the revolving platform as Daco considered his answer. "I believe we have found a home at the South Sea. It appears no one owns that land or has ever even visited it. The Jangles did not know what a fish was and that has become our main source of food."

"Fish – very healthy," Joshua said. "And you have met the biologists there?"

"We have," Daco said. "Thank you for allowing us to be the ones to tell them of our old planet's demise. I believe it was comforting for them to know we escaped as well."

"It could be seen as an act of cowardice on our part," Joshua said.

Daco smiled. "But we both know it was an act of kindness."

"It is kind of you to say so," Joshua said.

They stepped off at a high level and Daco saw cups of tea and a plate of fruit had been laid out on a table facing a view of Jangle and Sylvan pastureland. The grass almost glowed in its lushness. Those young skallon that had outrun the flood pranced about the tall grass, butting heads with other calves playfully. The adult skallon pulled out clumps of grass with their strong jaws, scanning the pastures with their eyes as they ate, always searching for possible threats.

Joshua pointed to a couch and Daco took a seat. "Have you come north to trade?" he asked.

"Yes," Daco said. We need skallon pelts for warmth and greens to supplement a fish-only diet."

"Yes, the mong leaves," Joshua said.

"You know about them?" Daco asked.

Joshua nodded. "A very nutritious plant. You should eat the roots as well."

"Thank you for telling me," Daco said.

Joshua smiled. "In time you will be growing plants at the South Sea in greenhouses."

Daco's mouth fell open. "You know this?"

Joshua shrugged. "It seems inevitable."

"Did you know the Brite and Flag representatives have asked to see the talking book you gave us?" Daco asked.

"We suggested they do so. They were very taken with Jonah's story."

"They're coming to our ship tonight for dinner. I have promised we will show them the book after we eat."

"Good," Joshua said.

"Perhaps you would all like to come as well? I am not sure how we would locate Jonah's story. It is a large book. I regret to say we have not as yet had time to explore its contents."

Joshua nodded. "You should perhaps make time for such an activity. You might find it helpful."

"Yes we will do that. Maybe you could give us some instruction on its usage?"

Joshua nodded. "Yes, I will come. Thank you for the invitation."

Daco wondered if that promise was a hint that it was time for him to leave.

"Have some tea and fruit and tell me about your new home at the South Sea," Joshua said.

Daco relaxed and was surprised by how comforting it was to hear someone speak of a new 'home'. "The South Sea is a wonder," he said.

"We believe it may hold the edge of a tectonic plate. There are active vents in the seafloor. Some emit black smoke carrying sulfides rich in rare ores. Others breathe white smoke and carry calcium and its like. It is a treasure trove for miners."

"And what does it provide for the biologists?" Joshua asked.

"For them, the vents are rich in all manner of sea life. The bacteria attract shelled creatures of every sort. And those shelled creatures attract the many armed cephalopods. The shrimp attract larger fish. The fish are many and varied. We are fortunate to be at home in the water. The Cold Land natives don't have our gill slits and seem unused to large bodies of water."

"Yes," Joshua agreed. "Your gill slits are a rare gift. Only a few of God's creatures are at home both on land and sea."

Daco nodded. "We had several such creatures back on Swage. It was a land of jungles and pools. A land thick with foliage and the most beautiful flowers. But we circled close to our star. Too close."

"I wish I could have seen it," Joshua said. "All of God's creations are wonders."

"You believe your God created Swage?" Daco asked.

"Most assuredly," Joshua said.

"Then why would he allow it to be destroyed? Why burn up such a beautiful creation?" Daco asked. He could not keep the angry tone from his voice.

"We don't know God's ways or God's thoughts," Joshua said. "But we can be assured God is good and he loves us."

"How can you be assured of that?" Daco asked.

"Because while we were dead in our own flawed natures, he made us a path for eternal salvation. And he did it out of love. We did not deserve his grace. That was clear."

"I suppose all this wisdom is contained in the book you provided?" Daco asked.

"It is," Joshua said. "But each story in the book has layers of meaning. It takes a great deal of study to ferret out the truth for most of us."

"We will make a beginning tonight," Daco said. "But I think those men from Brite and Flag will not be satisfied with hearing Jonah's story. They will likely want to hear all the stories it contains."

"Yes, they will," Joshua agreed. "My own story is there. The stories of all of us aboard the *By Grace*."

"That is the name of your ship? The *By Grace*?"

"Yes, Joshua said. "It will make sense to you by and by"

Daco sighed. "I suppose we could open the book up to others every time we come north to trade," Daco said.

"Yes, that is a good plan," Joshua agreed. "You might also consider opening a school where students of the book could come to study the book, and perhaps make copies to share with their clans."

"You think there will be that much interest?"

"I do," Joshua said.

Daco leaned back on his couch and took a drink of the tea which had grown tepid. He reached for a piece of fruit and was surprised again by its richness. "I wish we had a climate conducive to growing fruit at our new home," Daco said wistfully.

"In time, perhaps several years from now, you might consider a visit to the burned out husk of your old planet which still revolves in its orbit around your red star. All the life on its surface was burned away, but deep underground where the planet's past lies buried, there may be some traces of its early life still salvageable. I cannot promise such a miracle but seeds are by nature a miracle in and of themselves."

"You think there may be buried seeds that are still viable?" Daco asked.

Joshua shrugged. "One can always hope."

A realization flashed through Daco's mind. This fruit he was eating had no seeds. He finished his piece of fruit, almost in a trance, his mind far away on what remained of Swage. He looked up at Joshua. "You have given me so much to think about, I can hardly contain it all. I should probably leave now before my head explodes."

Joshua laughed. "I will bring some fruit with me tonight," he said. "I look forward to meeting more of your passengers."

"You will find them equally pleased to meet you," Daco said, standing up.

Chapter 48

Daco

Daco returned to his ship to find a storm of activity. Biologists were streaming in and out of the ship, their arms full of weeds, insects, nematodes and other bits of life. One even carried a dead ripcon which Daco hoped was not the result of an attack on either side.

The four men from Brite and Flag were there, early for dinner, but seemingly with nowhere else to go. They held baskets of dried skallon meat. The baskets were woven of dried mong leaves.

A few Jangles were there, too, waiting patiently. They held possible trade items in their arms. He saw Jhar among them holding a long rope made of dried mong leaves.

"Jhar," he said. "How good to see you. Have you come to trade?"

"Maybe," she said. "Do you need a rope?"

"Always," Daco said. "Please come aboard with me. I need to speak with you if we can find a quiet corner somewhere."

Jhar followed him through the open hatch, carrying her rope.

Daco led Jhar up to the navigation deck which was vacant now. He sat down in the pilot's chair and invited her to sit alongside.

Jhar set her rope on the floor. "I hoped to trade for a translator," Jhar said.

They both knew a rope was not enough for a translator. It would be worth several ropes. "If you're staying a few days, I can add more ropes and baskets to the trade," she said.

Daco knew that his brother, Bran, had already given Jhar a translator on a previous visit and he knew she was wearing it now. "Why do you need a second translator?" he asked.

"I was advised by one of the fruit givers to offer something of value to the council to better my chances of getting a favorable response to my petition. I know they want more translators. I also plan to offer what fruit I have left." She shrugged.

"I have heard about your upcoming council meeting," Daco said. "Your Sylvan man has asked to become a Jangle?"

Jhar nodded. "He wants to share a dugout with me. Without the required permission, it would be an offense punishable by death."

Daco was quiet for a moment. "I have spoken to your leader Cray. Our petition to trade with the Jangles will be discussed at the same meeting. I believe they have already made a decision not to accept your young man as a Jangle. They appear to be inflexible where any rules are concerned."

Jhar slumped. "I suspected as much."

"They will kill you both if you ignore their ruling," Daco warned.

"I know," Jhar said.

"Would your young man consider becoming a South Sea man rather than a Jangle?"

Jhar looked up. "A South Sea man?"

"No one owns the South Sea as yet so we are claiming it as our home. By we, I mean we miners and biologists formerly from the planet, Swage. But we could include you and your Sylvan as well."

"Won't you return eventually to your old planet?" Jhar asked.

"No, we will not," Daco said. He didn't want to tell anyone why just now. He especially didn't want to break down in tears as sometimes happened.

"Isn't the South Sea a death sentence to any who go there?" Jhar asked. "It's too cold outside pastureland to survive and there's nothing to eat."

"We've been there for some time now and as you can see we're still alive. There is a good source of food there called fish. We plan to continue to make translators for all the clans which we will trade for skallon meat, pelts for warmth, mong leaves to eat and make ropes. You would be useful there to show us how to make baskets, ropes and torches from mong leaves."

A small expression of hope returned to Jhar's face. "My young man, Dunk, is a tanner."

"I remember Dunk," Daco said. "His father is now leader of the Sylvans?"

"Yes. He's willing to leave his father for me even though they are very close. They have no other family."

"Dunk's father would be welcome to visit."

"You think we could both be useful there?" Jhar asked.

"I do," Daco said.

"I'll speak to Dunk about the possibility," Jhar said. "And I'll leave the rope as a down payment."

"A down payment on what?" Daco asked

"Our lives," Jhar said.

Daco walked back to the bottom hatch with Jhar. "You can give me your decision before the council meeting begins if you want, or you can wait and see which way the council votes first," he said.

Jhar nodded and walked through the open hatch.

Daco took a quick look outside to see if anyone else was waiting to be invited aboard, but no one seemed to be looking in his direction.

He heard a familiar voice calling his name from within the ship. He turned to see Mona, holding a bouquet of weeds.

"We've been testing all day and a few of these pasture weeds are edible, but the mong plant is still our best bet by far," she said.

"Is the mong plant plentiful?" Daco asked.

"Very," Mona said. "The skallon will eat it, but they prefer the grass. The Jangles use it, of course, but they have plenty to spare."

"How much do you suppose we could get for one translator in trade?" Daco asked.

"It might depend on whether we harvested it ourselves or the Jangles harvested it for us," Mona said.

"I'll add that question to tomorrow's agenda at the council meeting," Daco said. "Did you by any chance test the roots for nutrients?"

"Of course," Mona said. "They store most of the plant's starch. Very nutritious. Of course if we take the roots, the plant cannot regrow. But there are plenty to reseed themselves."

"Good work," Daco said. "We will have quite a crowd for dinner. Is anyone in charge of food?"

"I think Dray and Mica are," Mona said. "If you get too close to either one they will assign you work."

Daco laughed. "Thank you for the warning. Have you seen Onri?"

"Yes, he is still at the table, turning out translators. I believe he would like me to remove my microscope to give his workers more room."

"Leave your microscope where it is," Daco said. "We still have more biologists returning with things to be tested."

Mona grinned. "I had no intention of moving it in any case."

Daco smiled. "I need to count the number of translators that we have available to sell."

"All of us are wearing one, so we have that many at least," Mona said.

"Have you seen Aldo?" he asked.

"He's with Bran at the table, I think," Mona said.

Daco moved on to the big dining table on the second level of the ship.

"Dad!" Aldo called out. "I made a translator." He held up his prized achievement.

"Good," Daco said. "How many do we have now all together?"

"Around sixty, I would guess," Onri said.

"How many pelts do you think we need?" Bran asked.

"I think one pelt would clothe two people," Daco said.

"Yes, that sounds right," Bran said. The skallon are as long as a man, twice as wide, and each skallon has two sides."

"We'll need to use the rest of the translators to trade for mong leaves," Daco said. "I'll try to bargain for two pelts for one translator, but we'll have to establish that at tomorrow's council meeting."

"For now, we had best concentrate on tonight's dinner. Dray has threatened to sweep everything off the table if we don't shut down manufacturing soon," Bran said.

Daco nodded. "We need to keep the cook happy. Let's clear things up here."

"I need a word in private about the translators," Onri said.

"Of course," Daco said, leading Onri to a quiet corner in the sleeping area. When they were far enough away for privacy, he asked, "What have you to tell me?"

"I'm not sure you realize the capacity of the gift we have been given with these translators," Onri said.

"I know they have saved us from starvation and enabled us to make friends among the Cold Land clans," Daco said. "Is there more?"

"I believe they have given much more than that," Onri said.

Daco searched his own mind for possibilities and he took a moment to reply. "How so?"

"The mechanism digitizes brain waves and cross references speech centers with the speech centers of any who use soundwaves for speech," Onri said.

"I am still not seeing where this leads," Daco admitted.

"The same technology is capable of digitizing all of the information stored in our brains. We can gather all of our mind's activity and memories and either store that or transfer it to robots or avatars."

Daco nodded slowly. "Yes, I see what you are saying. We could design robots and send them to asteroids and possibly other planets while we control them from here. They could set up structures for us or mine metals for us."

"Exactly," Onri said. "The opportunities are far reaching."

"You must choose an apprentice to share your knowledge," Daco said. "Such technology must be guarded and preserved."

"Would you consider giving me Aldo?" Onri asked.

"I'll ask him when things settle down a bit. In the meantime, perhaps we should keep this new information between the two of us."

"Yes, I think that is wise. We have our immediate survival to think about just now."

Chapter 49

Daco

As soon as the cooked fish was laid out on the large miners' table, Daco went to the hatch and began welcoming guests aboard the *Bonanza*.

He showed the guests to chairs around the table and a few miners and biologists filled in the empty ones. All the others aboard filled their plates and then either sat or stood against the walls of the dining area.

Joshua's fruit, leader Cray's skallon, and the dried skallon from the Brite clan and the Flag clan were added to the table. Daco stood to say a few words. "This is a gathering of like-minded men and women willing to put aside their differences for the greater good. We welcome various clans and even those of other star systems to share what goods and knowledge we hold. Any foods that are new to you, please take in small quantities to judge whether they agree with your various constitutions. Now, welcome aboard the *Bonanza* and let's eat."

The fruit was soon gone, but everyone got at least one piece. The skallon meat was soon devoured as well. The fish were tasted by all except for one of the Flag men and had mixed success. Joshua pronounced it delicious, but Cray and his council members ate only enough to be polite.

Everyone had questions. Daco told them he and his group had made their home the South Sea and many of the clansmen predicted bad outcomes for such a choice.

"We have fish to eat and plenty of ice to melt for drinking water," Daco argued. "We will soon have the means to draw warmth from the waters of the sea."

"Have you not horids lying in wait to kill you?" Craig asked.

"We do have some large white predators. I'm not sure if they are the ones you speak of. But they feed on the large fish of the sea. They don't lie in wait for me or my people – though they will fight if provoked."

"What other creatures come out of the water?" Chai of the Brites asked.

"There are a few that come ashore to lay eggs and then return to the sea," Daco said. "We have not found them to be hostile and their eggs are edible."

"These are bird creatures?" Cray asked. "Only the birds lay eggs."

"No, these are not flying creatures," Daco said. "They crawl on land and swim while in the sea."

"What does this mean, to swim," Stan of the Flags asked.

"Different creatures have each their own means of propulsion through the water. Some wave their bodies, some push and pull with their arms or legs, some crawl along the seafloor," Daco said.

"How do you know these things?" Cray asked.

"We go in the water ourselves and observe these things," Daco said.

Cray paused with his piece of skallon halfway to his mouth. "You walk along the floor of the sea with water all around you?"

"Yes, or more often, we swim through the water looking around us at the various forms of sea life," Daco said.

"What demon behavior is this?" Swarm of the Flags asked.

"Do you call birds demons because they can fly?" Daco asked. "It is something we are able to do. Actually, you could do it as well if you learned how, but you would need to swim close to the surface to come up for air."

"It sounds unnatural to me," Swarm groused. He looked around for support for his words but found none.

"I should like to visit your South Sea home," Cray said. "I would like to see these wonders you speak of."

"Visitors are always welcome," Daco said. "I hope we can become trading partners, taking advantage of what resources we have individually to enrich all our lives."

"We would need to fly down on your ship to visit," Cray said.

"That could be arranged for a trade of goods," Daco said.

"Of course," Cray said.

"And we will be making regular trips north to trade," Daco said. "Perhaps once every thirty days?"

"The Brite clan would welcome you," Chi said. "We could perhaps send an emissary down with you to return in thirty days' time to trade with us?"

"Yes, that could be arranged," Daco said. "We would welcome a Brite emissary."

"And the Flags could do the same," Stan said, not to be outdone. "We could send someone down to study your book for a thirty day period. Someone to bring back stories to tell our clan. We have unique products to offer – unique among the clans."

"What products are those?" Cray demanded. "We Jangles have not heard of this."

"We Flags are separated from you by the Brite clan. If not for these new translators we would be unable to speak to you. But now with the Brites' permission, perhaps we could begin to trade," Stan said.

"Yes, we would very much like to see these new products you speak of," Cray said.

"We have always seen neighboring clans as enemies, eager to overtake our pastures if given the opportunity. But now I see that we could change our views to everyone's benefit," Stan said. "It is a new way of thinking, but perhaps a better way."

"I believe the old ways are always the best," Swarm grumbled. "They are tried and proven true by our histories. They keep things in balance."

"They can also keep progress at bay," Daco said. "If you allowed yourselves to learn new ways of thought and action you, too, could have ships that fly through the air."

A few guests gasped at the thought, but others seemed intrigued by the possibility.

"You would share your secrets of flight with us?" Stan asked.

"We are considering the idea," Daco said. "A wise man has suggested we open a school to students who wish to study the book we have in our keeping and perhaps to learn the steps toward a higher level of technology as well. And that man is here with us tonight. You know him as one of the fruit givers. A few of us know him by his name – Joshua."

Joshua nodded and smiled. "I am encouraged by the strides you are making here tonight to live as friends rather than enemies. It is in hope of such a transition that we have left our home to come here."

"What can you tell us of your home planet?" Cray asked.

"We are all of a body ruled over and cared for by our God, the creator of the universe. Our God is both our friend and a mystery. No one can know the mind of God, nor do we know why we are sent out until we arrive at our destination and seek out where we can be of use. Our home was built for us by God and delivered to our planet as one of God's beautiful creations. Our trees provide the major part of our food – the fruit you all seem to enjoy. Our God provides our light and we want for nothing. But in gratitude, we all live to serve him."

Everyone considered Joshua's words for a moment wondering at the perfection he described.

"Could we ever hope to visit there?" Cray asked.

"As I said, our God remains a mystery. Perhaps he has such a thing in mind for you, but I could not promise it."

"Does your God know about this book you have brought along with you as a gift to the miners?" Stan asked.

Joshua nodded. "God wrote the book and provided this speaking version for our mission."

"I think perhaps it is time we all gather to view and listen to this marvelous gift we have been given," Daco said. "And we are fortunate to have Joshua with us tonight to explain its workings to us."

On hearing these words, Dray and Mica began to clear the table to make a space for the book.

Chapter 50

Jhar

The night was very dark and Jhar hadn't brought a torch. She looked up at the stars and wondered if one of them was the home of the fruit givers.

"Dunk, are you here?" she said quietly.

"Yes, I'm here," came a voice she recognized.

Dunk was only a shadow against the star-filled sky but he reached out to touch her hair as he always did.

"Something is wrong," Jhar said. "I can sense it in your voice."

She heard him take a deep breath.

"As usual, Romm is trying to cause trouble," Dunk said.

"What kind of trouble?" Jhar asked

"He's trying to raise support against us. He plans to come to the council meeting tomorrow prepared to kill me for asking to become a Jangle."

"He is doing all this because he is angry about your father becoming leader?"

"Yes, he knows killing me is the best way to hurt my father."

"How did he ever become leader to begin with?" Jhar asked.

"He gave people gifts to vote for him and promised them special favors."

"He really is a terrible person," Jhar said.

"At least I have the satisfaction of knowing if he kills me, my father will find a way to kill him."

"That thought brings me no satisfaction," Jhar said.

"Maybe the Jangle council will not allow him entrance," Dunk said.

"From what I have heard they are more likely to help him," Jhar said.

"Truly? We have no support for our petition?"

"Cray would like to help us, I think, but he feels bound to follow the rules as the Jangle leader," Jhar said.

"What do you want to do?" Dunk asked.

Jhar decided to ignore that question for the time being. "Daco is back and this time he has brought more people from his planet. He has settled at the South Sea and calls that his home now."

"No one can survive living at the South Sea. Will they all live aboard their ship and grow their food in the ship as well? What will happen when they have children and no more room?" Dunk asked.

"He says they have a thing called fish to eat and they will soon have heat there in structures they will make."

"I would have to see it to believe it," Dunk said.

"Yes, why don't we go with him and see it?" Jhar asked.

"He has invited us to see it?" Dunk asked

"Yes, he has said we would be welcome to join him there. He says we would be useful."

"How could we be useful? These people know how to build airships and make them fly through the air. We are like skallon to them," Dunk said.

"He has come north to buy pelts and mong leaves. He says they have need of a tanner and someone to show them how to make ropes and baskets from mong leaves."

"He said all this?" Dunk's voice held a note of hope.

"He said it and he meant it. They need our help to survive," Jhar said.

"I would like very much to ride just one time on their spaceship," Dunk said. "Would you?"

"Yes," Jhar said. "I would like to do that."

"I have twenty-five pelts ready to offer to the Jangle council tomorrow," Dunk said.

"And I have four baskets of fruit still to offer," Jhar said.

"We could withdraw our petition and offer these gifts to Daco instead," Dunk said.

"I think that is our best choice just now," Jhar agreed.

"If we die there at the South Sea, we will at least have had our ride aboard the spaceship."

"Daco said your father is welcome to visit us there. He plans to fly north once every thirty days to trade. Your father could come for a thirty day visit and also have a chance to fly."

"He would like that, I know," Dunk said.

"We could go by Daco's ship tomorrow and ask for a bite of this fish he says we would live on," Jhar said.

"Yes," Dunk said, "and if the fish doesn't kill us, we will withdraw our petition."

"I think that is a good plan," Jhar said. "I like the idea of seeing more of our planet as well."

"Yes, this sea which spread out to try to drown us," Dunk said. "What a great body of water it must be."

"I can't imagine it," Jhar said.

"I could dig our dugout there. I would have to find a way to fuel a fire to melt the permafrost. That could be difficult with no skallon dung."

"Daco says there will be heat from the sea," Jhar said.

"Did Daco look close to dying of starvation?" Dunk asked.

"He seemed a little thinner but nowhere near starvation," Jhar said.

"What would we need to take with us?" Dunk asked.

"All the dried skallon meat we could find," Jhar said. "And lots of skallon dung and mong leaves."

"Yes," Dunk agreed. "A thirty day supply would be good."

Jhar could hear the smile in Dunk's voice and was finally able to relax a bit after so many days of facing a probable death. "I think I could manage that, although I may have to trade a bit of my fruit for the dried skallon meat."

"My father will make sure I have everything we need," Dunk said. "I'm sure he will want to fly down with us."

"Ask him to come to the council meeting tomorrow. The miners are on the list of things to talk about now. They want to ask permission to become permanent trading partners with the Jangles. Your father might want to set up trade rules for the Sylvans as well. The miners have many translators to trade."

"Yes, he'll want to establish trade with them," Dunk said.

"I'll tell my parents to come," Jhar said.

"They weren't planning to come to support you?" Dunk asked.

"I think they were afraid they would only be watching both of us get killed," Jhar said.

Dunk's voice dripped almost to a whisper. "I didn't realize Cray was so set against me."

"He sees his role as leader to be the one charged with enforcing the rules. He actually likes both of us and doesn't want to see us killed."

"How did he feel about us meeting secretly for so many years?" Dunk asked.

"I'm not sure he knows about that. Probably best not to mention it," Jhar said.

"Very well," Dunk said. "I'll meet you tomorrow early at the miners' ship. I'll offer one pelt for a meal of fish and let Daco know that I have twenty-four more. If we survive the fish meal, we'll go to withdraw the petition."

"Yes, and you should bring your father to the miners' ship. If he comes for a thirty day visit, he needs to know about the fish diet."

Dunk pulled Jhar close into a hug. "Is there a chance we will live to be together?" he asked.

"Yes, I think so," Jhar said, hugging him back. "I hope so."

Chapter 51

Daco

Daco set the wooden box on the table and the guests stood around it, watching. "Joshua, will you sit and show us how the book is made to speak?" he asked.

"Of course. Is there something particular you would like to hear?"

Stan of the Flag clan answered before Daco could respond. "We from Flag would like to hear Jonah's story."

Joshua took a seat in front of the wooden box and lifted the lid. He picked up the leather-covered book and laid it open to reveal the pages marked with small inked letters.

"Good book," he said. "Go to Jonah."

The pages began turning as everyone crowded closer to view this marvel.

The pages stopped moving and as Joshua's finger slid over the words, a deep voice began to speak. The voice seemed to be coming from somewhere within the book.

"The word of the Lord came to Jonah son of Amattai: go to the great city of Nineveh and preach against it, because its wickedness has come up before me."

Joshua lifted his finger and the deep voice fell silent.

Stan was speaking to his fellow clansman Swarm in a loud voice. "It is just as Jonah told us. Nineveh was his enemy and he was sent by the Lord to warn them."

"Yes," Joshua said. "Jerusalem and Nineveh were mortal enemies."

"It was wrong of the Lord to ask him to warn his enemies," Swarm contended.

"Did Jonah not wish to come here to defend his actions?" Stan asked.

Joshua smiled. "I think perhaps he does not enjoy hearing of his past actions."

"Because they were wrong?" Stan asked.

"It is a story," Joshua said. "I believe it is up to each who hears it to consider all sides of a story and decide what is right or wrong."

"Yes," Chai of the Brites said. "There is more to the story. You should listen."

Joshua nodded and began moving his finger over the words below.

"But Jonah ran away from the Lord and headed for Tarshish."

"Wait," Stan said.

Joshua lifted his finger and looked at Stan.

"What is it?" Chai of the Brites asked.

"We need to know why he chose to go to Tarshish. Was this city a friend or another enemy?" Stan asked.

"Tarshish was a great trading city and one rich in metals – gold, silver, iron and the like," Joshua said. "They traded with Jerusalem but they traded with Nineveh as well. I believe the most important fact here might be that Tarshish was in the opposite direction from the city of Nineveh."

"Yes, that makes sense," Chi said. "Go on and everyone, stop interrupting."

Joshua moved on in the book.

"He went down to Joppa where he found a ship..."

"Wait," Chi said. "There are flying ships there in Joppa?"

Joshua stopped to look at Chi. "No, this was a very long time ago, and there were no flying ships at that time – only ships that sailed atop the waters of the sea. Those who made their living as traders either had to load their wares atop a pack animal or aboard a ship."

"They could not just carry them?" Swarm asked.

"Yes, or carry them," Joshua amended.

"What is a pack animal?" Cray asked.

"Animals like skallons," Joshua said. "They would tie their wares in bundles and load them on the backs of skallon-like animals – they would keep them in place with straps."

This statement drew loud laughter from all the Cold Land clansmen. "Those animals were nothing like skallon," Cray said. "A skallon would die before it would allow such an insult." All those around seemed to agree with this observation.

"It doesn't matter," Chi complained. "We need to get back to the story."

"You were the one who interrupted," Stan pointed out.

"Yes," Chi admitted. "But it is good we now know of ships that move on the surface of the water."

Joshua resumed his skimming motion.

"Bound for that port," the deep voice continued, "after paying the fare, he went aboard and sailed for Tarshish to flee from the Lord."

Joshua lifted his finger. "No questions?" he asked.

"No, this is as Jonah told us," Stan said. "He did not want to go to Nineveh."

"Good book, continue," Joshua said. This time the book began speaking without his finger's help.

"Then the Lord sent a great storm on the sea, and such a violent storm arose that the ship threatened to break up. All the sailors were afraid and each cried out to his own god. And they threw the cargo into the sea to lighten the ship."

"Stop," Stan said.

"Good book, pause," Joshua said, looking at Stan. It seemed the book obeyed both verbal commands and a finger's movement above the words.

"This is confusing," Stan said. 'How did each man cry out to his own god if there is only one God who created the whole universe?"

"Yes, that is confusing," Joshua agreed. "At that time, long ago, many people did not believe in the one true God. They worshiped idols which were nothing more than bits of wood or stone carved into mythical gods – as though the man-made carving carried power within it. Almost every city had its own carved god or even several different gods that they would adorn with flowers or bits of food in hopes of having their prayers answered."

"What is a prayer?" Cray asked.

"It is a plea for help or a hope of attaining some benefit," Joshua said. "Many who were sick would pray for their ailment to leave them."

"It seems that a God who speaks as Jonah's God did would be a better choice," Cray observed.

"It seems so to me as well," Joshua said. "Good book, continue," he said.

"But Jonah had gone below deck, where he laid down and fell into a deep sleep. The captain went to him and said, how can you sleep? Get up and call on your God! Maybe he will take notice of us so that we will not perish. Then the sailors said to each other, come, let us cast lots to find out who is responsible for this calamity."

"Stop," Swarm said.

"Good book, pause," Joshua said.

"What is this casting of lots?" Swarm asked. "Is this some evil magic?"

"Casting lots is like a game of chance," Joshua said. "When no argument seems to carry a solution and a choice cannot be made easily, some prefer to throw a die or pick a straw to avoid making a decision."

"Ah," Cray said. "We call that leaving the matter to fate. We throw up stones to see how fate answers."

Joshua nodded. "Good book, continue."

"They cast lots and the lot fell on Jonah. So they asked him. Tell us, who is responsible for making all this trouble for us? What kind of work do you do? Where do you come from? What is your country? From what people are you?"

These questions were close to those that could be leveled at Daco and he considered putting a stop to proceedings, but decided to wait a little longer. He continued to listen.

"He answered. I am a Hebrew and I worship the Lord, the God of heaven, who made the sea and the dry land.

This terrified them and they asked, what have you done? (They knew he was running away from the Lord, because he had already told them.)"

At a sign from Daco, Joshua asked for another pause.

"I believe it is quite late," Daco said. "This is obviously an important story and we know it is one Jonah has lived to tell. I can see why he would not enjoy hearing it. We must close the book for tonight and continue tomorrow night if you are willing. Tomorrow morning we South Sea residents must be rested and ready for trade talks at the Jangle council dugout."

"You will stay to finish the story tomorrow?" Stan asked.

Daco smiled. "Yes, we will stay and I hope Joshua will return tomorrow as well."

"It would be my pleasure," Joshua said.

With that, Daco began to usher out his guests who were still debating Jonah's actions among themselves.

Chapter 52

Jhar

Early the next morning, Jhar, Dunk and his father Darp stood outside the miners' spaceship. They didn't have to wait long. The hatch opened and several young men and women walked out carrying bags made of some unknown material, laughing and calling out to one another.

Jhar had her translator on and asked if Daco was aboard.

"Yes, go on in," a young man said. "We are off to collect weeds from the pasture."

Jhar wondered why anyone would want to collect weeds but did not ask.

The three stepped aboard the ship and began to call out. "Daco? Are you here Daco?"

Daco came down a stationary set of descending blocks, not moving ones as on the fruit givers' ship.

"Jhar," Daco said. "Is this your young man with you?"

"Yes," Jhar said. "This is Dunk and his father Darp who is leader of the Sylvans."

"Actually, we have already met. We came here together after the flood," Daco said, smiling. "Please come up to our dining area. We are just finishing up a morning meal."

"Do you have fish to eat?" Jhar asked as they climbed to the next level.

"Always," Daco said. "Would you care to try some?"

"It is what we have come for," Jhar said. "Before we agree to fly with you to take up residence at South Sea we need to know if we can eat your food and survive."

"Very wise," Daco said. "Does this mean you intend to become permanent residents?"

"Yes," Jhar said. "Dunk and I do. Darp only wants to come for a visit."

"I see. Then let's not waste any time. We have three kinds of fish."

"I have brought a pelt to trade for the fish we will eat," Dunk said, holding out his gift.

Daco spread the pelt out at one end of the table. "This is a very fine quality," he said, running his fingers through the thick skeleton fur. "This pelt will shield two men from the cold."

"Yes," Dunk said. "I have brought twenty-four more to offer as a gift for you to accept us into your clan."

"That is most generous and much appreciated," Daco said. "I certainly hope the fish agrees with you."

They all sat on chairs at the table and Daco gave each one of them a thing he called a plate. Jhar couldn't identify the material it was made from or why it was necessary for eating fish.

Daco pushed a very large plate containing beige lumps of food in front of them. "The little round ones are a form of shell fish. They are new to us as well, though we had similar shelled sea animals on Swage."

"Swage is your home planet?" Darp asked.

"Yes," Daco said without elaborating.

"Is there any particular reason you have decided to live here on Cold Land instead?" Darp asked.

"Many reasons," Daco said. "But I assure you we plan to stay here on Cold Land. We don't plan to return to Swage."

Darp nodded and transferred his attention to the platter of fish.

Daco used a knife to point to the second type of fish. "This fish is, in my opinion, the tastiest. It is so reminiscent of a fish we called a skipper on Swage, that we have decided to call this one a skipper as well. The last," he pointed to a strange shape that looked like that of very large insect, "this is some kind of crustacean. You must remove the outer shell to get to the meat."

Jhar, Dunk and Darp each took a small portion of all three fish and began to eat.

Jhar thought the shellfish and skipper rather bland but she liked the taste of the crustacean even though it required the most effort – breaking open the shells and pulling out little bits of the fish inside.

They all waited silently after eating, wondering what might happen to their bodies if this experiment proved deadly.

"We have a council meeting scheduled today at the Jangle council dugout," Daco said. "We plan to ask for a formal trading agreement with the Jangle clan. Mostly we will be bringing translators to trade for mong leaves and skallon pelts. Might your Sylvan clan like to establish such an agreement as well?" he asked, looking at leader Darp.

"Yes, we would. I look forward to seeing what other trade goods the South Sea has to offer," Darp said.

"Are you in favor of this plan for your son to live at the South Sea?" Daco asked.

"I am in favor of any plan that does not result in his death," Darp said.

"Yes, Cray seems to be a stickler for obeying rules which may no longer be necessary," Daco said. "Have the clans any mechanism to change rules that no longer apply?"

"No," Darp said. "For the most part nothing changes here on Cold Land. Your coming and the coming of the fruit givers is the first change we have ever had to deal with."

"Change is always difficult. It has been difficult for those of us from Swage as well. But change can sometimes be for the better," Daco said.

"Would you say coming to Cold Land has been a change for the better for you?" Darp asked.

Daco took a deep breath. "I see you want to know why we are here so I will tell you the truth. While we were busy mining for metals on the asteroid that caused the flood, we watched the destruction of our home planet, Swage. A huge fireball flared out from our red star and destroyed Swage. We have no planet to return to." A tear escaped from Daco's eye and ran down his cheek. "I don't like to speak of it, but you have a right to know."

"I thank you for trusting us with this terrible information. We will not speak of it to others," Darp promised, with a warning glance at his son and Jhar. "Such information could put you in a weaker position here on Cold Land."

"Thank you," Daco said. "I can see that the Sylvan clan is lucky to have you as their leader."

"I think that we seem to be able to eat fish and live," Darp said. He looked at Jhar and his son. "Any sign of sickness?"

"I feel fine," Jhar said.

"As do I," Dunk said. "I think we will be ready to leave for our new home whenever you are."

"I am pleased to hear it," Daco said. "I'm sure you have as much to teach us about survival on Cold Land as we have to teach you about Swagian technology."

"We are going to go now to withdraw our petition to make Dunk a Jangle," Jhar said.

"We will be honored to have both a Jangle and a Sylvan living among us," Daco said. "But please plan to come to the council meeting even though your petition is withdrawn. You can help us decide what constitutes a fair trade in pelts and mong leaves for a translator."

"It would take a lot of mong leaves to equal a translator," Dunk said.

"I hope Cray agrees with you," Daco said.

Chapter 53

Daco

Daco, Bran, Jhar, Dunk and Darp all left early for the Jangle council dugout. Daco took twenty translators, ready to trade immediately should a good opportunity present itself.

The fact that Dunk was already gifting them with all of his pelts would go a long way. He judged that one translator for one day's gathering of mong leaves would be a fair trade.

The council dugout had been cleaned and decorated for the day's council meeting. Two guards in their green capes stood on either side of the entrance. The hair on their capes had been brushed to a shine and their facial hair had been combed and braided into pleasing patterns. Green flags flew around the cave's opening.

Inside the dugout, torches burned, raising the temperature. Around the large fire pit, skallon rugs had been set out for all. The smell of roasting meat filled the air.

They found Jangle leader Cray already at the council dugout speaking to his council members. He looked angry.

When Cray saw Jhar coming into the dugout, he shouted at her. "Why are you forcing us to do this terrible thing?"

"I wish to withdraw my petition," she said.

Cray's eyes grew large with surprise. "You do?"

"Yes," Jhar said. "Dunk no longer wants to become a Jangle."

Cray beamed a smile and clapped his hands together. "Your petition is officially withdrawn. We will speak no more of it. Cray looked past Jhar and noticed the others in the group. "Leader Darp, welcome. I am so relieved you have been able to convince your son to rethink this foolishness."

"Yes," Darp answered. "I am relieved as well."

"We are all of us quite relieved," Cray said, nodding at his council members. "Jhar is a valued member of our clan and you needn't worry for her care. My nephew has offered to dig a dugout for her to share."

"I believe Jhar has made a different choice," Daco said. "You need not concern yourself. She and Dunk and Darp are here today as trade advisors to me and my brother."

"Trade advisors?" Cray said. "Oh, yes, we have established some guidelines ourselves that I am sure you will feel are fair."

"We look forward to hearing your proposed guidelines," Daco said.

"We have some time before the meeting begins," Cray said. "Will you all join us at the fire pit?"

"Thank you," Daco said.

When they were all seated on the rugs around the pit, Cray stirred the burning coals to life and exposed a few hidden mong leaves wrapped around small pieces of skallon meat. "Anyone hungry?" Cray asked.

"We have been testing our tolerance for fish," Darp said. "We already have full bellies."

"Yes, fish," Cray said. "We tasted it last night and found it adequate, but I fear there will be no great demand for it in trade."

"It is an acquired taste," Daco said.

"I liked the crustacean," Jhar offered in defence of her new clan.

Daco smiled. "I favor those as well."

"Your most valuable trade item by far is your talking book," Cray said. "It is the most amazing thing I have witnessed in my many years on Cold Land. You could charge almost anything and people would still come to see it and hear it."

"Since it was a gift to us from the fruit givers, I would not feel right about charging others to hear its words," Daco said.

Cray shrugged. "You may change your mind if you run out of skallon meat."

A commotion at the entrance to the dugout garnered their attention. They stood to see what was happening. The two guards who sat at the entrance were wrestling with three men trying to get past them.

"What is the meaning of this intrusion?" Cray demanded.

Romm pushed a guard aside and came forward. He and his two men had come armed with clubs made from the dried leg bones of skallon. "We have come to kill Dunk. He has made petition to become a Jangle. We will not abide such an insult. He must die. It is the rule."

"There is no such petition," Cray said.

"What?" Romm said. "You would lie to a clan leader?"

"I think you are no longer a clan leader," Cray said, "but even if you were, you would hear the same truth. There is no such petition. These two men from the Sylvan clan have come here today as trade negotiators. Today's agenda calls for setting trade standards with those now settled at the South Sea."

Romm glared at Darp. "You have come to trade with the aliens?" he shouted.

"We are here to advise them of what constitutes a fair trade. But we may trade for translators as well. It is not your concern," Darp said.

"I believe it is my concern," Romm said. "Our clan needs to know if you are making secret agreements without consulting our council members."

"You are welcome to stay," Cray said, "as long as you don't cause trouble or try to disrupt our meeting. If you do, you will be asked to leave. If you refuse to leave you will be killed."

These last words issued in a calm voice seem to have an effect. Romm lowered his club and gestured to his two accomplices to stand down.

"Come and sit," Cray said. "We were just discussing the talking book that the miners have in their possession."

"What is this talking book?" Romm asked, his face a mask of suspicion.

"It tells the stories of the fruit givers," Cray said. "We heard a bit of Jonah's story last night and it caused a lot of debate among the Brites and Flags about who was right and who was wrong."

"The Brites and Flags are here as well?" Romm asked.

"Yes," Daco answered. "They have a great hunger to hear the stories held within the book. They may wish to come to our South Sea residence to hear more of what the book has to tell."

"I would hear these stories," Romm said. "They may not be proper for the clans of Cold Land."

"Do you really think you are the one to decide that?" Cray asked.

"Who else?" Romm asked.

"Well, your clan leader, for one, who is sitting right here," Cray said.

"Did you hear these stories?" Romm asked.

"No, I did not," Darp said. "I came here to taste the fish that they have to trade. Dunk and I ate some this morning and found it interesting. It serves to staunch one's appetite, but has a very different taste from the skallon meat we are used to eating."

A few more people arrived at the entrance to the dugout. Daco was surprised to see Jhar's family members come walking in.

Jhar's mother rushed to hug her daughter. Jhar whispered some words into her mother's ear which her mother quickly passed on to Jhar's father and brother.

Just before the meeting was scheduled to begin, the representatives from Brite and Flag came in wearing their distinctive red and blue capes.

When all were seated in double rows around the fire pit, Cray stood and said, "This council meeting of the Jangle clan is now open.

Today we meet to negotiate trade standards with the South Sea clan represented by Daco, leader of the South Sea clan. Leader Daco, please state your concerns."

Chapter 54

Jhar

As soon as her family had come into the dugout, Jhar had whispered to her mother, "We have withdrawn our petition, but don't even mention the word petition. Former leader Romm of the Sylvans is looking for any chance to kill Dunk."

Her mother had nodded and then passed the message on to her father.

Now that the meeting had turned to trade standards, Jhar breathed a little easier. She thought perhaps this whole arrangement of moving to South Sea with the miners might actually work. If Darp was allowed to visit his son there, perhaps her family might be able to come for a visit as well. Maybe she would be able to fly back in their ship to visit her family in Jangle's pastureland. The tightness that had settled in her chest for the past week began to ease just a little.

Now she was an advisor on trade negotiations. Daco stood to speak. She needed to take this new job seriously and make sure the miners struck a favorable deal. She prepared to listen closely to his words.

"We mean to be fair in our dealings with the various clans. So far we have met only four – the Jangles, the Sylvans, the Brites and the Flags. All seem interested in obtaining translators, so we will start by concentrating on the value of a translator to each clan."

Daco looked at those seated around the fire pit. "I see that the translators have already opened up the possibility of more trade between the clans and a flow of ideas as well. This is no small thing."

Daco smiled before continuing. "We had representatives from four clans on our ship last night for a meal and we had a very enjoyable evening."

Several men nodded in agreement.

"The main items we need just now are mong leaves for nutrition and pelts for warmth. Might I have some bids on the ratio of one translator for pelts?"

"One translator for one pelt," Romm said. "A good deal of work goes into the tanning of a pelt."

"Any other thoughts?" Daco asked.

"The skallon must be killed for food," Jhar said. "We all have plenty of pelts as a result. It is true that tanning is a long process but the knowledge needed to make a translator should also have value. I think two pelts for one translator would be a fair trade."

Chai of the Brites stood to speak. "I believe two pelts for one translator is a fair trade, but since the Brite clan is eager to trade with the South Sea clan, we will offer a one time trade of three pelts for one translator."

Stan of the Flags stood as well. "And we Flags will match the Brites' offer for our initial trade," he said.

Daco appeared stunned. "Thank you," he said. "My South Sea clan thanks the Flags and the Brites for this generous offer."

Daco gave a small nod of thanks to Jhar as well. "I will move on to the matter of mong leaves. We are able to send out our people to harvest the mong leaves on your pasture, but if you object to having such an arrangement, we could trade for the mong leaves harvested by your own clan members. Which arrangement would you prefer?"

Swarm of the Flags stood to speak. "Only Flags are allowed on our pastures. We would need to harvest the mong leaves and trade them."

Others seated around the fire pit seemed to be in agreement.

Cray stood to speak. "Your young people have been out gathering weeds but have been respectful of our property. They have not interfered with our herds or bothered our shepherds or those gathering dung for fires. We Jangles would allow either option. If we do the gathering we would demand more in trade than if one of yours did the gathering."

"Thank you for your trust in our young people," Daco said. "Might I send out our young people tomorrow and set them to gathering?"

"Yes," Cray said. "Shall we set the value as all the mong leaves that one person can gather in a day for one translator?"

Again, Chai stood. "We will put the same value on what one of our own shepherds can gather in a day," he said.

"We Sylvans will offer the same," Darp said.

Stan was the last to agree as he stood and said, "Flag agrees."

"Good," Daco said. He was quiet for a moment. "We have a limited number of translators to trade. I will send ten of my young people out tomorrow at dawn to collect here on Jangle. I will also trade for the work product of ten gatherers from Flag, from Brite, and from Sylvan clans. That is forty in all. I will give an extra translator to the group which gathers the most. If that group is my own people, no extra translator will be awarded."

Those gathered seem to be eager to engage in what had now become a challenge. Which clan would win the prize?

Stan stood to speak. "We must set rules for this competition. "When does the day's work begin and end? Will we have referees to monitor the event?"

A good deal of discussion between the clans followed with Jhar, Darp and Cray all working to keep the arguments civil.

Cray consulted with Daco and Darp before continuing. Then Cray stood to speak. "This is what we propose. The day will officially begin when our star is completely above the morning horizon. The day will end when our star touches the rim of the evening horizon. Each clan will send one person to monitor the event, so four people will be watching the ten participants, making sure they fill their baskets only with mong leaves."

Daco nodded his agreement before speaking. "My ship will fly to each pastureland with representatives from each clan," Daco said. "We will dump the baskets and sacks of leaves into the bins on our ship at the end of the day and measure the height of each. All the representatives will be there to witness the height of the leaves. The leaders of each clan will fly with us. At the end, we will give each leader ten translators and an eleventh to the winner. Is this agreeable to all?"

The various leaders nodded their assent and Cray stood to speak. "I think we have made a good beginning today in establishing not only a trading relationship with the South Sea clan, but with one another. As we gather more translators, I believe we may begin to set standards for trade within our traditional clans. Now I will adjourn the meeting so that Daco can fly you back to your pasturelands and we can all make preparations for tomorrow's event."

Daco turned to his trade negotiators and smiled. "This went better than I had hoped. Thank you all for your help."

"Can we fly with you to the Flag pastures?" Dunk asked.

"Of course," Daco said. "You are part of our clan now."

Dunk looked at Jhar and smiled. Jhar moved closer and took his hand in hers. She had never been so happy and so relieved in her life.

Chapter 55

Daco

The days and nights were long on planet Cold Land. Due to the slower rotation, Daco had set his time keeper to adjust to the new definition of day and night. He judged he still had time to drop off the Flag and Brite men near the border of their pastures and return to Jangle in time for a communal evening meal. He had promised they would return to the book tonight and the conclusion of Jonah's story.

Leader Darp of the Sylvans had already left for Sylvan pastures where he would organize his harvesters and return with his referees. This was the next step for Daco as well.

He entered his ship with the men from Flag and Brite. "Make yourselves at home," he said. "I will just find out who is available to harvest tomorrow for the South Sea clan. Cray will take care of the referees from the Jangles."

"I'll bet he is regretting letting your people represent Jangle," Swarm said.

"Why would you say that?" Daco asked.

"Because your people are not familiar with every patch of mong leaves as ours are," Swarm said.

"Your shepherds know where every patch of mong leaves are on Flag land?"

"Yes, of course," Swarm said. "We all do. It is our land. We know it as we know those who share our dugout."

"That is amazing," Daco said. "Yes, I suppose that puts us at a disadvantage."

Swarm laughed. "That guarantees your loss, would be the truth."

"Most likely. Still, we will be the ones to go hungry if we don't harvest enough," Daco said.

"A good incentive," Stan agreed.

"Yes, well, I will leave you to entertain yourselves," Daco said. "If you think you know enough to give commands to the book, you may go ahead with Jonah's story on your own."

Stan's face lit up. "We have your permission?"

"Yes," Daco said. "I look at the book as a gift to all of us. We miners are only the stewards."

The Flags and Brites hurried to the large dining table as Daco looked for volunteers.

He found a group of four students pulling specimens from their baskets to hand over to Mona who had set up a receiving table of sorts next to a platform that held their microscope.

"I need volunteers," Daco said.

"What is the mission?" Soma asked.

"I have set up a contest between clans," Daco said. "We will be representing the Jangle clan. It is an honor bestowed on us due to your good behavior while gathering weeds and your respect for Jangle's skallon and Jangle's shepherds."

"What sort of contest?" one of the other students asked.

"A mong gathering contest. We will be paying one translator for the work product of one person's gathering from sunrise to sunset. Each clan will have ten gatherers. Whichever clan gathers the most will receive a reward of one extra translator."

"And if we win?" Soma asked.

"I will award a translator to the one among you that gathers the most. You can keep it or trade it as you will."

"I volunteer," Soma said.

The others with him volunteered as well.

"Go out and find me six more volunteers," Daco said. "Then come back to the ship as soon as you can. We must fly the Brites and Flags back to their pastures so that they can get ready for tomorrow's event."

The students went out in a rush and Daco was left alone with Mona. "You don't wish to volunteer?" he asked.

Mona laughed. "I don't think my volunteering would improve our chances of winning. I am better suited to manning the microscope."

Daco laughed with her. "We all have our strengths. I doubt that my volunteering would improve our chances either. I am told that shepherds here know where every patch of mong leaves lie within their pastures."

"We may soon know quite a bit about our own new land, the South Sea, where the different fishes gather. We'll know the location of each vent, the fault lines that divide the plates, the secret places where predators lie in wait."

"Yes," Daco said. "There is a lifetime of discoveries awaiting us. It is a thing that excites me."

"And me as well," Mona said.

Daco nodded and felt a kindred spirit in the young student. "Well, I must check on our bins. We will need four of like size completely empty to hold the gatherings of the four clans tomorrow."

As he passed by the crowded dining table, he heard the deep voice of the book saying, "I will say, salvation comes from the Lord. And the Lord commanded the fish, and it vomited Jonah onto dry land."

The two Brites and the two Flags were huddled around the book, their eyes mirroring their fascination.

Daco was cleaning out the fourth bin when Jhar arrived with her family. Her mother, father, sisters and brothers, were all carrying something – baskets of fruit, skallon pelts, mong leaves or skallon dung.

Jhar's mother placed a basket of fruit before Daco. "Thank you for saving our daughter's life," she said.

"We are fortunate to have her and Dunk with us," he said. "You didn't need to bring all these gifts."

"These are gifts from Dunk and Jhar," the woman said. "We are only here to transport them."

"You know you are welcome to visit them any time. We will be making trips north every thirty days."

"I want to visit," a small boy said.

Jhar's mother smiled. "This is Sim. He will miss Jhar very much."

Daco picked up the small child. "Then you will have to be first to visit. Would you like that?"

"Yes," Sim said.

"Good. We will look forward to your visit." He set the child down next to his mother. "Where is Dunk?" he asked Jhar.

"He went back with his father to Sylvan land. He needed to pick up some of his tanning supplies. My father will be flying with us to the Flag pastures. He has been selected by Cray as one of Jangle's referees."

"I'm called Singe," the man said. He was a big man with pale blue eyes and long blonde braided facial hair. He wore a green fur cap on his head.

"I'm honored to meet Jhar's father," Daco said. "I am Daco, leader of the South Sea clan."

Singe nodded. "We will miss our daughter very much, but we trust that you will watch over her."

"She will also be watching over us – showing us how to dry the mong leaves and turn them into baskets and ropes. We value her skills and those of the Jangle people."

"Thank you," her father said.

Chapter 56

Jhar

The *Bonanza* lifted off a little after midday with the referees from the Sylvan and Jangle clans on board. They would land close to the border between Flag and Brite. Then, after the leaders chose their gatherers and referees, they would return to Jangle.

Jhar sat between her father and Dunk strapped down on a couch. The ship was so full they had to share restraints.

"Look there," Daco said, his excitement making him grip Jhar's hand too tightly. He pointed toward the portal that offered a view of the boundary marker between Jangle and Sylvan pastures. "Our meeting place."

Jhar wondered if he had forgotten that her father sat beside her. Dunk seemed to be overwhelmed by his excitement of flying through the air on a ship. If not for the restraints she imagined he would be jumping up and down in his seat.

"I'm glad my father did not appoint me as one of the harvesters. I wouldn't have wanted to miss this."

"You could hardly be appointed one of the harvesters for the Sylvans since you now belong to the South Sea clan," her father pointed out.

"Right, I suppose that's why he didn't choose me," Daco said. "I would have been a very fast harvester."

"I'm sure," her father said, with a smile in his voice.

"I plan to dig a dugout there by the sea," Dunk assured her father. "Even if they give us a stone residence, I will still dig a dugout beneath it. I will not forget the old ways."

"You should perhaps clear it with your new leader, Daco, first," her father said.

"Yes, of course. My father is coming with us, you know. He can help me dig."

"Your father will spend a month away from his clan?" Singe asked.

"Yes, he has appointed Gerd to act in his place until he returns," Dunk said.

Singe nodded as Dunk said – "We are over the ice of the north now. Look, see how it freezes into peaks?"

It was indeed an amazing sight to see. The ice formed into towering shapes with deep crevices in between.

"And now we are going down. Do you feel it?" Dunk said.

Singe laughed. "I do. It is an uncommon thing to experience flight."

"It is a wonder," Jhar agreed.

The *Bonanza* set down near the boundary marker between Flag and Brite. Even though the pastures would have likely looked no different from those of the Jangle's and the Sylvan's to the miners, Jhar, her father and Dunk noticed innumerable differences.

"Look at that rock formation. That is no doubt their boundary marker. It is large as a horid," her father said.

Neither Jhar nor Dunk had ever seen a horid face to face, but they both nodded their agreement.

"And the grass, see how a dark place grows near the border?" her father continued. "A lot of mong leaves grow there to give it the darker color. Having a large area so close at hand will give both clans an advantage in the contest."

"I wish I could be competing," Dunk said wistfully.

"I am sure you will have opportunities to shine in our new home," Jhar said.

"Do you really think so?" Dunk said. "The aliens seem to know so much more than we do."

"But they don't know more about our own planet," Jhar said. "Cold Land is new to them."

"This is true," Dunk said. "Surely they must know a dugout provides more warmth than any shelter above ground."

"They don't seem to know that – yet," Jhar said.

Dunk nodded. "Yes, and I am sure none of them has ever tanned a skallon hide."

"I must leave you now," her father said. "I will be the Jangle's referee for the harvesters in Flag."

"I will see you tomorrow at the end of the contest," Jhar said, hugging her father.

"Yes," Singe said. "Hopefully the Flag clan will play by the rules and I will not have to censure anyone."

Jhar and Dunk looked at one another, grinning, after her father left. "This is really happening," Jhar said. "We have flown on a ship – our own ship now that we are members of the South Sea clan."

"Yes," Dunk said, hugging her. "If we can fit in, what other wonders lie ahead?"

"I can't imagine," Jhar said.

They walked out of the ship with many others, looking around at the familiar landscape but noting the differences.

"Don't go far," Daco warned the group. "We will only be here long enough for the leaders to appoint their gatherers and bring their referees on board. Then we will lift off to return to Jangle."

Jhar noticed the biologists were already scouting these new pastures for any new weeds they could find.

"Why are they so interested in weeds?" Dunk asked.

"They are looking for anything edible," Jhar said. "Nothing grows at the South Sea. It is too cold."

"I'll miss the grasslands," Dunk said. "Shall we attempt to learn to swim?"

"Yes, I think we should," Jhar said. "Daco says it is possible if we stay near the surface of the water."

"It's a little unsettling, knowing all those fish are alive and swimming below you," Dunk said. "But I want to try it."

"Yes, we should both try it. Maybe the skins of the large fish can be tanned," Jhar said.

"I had not imagined that, but you could be right," Dunk said. "That would be a thing we could trade. Fish skin capes."

"We have so much to discover," Jhar said.

"Everyone back on board," Daco shouted. "I can see leader Stan and leader Chai returning with their referees."

"Tonight we will see the talking book," Jhar said.

"Yet another wonder," Dunk said.

The referees from Flag and Brite seemed relieved to see other natives from Cold Land aboard and made their way over to where Jhar in her green cape and Dunk in his purple cape were standing. "You are one of the Jangles and one of the Sylvan clans," a referee said.

"No, we are of the South Sea clan," Jhar said. "But the South Sea clan has yet to pick a color."

"What is this South Sea clan?" the man asked.

"Come with us," Dunk said. "We will show you how to strap in for take off and then we will tell you all about the South Sea clan."

"Good," the man said. "Perhaps you can begin by telling us how it is we can understand one another's speech?"

Chapter 57

Daco

The *Bonanza* touched down on Jangle pastureland just as their red star touched the horizon.

Daco released his restraints and went about the ship telling everyone that they would soon be cooking fish and all aboard were invited to eat with them. Dray and her daughter, Mica, followed in his wake gathering volunteers to help with the meal from among the students. In some cases they physically pulled female students with cooking experience bodily away from the men vying for their attention.

Daco knew things were getting tense as too many miners sought the hands of too few female students. He noticed that those who tried for Mona's affections were all politely but firmly rebuffed.

The *Bonanza* had landed close to the *By Grace* and Daco kept peeking out the open hatch to see if Joshua might be on his way. He was finally rewarded with a view of the medium-sized man with brown hair, a brown beard and tan complexion, heading for the *Bonanza*. He went out to meet him.

"I didn't know if you would make it back in time for a meal," Joshua said. "You have had a busy day."

"And it just keeps getting busier," Daco said. "We have aboard our ship people from four clans – five if you count our own newly formed clan of the South Sea."

They walked through the cargo area, now covered with rugs scattered around raised eating areas to handle the large dinner crowd. They continued up the stairs to the galley/dining area filled with bustling activity as Dray and her galley workers ran from galley to dining table with large platters of food. Smells of cooked fish and roasting meat filled the air. Daco and Joshua took seats at the large dining table.

"You plan to make the South Sea your home then?" Joshua asked.

"Yes, we will be returning there after we have our pelts and enough mong leaves for a month," Daco said.

"And what of Jhar? Rahab was most insistent that I ask about her," Joshua said.

"Jhar and her young man, Dunk, have become members of our South Sea clan. Dunk's father, Darp, will be returning to South Sea with them for a thirty day visit."

"Rahab will be pleased," Joshua said. "And Jonah wishes to know if his story has had any effect?"

"His story will continue to its end tonight. So far it has produced a good deal of debate from all those who have been listening to it. Debate within clans as well as debate between clans."

"Jonah will be pleased to hear it," Joshua said.

"Debate is a good thing?" Daco asked.

"Yes, it is the best way to question our thinking and find consensus," Joshua said.

"I hope Rahab and Jonah realize our invitation to dinner was meant to include them as well," Daco said.

"Yes, we have our own debate going on and the others are immersed in it," Joshua said. "Some feel our work here is done and some feel we need to stay a while longer."

"Who has the deciding vote?" Daco asked.

"I do," Joshua said.

"And what is your thinking?" Daco asked.

"I will decide tonight," Joshua said.

"I feel it might be in our best interests to appear helpless and distraught, if that would serve to keep you here longer," Daco said.

Joshua laughed. "You might think so, but humility is actually a thing God values. I will admit we ambassadors like to see signs of self-sufficiency, but we are not your creators or sustainers. Only God has that power."

"It is difficult to outwit you," Daco said. "You seem to have a mastery of the inner workings of the minds of all creatures."

"We have been ambassadors for a very long time."

"How long?" Daco asked.

"Time is relative," Joshua said. "You must have noticed a day of time on Cold Land is different from a day of time on Swage."

"Yes, our bodies have not yet adjusted," Daco said. "Is your planet one with long days and nights?" Daco asked.

"We do not revolve around a star," Joshua said. "Our light comes from our God, the High King."

"How remarkable and unimaginable," Daco said, unable to find a place in his mind to store such a concept. "It looks as though dinner is about to be called."

Joshua nodded as he surveyed the table, now full of steaming platters.

Daco and Joshua fell into the makeshift line, waiting their turn at the buffet. The table held various kinds of fish, fruit and skallon meat wrapped in mong leaves.

They all took their plates of food down to the cargo hold for a communal meal, talking about the competition that would take place tomorrow beginning at dawn.

"All those interested in hearing the conclusion to Jonah's story from the talking book can gather around the dining table at the conclusion of tonight's meal," Daco called out.

The cargo hold was filled with the sounds of eating and talking with a good deal of flirting between courting couples.

At the end of the meal, about half those assembled moved up to the dining level to hear the talking book. Daco and Joshua followed them.

After washing his hands Joshua took the book from its wooden box. He let it fall open on the table.

"Good book, continue," he commanded.

"Jonah had gone out and sat down at a place east of the city," the deep voice from within the book said. "There he made himself a shelter, sat down and waited to see what would happen to the city. There the Lord God provided a leafy plant and made it grow up over Jonah to give shade for his head to ease his discomfort and Jonah was very happy about the plant. But at dawn the next day God provided a worm, which chewed the plant so that it withered. When the sun rose, God provided a scorching east wind, and the sun blazed on Jonah's head so that he grew faint. He wanted to die, and said, it would be better for me to die than to live.'"

"Stop," Stan of the Flags said.

"Good book, pause," Joshua said. "What is your concern, Stan?"

"Why did God give him a plant only to take it away again?"

"Let us find out," Joshua said. "Good book, continue."

But God said to Jonah, is it right for you to be angry about the plant?

It is, he said. And I'm so angry I wish I were dead.

But the Lord said, you have been concerned about this plant, though you did not tend it or make it grow. It sprang up overnight and died overnight. And should I not have concern over the great city of Nineveh, in which there are more than a hundred and twenty thousand people who cannot tell their right hand from their left – and also many animals?"

Joshua closed the book. "Thus ends the story of Jonah."

"That is the end?" Stan asked.

"Yes," Joshua said.

"That does not seem like the end," Stan said. "Did Jonah live or die? Did he return to his people?"

"We know he lived," Chai said. "We talked to him only two days ago."

"But what have we learned about God from this story?" Stan said.

Joshua smiled. "That is the question we must ponder, isn't it? What does this story tell us about God?"

Stan continued to grumble and others spoke up with their opinions about what God's message was.

Daco felt Joshua's eyes on him and turned to face him.

"I believe our work here is done," Joshua said.

"I was afraid of that," Daco said. He looked down at his feet before looking back up to meet Joshua's eyes. "I truly believe now that there is a God who watches over us and that he sent you to save us. I can never thank you enough for all you have done."

"Keep those words in your heart and you will thrive," Joshua said.

The two men hugged one another and Daco could not stop several tears from falling as he watched Joshua walk away.

Chapter 58

Daco

Daco woke before dawn and left the ship to find the *By Grace* gone. He looked to the sky just tinged with the color of a new day and silently wished the ambassadors well. Their gift of fruit, translators and the talking book had been pivotal in securing a new home for his planet's few survivors.

The student harvesters representing Jangle were already assembled outside the ship where the referees stood gazing at the spot on the horizon where the star always rose. Daco could see a small red bubble emerging from the halo of dawn's light.

"Just a bit longer," the Jangle referee said. "The whole body of the star must clear the horizon."

The students shivered as they held their bags, needing to move to keep warm.

"Now," the referee shouted, "you may begin."

The students were off and running. It would be a long day and others had been appointed to keep providing the harvesters with food and water throughout the allotted time.

Daco's brother, Bran, came to stand beside him. "Do you think we have a chance of winning?" he asked.

"I suppose there is always a chance," Daco said, his true opinion evident in his tone.

"I have good news," Bran said. "One of the students, Lila, has agreed to be my wife."

"What?" Daco said. "Lila? How did I know nothing of this?"

"We tried not to be too obvious. There were others hoping her decision would go their way," Bran said.

"I am so pleased for you. I admit I don't know Lila. I have had so little time to come to know all the students by name," Daco said.

"She usually wears her hair in a braid that circles her head," Bran said.

"Yes, I noticed her," Daco said. "She is very pretty."

"Of course I think so, too," Bran said. "Will you not try for a bride?"

"Me?" Daco said. "No, I am too old and I have had my true love. I still have the son she gave me. It is enough."

Bran shrugged. "We plan to rush out with empty bags to exchange for full ones as the day goes on. The referees assured me that isn't against the rules."

"A good plan," Daco said. "Will you have some breakfast with me?"

"I've already eaten," Bran said. "Stan of the Flag clan asked if he could fly with us to South Sea to give him an opportunity to hear more stories from the book. He says he will put Swarm in charge while he is gone."

"What did you tell him?" Daco asked

"I told him I would ask you."

Daco nodded. "I'll go and speak to him. I suppose it would be all right. We'll be flying back to Flag at the end of the day. He could pick up what he will need for thirty days at his dugout there."

"I'll let you tell him. I'm going to scout out pastures of mong leaves for our harvesters."

Daco smiled. "Best check with the referees first."

Daco found Stan eating fruit at the dining table. "You wish to accompany us back to South Sea?" he asked.

"Yes, I'm convinced by all the impossible things I've witnessed aboard the *By Grace* and the *Bonanza* that there is a God who cares for us. I need to find out more about him if I am to continue as leader of the Flags."

"A commendable goal," Daco said. "We will welcome your company."

"Thank you," Stan said. "I'll provide my own food. I don't wish to be a burden."

"As you will, though the South Sea provides an abundance of fish."

"I don't wish to insult your fish but I will be bringing skallon meat aboard," Stan said.

"No insult taken," Daco said. "Many others aboard share your preference."

"I'll bring extra," Stan said.

Daco smiled and reached for a piece of fruit.

He walked about the nearly empty ship and was surprised to find Mona still aboard, working at her microscope. "Aren't you interested in the competition going on outside?" he asked.

"Yes, I'll go out in a bit. I just have a few more weeds to test in case we may wish to take some with us for further study."

"You are very dedicated to your work," Daco noted.

"Of course. It's a matter of survival, isn't it?"

"Yes," Daco agreed, "though many of the students and miners seem to be more occupied with picking a partner for our life here on Cold Land."

"Yes," Mona said, smiling. "I've had some offers as well."

"But none you accepted?" Daco asked.

"I'm only interested in one man," Mona said, "and he has not asked as yet."

"I'm sorry to hear it," Daco said. "Do you believe he has paired with another?"

"No, I don't think so," Mona said.

"You must realize that the men outnumber the women by a sizable margin," Daco said. "If he knew your feelings I am sure he would be happy to choose you."

"Do you think so?" Mona said.

"I'm sure of it," Daco said. "No man wishes to spend his life alone."

"What about yourself?" Mona asked. "You seem content to remain alone."

"I've been married. I have a son. I don't wish to be greedy."

"That is a problem for me then," Mona said.

As realization finally dawned, Daco grew flustered. "Me? I am the man who interests you?"

"The only one, I fear," Mona said.

Daco's face erupted into a smile as he reached for Mona. He pulled her into a hug and said, "I can hardly believe my good fortune."

"Nor I, mine," Mona said.

"We must tell Aldo. You don't mind that I have a son?"

"I look forward to being his friend. I am eager to replace my old family of cousins, siblings, aunts and uncles, with a new one. The more the better," Mona said.

That evening the *Bonanza* took aboard the product of the Sylvan and South Sea harvesters. Though the students had made a great haul, the Sylvan bin was clearly higher.

The *Bonanza* took off at twilight to gather aboard the mong leaves collected by the Flags and the Brites.

As the Brites and Flags brought out their bags of leaves by torchlight, Daco stayed aboard to monitor the emptying of the bags into the proper bins.

The Flag bin was just a little higher than the Brite bin, but between the Sylvan bin and the Flag bin, it was too close to call.

Daco handed out eleven translators to referees of the Sylvan and Flag clans and ten each to representatives of the Jangle and Brite teams.

As soon as all were aboard who would return to Jangle, the *Bonanza* made ready to take off. Those aboard waved to the harvesters and referees that had worked so hard for their respective clans.

As Stan stepped aboard he saluted those holding torches from the Flag clan. "I will return with many stories to tell," he shouted.

Daco went to rest with his family which now included Mona. He felt himself a blessed man.

Chapter 59

Daco

The morning after the mong gathering contest, the *Bonanza* flew to South Sea carrying the Flag leader, the Sylvan leader, Jhar and Dunk. It was hard to say who was the most anxious to arrive – the miners and students or their guests. The flight was a mix of acceleration and deceleration, an up and down trip that made restraints necessary and conversations problematic. He slept most of the way, tired after all the excitement of his two days racing between clans. He dreamed of Mona.

As they closed in on South Sea, the sky was its usual overcast gray color and the sea a dark forbidding expanse of water. Landing close to the sister Swagian ship, the *Seeker*, the *Bonanza* set down.

When the hatch opened, Daco immediately noticed a new sound. The sound of their generator, installed and producing electricity. Holding Mona's hand in his right hand and his son Aldo's hand in his left hand, the three ran to the stone structure that housed the generator.

"It is up and running," Pheebs sang out. "We have heat in two rock structures."

"Well done," Daco said. "I have a surprise as well. Mona has agreed to be my wife."

"Well, you have been busy," Pheebs said with a grin. "Welcome to our family of miners, Mona."

"Thank you," Mona said. "I'm accustomed to having a large family. This suits me well."

"What is the news here?" Daco asked. "Besides the working generator."

"Not good, I fear," Pheebs said. "Professor Stern has succumbed to a heart attack. We tried to revive him but were unable."

"I'm sorry to hear it," Mona said. "I think his spirit died when he realized he had lost all he held dear on Swage."

"I'm sorry as well. We could have used his vast knowledge of biology. But he has left a legacy of dedicated students." Daco looked back at Pheebs. "You say you have heat in two structures?" he asked.

Pheebs curled his hand in a forward motion. "Follow me."

Pheebs led them to a large rock structure with a concrete floor and rock walls held together with cement. An orange tarp formed the roof.

"Lucky we had that limestone from the asteroid," Pheebs said. They both knew limestone was a necessary element in the production of both concrete and cement.

Inside the structure, warm air was coming up from vents attached to an underground pipe.

"This is wonderful," Mona said. "A place we can always come to warm up."

Daco nodded. "It's large enough to hold us all for meals or meetings."

"Yes," Pheebs said. "Most of us crowd in here with our cots to sleep at night."

"Any other events?" Daco asked.

"The biologists have some news, but I didn't understand what it was," Pheebs said.

Mona let go of Daco's hand and raced out of the building. "I'll find out," she said.

Daco moved around the room, cherishing its warmth. "Should we move the big table here?" he asked.

"No," Aldo said. "It's too far from the galleys of both ships."

"Yes, you're right," Daco said, smiling at his son. "I can see I need to make you my chief advisor."

"We continue to pile up stones," Pheebs said, but some prefer the familiarity of living aboard the ships."

"We have Dunk and Jhar with us," Daco said. "They will be permanent residents. Dunk is determined to live in a dugout as is customary with the clans."

"How does he hope to dig through the permafrost?" Pheebs asked.

"He plans to melt his way through with a series of fires," Daco said.

"What will he use for fuel?" Pheebs asked.

"They have brought skallon dung along," Daco said.

Pheebs shrugged. "It won't be long before we have a village of heated rock homes. Perhaps he should reconsider."

"Actually I'm glad he is determined to try it. I say try everything and see what works best. We aren't accustomed to living above permafrost and he's not accustomed to living without skallon. We'll all have to adjust and adapt."

They were just leaving when Mona rushed back again, breathing hard. "We have found edible seaweed. We are saved."

Daco laughed. "We cannot make the jump as you are able to. How does edible seaweed save us?"

"It is full of vitamins and nutrients the body needs. This is revolutionary," Mona insisted.

"We have a lot to celebrate," Daco said. "So many new unions of marriage and now our survival, thanks to seaweed. Will we be able to include it in tonight's meal?"

"Yes," Mona said.

"Then I propose we celebrate multiple unions, new members and guests with a meal in our new heated structure. How does that sound?"

"It sounds perfect," Mona said. "I'll go and arrange things with Dray and Mica."

"Excellent," Daco said. "We'll put together something approaching a dining table and benches here in the warm air."

That evening all of the South Sea clan and its guests gathered in the new stone building. Daco, Pheebs and Aldo had moved forty cots from the ships to this building. They had stretched a heavy tarp over twenty cots and set another twenty alongside it to form a table and benches long enough to hold everyone.

Both ships' galleys had been utilized to cook fish wrapped in mong leaves and seaweed. Cooked skallon brought along by Stan and Darp was added. Fruit from Jhar had been mixed with melted snow to make a sweet drink.

After everyone was seated, Daco raised a glass of fruit juice. "We are celebrating many new marriages tonight, my own included, so I will begin and I want each new couple to rise and introduce yourselves. "Aldo and I wish to welcome Mona to our family. We will henceforth be known as Daco, Mona and Aldo South Sea." The three raised their glasses to cheers from the crowd.

And so it went with fifteen new couples added to the South Sea list. Jhar and Dunk were the last to stand. "Jhar and I thank you all not only for accepting us into your clan but for saving our lives," Dunk said. "Our own clans were ready to kill us for wanting to be together. You have adopted us and treated us as family. You will always be welcome in our dugout, which I have yet to dig."

A few smiles and laughter followed that admission.

"We will henceforth be known as Jhar and Dunk South Sea," Dunk concluded.

After all the introductions had been made, everyone settled into their meal. Daco found he liked the taste of fish wrapped in seaweed and determined he would soon be putting back some of the weight he had lost.

"What do you think of our new diets?" he asked Mona.

"I think we will all become quite healthy and brilliant. Fish is food for the brain, you know."

"Another thing I didn't know," Daco said. "I'm lucky to have you and Aldo to advise me."

Mona laughed. "I see you have some experience at being a husband."

Daco laughed as well. "It's coming back to me."

At the end of the meal, Daco stood and said, "Sleep well, all of you. Tomorrow it will be work as usual. Anyone who wishes to spend a warm night is welcome to sleep here on the cots that make up the table and benches."

And most did just that, sleeping soundly within the comfort of their clan.

Chapter 60

Joshua

Joshua faced his brothers and sisters in the Body of Christ with a sense of satisfaction for a mission accomplished in the name of their God and King. Daniel, Deborah, Jonah, Rahab and Lydia stared back at him. He sensed they still had questions.

"Are you sure it was enough?" Lydia asked. "The Cold Land clans were only beginning to question the infallibility of their laws, and as to that, not all of them, but only a few."

"But the important few," Joshua said. "Their leaders. Did you see how moved Stan of the Flags was on hearing Jonah's story? He even went with Daco to South Sea to learn more stories from the Book. He wants to take the stories back to his people. He just felt it was the right thing to do. That feeling had to come from God."

Lydia smiled. "I am familiar with following such a feeling rather than living by rules and traditions. But it was easier for me to be led by the Spirit. I lived in Thyatira, where new ideas were encouraged and embraced. The rest of you valued your laws and traditions, even above God's words."

"Sad but true," Joshua said. "We Jews should have recognized Christ when he came into Bethlehem as a newborn. It was all prophesied. But back then the Jewish nation was expecting a king to come with visual power and strength, with all the accoutrements of royalty. Not a poor and humble person out of poverty-stricken Nazareth."

"And Jews have always been an obstinate people," Jonah said. "None more so than I myself."

"But look how Stan and Chai and Chi, and especially Grum, were able to relate to your story," Joshua said. "They recognized right away that your experiences had some important truth for them. Stan is still working on trying to unearth that truth."

Jonah shrugged, aiming an annoyed glance at Joshua. "It is embarrassing to know that my story helps others to see their flaws so easily. It must be comforting to know that your own story makes you a hero to all who hear it. You were God's champion. A shining example of what faith in God can achieve."

"I hardly think believing God – taking him at his word – makes me a hero," Joshua said. "Believing what God says seems to me to be the sensible thing to do."

Deborah nodded. I agree. Many see me as a hero among women – ready to fight when others turned away from God's commands. But really I was only stepping up because no one else would. I kept thinking others would finally come around and finally they did."

"I think stories are key," Daniel said. "Many have difficulty holding on to some of the more abstract truths of God's grace. But stories, they can relate to. Stories, they can remember. When I tell them I was able to interpret dreams with God's help, they remember that, because they all dream and they all wonder if their dreams have import."

"I know your telling Jhar that you treated your enemies kindly – even those who captured you and took you into a foreign country – had a profound affect on her," Rahab stated, looking at Daniel. "She then had an example of someone else who had caring feelings for an enemy. And, it validated her feelings for Dunk, who came from an enemy clan."

Daniel laughed. "Not as much impact as your own story did. You were not only friendly – you hid the spies Joshua sent in. You chose their God over your own and became the ancestor of God himself through your son, Boaz. Jhar will read your whole story one day and be amazed."

Rahab shook her head. "God favored me for no reason I could fathom. It was my fear of a God who was powerful enough to hold back the waters of a mighty river that determined my choice."

"Yes, a healthy fear of God is an important consideration," Joshua agreed. "Some of us are so taken with the love of God and his great mercy that they lose sight of his great power."

"But will they really be able to ferret out all the truths from the Book?" Lydia asked. "Will they see that their laws are holding them back? Will they see that they too can have the real laws of God written on their hearts when the Holy Spirit takes up residence within them? I wonder if we should not have stayed longer to turn their questions back to the Book for answers."

"There will be a lifetime of cold nights when the South Sea clan huddles together for comfort and turns to the Book for inspiration," Joshua replied.

"And others from all the clans will eventually find their way to South Sea for a hearing of the Book," Daniel assured them. "Some will eventually establish schools, where they will decipher the ancient writing. Those who master the knowledge held within will take it back to their clans."

"And they will advance in technology as well," Deborah added. "They will learn all the refugees from Swage have to teach them and they will begin to build their own spaceships and explore their star system taking their technology and their beliefs with them."

"I suppose so," Lydia said. "But there may be wars and lean years along the way. What if their population begins to overwhelm their resources?"

"I did hint that there may be latent life in the form of seeds buried underground in the remains of their planet Swage," Joshua said. "I am sure, in time, they will return to have a look at what remains."

"Still, I feel as Lydia does," Rahab said. "I wish we could be there to see them through the dark times and celebrate with them on their victories."

"What of the trillions of others on planets in other star systems in other galaxies?" Daniel asked. "Do they not need our help as well?"

Deborah laughed. "God is prolific."

"Yes, he is," Joshua agreed. "I sensed it was time for us to leave and I always trust the Spirit within. But now look where Uriah has brought us. Is that the New Earth of New Jerusalem emerging from the clouds?"

Everyone's attention turned to the observation portal. They watched, spellbound, as their landing platform came into view.

"Ah, Jerusalem. How I have missed you," Lydia said.

"What will you do first?" Rahab asked. "I myself will go to visit Boaz and Ruth and others I have missed."

Lydia tilted her head in a thoughtful pose. "I think I will just walk along the river and take in the warmth and the light. And the singing. I have missed the music so much."

"I will make my report," Joshua said. "And I thank you all for your input. It will make my task easier."

"I plan to stay atop the city for a bit and go for a nice, long swim in a rooftop pool, where I can look up and see all God's creation above me," Deborah said. "What of you two, Jonah and Daniel?"

"I think I will relax with a nice game of chess," Daniel said. "Are you interested, Jonah?"

"That sounds perfect," Jonah agreed "Though I have lost to you too many times already to hope for a victory."

Daniel smiled. "Never give up hope."

Milton Keynes UK
Ingram Content Group UK Ltd.
UKHW030911121124
451094UK00001B/139